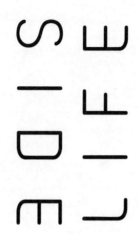

SIDE LIFE

Also by the author

Join

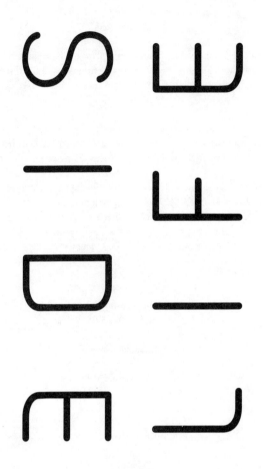

SIDE LIFE

STEVE TOUTONGHI

SOHO

Lyrics to the song "Itsi Bitsi" by Eik Skaløe,
are reproduced with permission. The full lyrics are available from
Dansk in the volume *Trip - Tekster fra tresserne*.

Excerpt from "To Daphne and Virginia" by William Carlos Williams, from
The Collected Poems: Volume II, 1939–1962, copyright © 1953 by William Carlos
Williams. Reprinted by permission of New Directions Publishing Corp. (in the US,
its territories and Canada). Reprinted by permission of Carcanet Press Limited (in the
British Common Wealth, excluding Canada).

Published by
Soho Press, Inc.
853 Broadway
New York, NY 10003

Library of Congress Cataloging-in-Publication Data

Toutonghi, Steve, 1964–
Side life / Steve Toutonghi.

ISBN 978-1-61695-889-3
eISBN 978-1-61695-890-9

1. Virtual reality—Fiction. I. Title
PS3620.O923 S55 2018 813'.6—dc23 2017044466

Interior illustrations © Dasha Bertrand
Interior design by Janine Agro, Soho Press, Inc.

Printed in the United States of America

10 9 8 7 6 5 4 3 2 1

We've evolved not to see the truth but to hide the truth.
The truth is too complicated. We don't need to know it.
[This] gives us a fiction of causality.

—Donald Hoffman

A new world

is only a new mind.

And the mind and the poem
are all apiece.

—William Carlos Williams, "To Daphne and Virginia"

PART

Nerdean

CHAPTER 1

The Axis on which It Turns

> *If I have to fill my days with dreaming, my dreams will be lucid.*

The man was defying traffic, striding slowly down the center of the merge lane that Vin and the line of cars behind him were waiting to use. The man was big and lean in a black T-shirt and black denim jeans, a long dark mane flaring like a sadhu's, a full beard softening his heavy jaw; and he looked preposterously confident, as if he were separate from the world and impervious, as if he were parting illusion. One lane over, cars flew by, their wakes gently tugging his long hair while he walked within two feet of Vin's new Tesla S and didn't even tilt his head to acknowledge the driver or the machine. Eyes forward, fixed on a vague middle distance, a derisive smile tightened the corners of his lips.

"Shithead," Vin said under his breath, one hand poised on the horn. He began to ease into the merge lane but couldn't stop watching the man, who was now stepping directly into the first lane of oncoming traffic. Cars slowed to negotiate a way around him but, incredibly, no one honked. Perhaps his riveting indifference silenced them; maybe he was violent; maybe he didn't believe he could be hurt.

He strode across two more lanes to the concrete barrier. Vin was glancing in his mirrors now as he accelerated past the tangle of spring greenery erupting from the northeast slope of Queen Anne Hill. Before him was the clear span of the Aurora Bridge, its sides railed by a high suicide barrier. The man hopped onto the concrete median and swayed precariously toward southbound traffic.

"Shithead," Vin said again, worry stabbing at him.

Yet his impulse to do something was already fading. Turning around would mean exiting, crossing under the bridge and driving back in the southbound lanes. And then what? There was no place to pull over. If he did find one, he would have to walk across express lanes to reach the man. And the man seemed altered, probably high. And Vin had already driven away.

HE PARKED WEST OF THE stained and stately Guild 45th Theater, a favorite holdout from the Seattle he'd grown up in. Over the last few years, as he was finishing his PhD and starting his company, Sigmoto, the region's economic titans had been transforming the city, unleashing forces that sparked flaring skyscrapers and culled weak businesses. Running his own company had protected him from the arrogant beauty of new things; it was how he had fought feeling lost and small among the stone-footed pedestals and high shells of evening light. But in the weeks since his ouster from Sigmoto he had begun to feel useless again, as if he had fashioned himself into a complex and intricate piece of living machinery, closely engineered for a now obsolete purpose.

His meeting with the guy who replaced him as CEO would be a courtesy, and Vin planned to keep it short. He was done volunteering information. It had been Vin's interest in cliodynamics and statistical physics, his understanding of big data, his focus on user experience and his design insights that had birthed the first iteration of Sigmoto's "Decision Turbines" (an absurd but actually kind of descriptive name that his investors basically stuck him with). And it wasn't an exaggeration to say that he had probably been the only person capable of guiding the company to its true potential. Sigmoto should have been a new kind of data aggregator, forging the tools needed to finally bring shape and weight to opportunity costs—the options unchosen, the things that didn't happen. But after a slower than expected start, the board said they had diagnosed the company's problem and they removed him.

He passed a handful of twenty-somethings wearing lanyards with ID cards and swatting jokes and fragments of sentences at each other—"whatever they need"; "he's such a bozo"; "Stan's going to fire him." Vin picked a lane through their scrum and ignored the templated *bonhomie*.

Hiring and managing a team at Sigmoto may have been the first time in his life that he felt fluent in friendship. But while selling the product he'd also had to fight unnervingly poor execution by his technical hires, and he'd slowly come to see a painful truth: if Sigmoto's Decision Turbines hadn't existed, the world wouldn't have noticed. That realization punctured his self-confidence, and then, worn down by conflict with his investors, he hadn't effectively resisted a "strategic pivot" toward gesture recognition. After that, all of his best ideas were off the roadmap and Sigmoto's potential was lost forever. So he didn't have a team anymore and he was feeling overwhelmed by the ambiguity and scope of his own ambition. But the challenge of motivation is only one part of the raw difficulty of doing something worthwhile. The answer is to work harder and smarter. It always is.

His phone started buzzing just before he reached for it. "Son!" His father, who smelled like sour white wine and described himself as a "Gaelic hustler," worked to make his voice a goad toward action. "I have a deal for you. Meet me for lunch at Fadó. I'm going to bring my friend, a very well-connected attorney by the name of Joaquin Brooks, who's looking for a house sitter." His father gave the name a conspicuous flourish. He wanted something from Joaquin Brooks.

"Why?"

"You don't have an income. You shouldn't be paying rent."

"I'm doing fine."

"Look, I didn't mind helping when you were building something."

Vin had asked his father for help with seed funding, to get Sigmoto off the ground, but his father had done nothing. Then, after Vin raised enough money to get started, his father had introduced him to two bankers, one of whom eventually helped out. After that, his father acted as though he had personally saved Vin from disaster.

"Okay, so you're young," his father was saying, "you were a bit too reckless. No surprise. But now you don't have a job anymore, so you have to move on. You have a chance to start again. And to focus this time."

"That's what I'm already doing."

"Meet us at noon, at Fadó. Or will you be gardening?" Vin's mother loved gardening. After a bitter divorce, his father started using it as shorthand for a low-priority activity.

"Gardening improves quality of life."

"You can worry about quality of life when you're dead."

THE NEW CEO DIDN'T ASK many questions. Instead, he avowed enormous respect for Vin's technical vision and skill, and offered to reach out to his own contacts on Vin's behalf. Within moments of their morning glory muffins arriving, Vin found himself describing his hopes for Sigmoto with a sloppy passion that embarrassed him even as it unshackled an ache in his gut. The guy changed the subject and started talking about other "interesting projects" in their "formative stages." But Vin knew he could find a job. People were in awe of what he could do. He got off a few decent barbs about rudderless, generic "innovation" (he used air quotes), without impugning anything specific. The guy listened calmly and replied with a grounded sympathy that made Vin feel ludicrous.

The morning was faded and blustery by the time he recrossed the Aurora Bridge. He was distracted by the odd wobble of a hunched and hairy man standing on the other side of a swiftly approaching bus stop. Despite the serrated chill, the man appeared to be wearing only black jeans and a T-shirt. Vin slowed his Tesla. The guy was rocking, nearly pitching forward from his spot on the curb. Beneath a thick beard, his jaw moved as if he were chewing air. It was the same man who had been jamming up northbound traffic only an hour earlier.

He punched the Tesla's control screen and told his phone to call 911. When a dispatcher answered, Vin got worked up by the possibility that the man might tip himself into the busy street and he started to yell. The dispatcher was patient. She needed more information about where exactly the man was standing. Vin calmed himself and told her where the bus stop was. He told her that the man had been crossing traffic only an hour earlier as if he were Moses parting the Red Sea. Only this Moses hadn't been leading anyone out of bondage but just might wreck cars and kill innocent people because he wanted to part the goddamn Red Sea for no good reason when he didn't have a safe way to do it. The dispatcher still didn't understand where the man was. Vin concentrated on clearing his anger and answering her questions.

AT THE LUNCH WITH HIS father, Joaquin Brooks offered Vin a house-sitting job for at least a few months, but possibly much longer. The house had been custom built to the exacting specifications of a client, a woman named "Nerdean" (no last name), and Joaquin said it was worth a visit even if he didn't want the job. That evening, Vin arranged to meet his friend, Bill Badgerman, at a Caffé Vita near the house and they walked over together.

Bill showed up late, per usual, and wanted to hang out first and "decompress." While Bill downed two macchiatos, Vin got excited explaining what had been lost when he left Sigmoto and he accidentally backhanded his twelve-ounce triple latte. A barista rolled out a bucket and mop to clean up while Vin was throwing paper napkins on the floor in an attempt to help. After the barista fended him off, Vin took the last quarter inch of unused paper towels from the counter and dropped them into the compost, then wiped his hands on his jeans and joined Bill outside.

"Why did you do that?" Bill asked.

"What? It was an accident." He didn't want to defend the spill, but he would if Bill was going to make a big deal out of it.

"Why did you throw away what was left of the paper towels? Those were perfectly good."

"Oh. I guess the spill seemed important enough to use the whole pile."

"It wasn't, man. That was just you." Bill seemed annoyed at being embarrassed in front of a new barista, Charlotte, whom he'd been trying to flirt with. Bill and Vin had been friends since third grade and though Bill could be painfully shy, he was always thinking about women.

Vin was slimmer than Bill, his shoulders narrower, his skin a little darker. Vin's mother was the reedy youngest daughter of a dermatologist from a village in Gujarat. Bill knew nothing about his own biological parents, beyond the fact that his mother was Native American and had given him and his sister up for adoption. He was narrow eyed, with jet-black hair and broad, muscled shoulders. He asked, "You going to see Beth later?" as they started walking toward the house.

"No. Like I told you earlier, she doesn't want to see me anymore."

"I guess I don't remember. If you did tell me." Bill was dragging the pace, showing he wasn't fully placated on the subject of the spill.

Vin said, "You know, I think about her every once in a while," and regretted it right away when he saw Bill's fractional wince. His own pulse jumped.

Bill said, "Who do you mean?" Pretending he didn't understand. Vin changed the subject.

• • •

TOURIST LITERATURE OFTEN DESCRIBES SEATTLE as a "city of seven hills," entertaining the notion that the city's geography connects it to a magisterial if somewhat dilute international tradition whose archetype is Imperial Rome. Vin knew contemporary Seattle had more than seven large hills and that there was some debate about which were the main seven, but he believed that every list would include Queen Anne Hill, whose southern slope defined the northern edge of downtown and provided iconic views of the Space Needle in the foreground and the misty prominence of Mount Rainier's volcanic cone behind. They found the huge house snugged into the western slope of Queen Anne Hill, beneath the lookout benches at Marshall Park and facing Puget Sound. The house's exterior was armored in broad rectilinear panels of aluminum and teak. Inside, three stories were stacked above a half-basement, all in cool creams and schist-textured grays; aluminum plating was embedded in the walls as if it were hanging art.

"It's almost eerie, man." Bill strutted in and quickly left Vin behind as he circulated through the open rooms of the first floor, including the big modern kitchen, separated from an expansive dining area by a generous island counter. Except for a single card table near the island and four small folding chairs, the dining room's golden hardwood floors were unburdened by furnishings. On the west side of the room, a wall-to-wall picture window framed a full view of the evening sunset as it spread its deep orange glow over the islands and water.

Vin followed as Bill, straight-backed and with his chest pushing forward like a pigeon's, circled the first floor before inspecting the refrigerator. Vin had always thought the rigid way Bill held himself wasn't just cocky but also had a kind of showy rectitude. It was Bill serving notice that he'd make his own choices.

Bill slid the crisper drawer closed. "No food. There's not even carrots. There's a beer though. One. Guess you don't get one."

Vin said he was going to check upstairs, which was also unusually uncluttered. The second floor had three large, empty bedrooms and a shared bathroom. There were a few bits here and there, a brush with the sales tag still glued to it, a couple of cheap pens in one empty bedroom and a chewed paperback titled *Life in a Medieval Castle* in another. On the third floor, the spacious master bedroom held a queen-size bed, tightly made up with crisp white sheets and two thin, rust colored blankets. A black, cheap looking media cabinet supported a sixty-inch TV with a blizzard of connected devices—a PlayStation, at least one Xbox, an ancient Wii, a Switch, a couple of ancient TiVo-branded boxes, an Apple TV, a cable box, a Chromecast, an Amazon Fire, a satellite box, and some other things Vin didn't recognize. All of the devices were on, various LED lights signaling oblivious electronic commotion. A remote control with a touchscreen rested on the cabinet. Vin thought, there's your artificial intelligence.

Back downstairs, Bill was gazing out the picture window while finishing off the beer. "This place is a mansion." He glanced over his shoulder at Vin. The waters of Puget Sound were beginning to purple. "With this view, you're actually obligated to party. Regularly. It's almost as if you really made a bunch of money with your company." He laughed at his own joke, the "heh heh" laugh. "It's like you bought yourself a dream home. Oh, sorry man."

"Yeah. I'm house-sitting. I'm a house sitter."

"You said they didn't know when she was coming back, right?"

"No. I don't think they even know where she is."

"See. You could lose all this anytime, maybe next week if you're really unlucky. And you have been. So you've got to get started."

Bill thumped up the staircase. Vin sat in one of the folding chairs beside the card table. Sitting made the huge room feel even bigger.

"I thought she was supposed to be a genius," Bill called down the staircase awhile later, as final light bled up from behind the mountains and the sparks of the city wavered on cooling charcoal water.

"She is," Vin yelled.

"Well, why aren't there any computers, anywhere?" Bill shouted.

And that was kind of interesting. No electronics other than the cluster of devices around the TV that Joaquin Brooks had said was supposed to stay on all the time. There were a handful of cups, bowls, and plates in the kitchen, a cheap set of flatware in one of the drawers. For a house she meant to come back to, this "Nerdean" sure had cleaned the place out.

CHAPTER 2

The Missing Girl

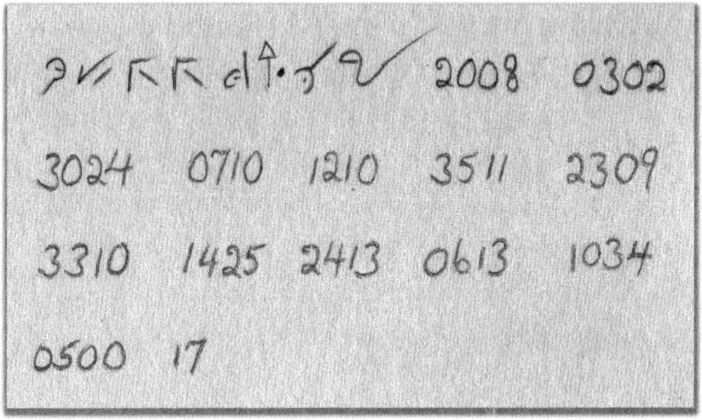
2008 0302
3024 0710 1210 3511 2309
3310 1425 2413 0613 1034
0500 17

The electronics that were supposed to remain powered made the master bedroom feel inhabited. Rather than sleep there, Vin put an air mattress in a bedroom on the second floor.

After his second night in the house, the puzzling birdcall of the doorbell rang in the early morning. Vin, in khaki shorts and his brown "Faux Museum" T-shirt, found Joaquin Brooks standing on the white cement porch, a thick leather portfolio tucked under one arm.

"Good morning, Vin." Joaquin was a heavy-set, middle-aged man about Vin's height, with darker skin and short brown hair.

He was wearing a tan, impeccably tailored suit and black leather loafers with small tassels that looked soft despite their high shine. He smelled good. "May I come in?"

When they'd met, Vin hadn't talked much because he'd wanted to listen to Joaquin, who'd clearly spent a lot of time honing his speech. His lack of an accent was so pronounced it was almost a kind of accent, maybe a variant of Network English, which Vin had read about. Joaquin had the glowing bass of a news anchor and his unhurried, melodic cadences coaxed syllables apart in surprising ways. His diction should have sounded affected, primarily because he avoided contractions and used unusual constructions and "whom" rather than "who" for the objective case. It shouldn't have worked, but combined with his unusual inflections it did, and produced a calming, almost hypnotic effect.

Vin stepped aside and Joaquin nodded as he passed. They sat on the flimsy plastic chairs at the card table.

"So, how are you finding the place, now that you have had a little time to settle in?" Joaquin asked.

"It's beautiful."

"And, do you believe you will be willing to stay?"

"I like it." Vin nodded.

"Oh, I am very pleased. Of course, as I once mentioned, you can bring in a few pieces of your own furniture. Or purchase one or two new pieces. Nothing too elaborate, but I can provide a small expense account. I will appreciate your consideration of reasonable limits."

"Thanks. I'm okay right now though. I kind of like the openness."

"I see."

"And that great view is like furniture too, in a way, isn't it?"

"Is it?"

"And we're not sure when she's coming back, right? Maybe she should find it the way she left it."

"I see. I appreciate that, Vin, but Nerdean has given no indication that she will return at any specific time. Frankly, I consider it a possibility that she may not ever be back. I believe that if she does return, it will not be for a long while. At least a few more months."

"Yeah. This place has so many curious things like that attached to it. When will she come back? Where has she gone? I like that."

Joaquin's smile was almost condescending. Vin said, "You said that she didn't want you to install an alarm system?"

"No. That is correct. Of course, that was why I felt that it would be very important to find a house sitter, after the break-in that occurred next door." Joaquin was a rendering of the human male as a shiny object, whole and separate from his environment, with no intimation of what might be happening in the spaces within. Vin almost felt sorry for what he was about to do, for touching Joaquin's smooth surface and causing ripples.

"Well, I think I may know something about that."

"Oh?"

"I think she didn't want a house sitter because she didn't want anyone looking at the electrical system. That might also be why she didn't want you to install an alarm."

"Really? Why do you imagine that she would be concerned about the electrical system?"

"You've been upstairs, right? And you've seen all those devices connected to the television?"

"Yes, of course. Though she left clear instructions that I should not stay in the house, I have walked through it regularly.

She contracted for an ongoing measure of my attention. It will be a relief to have you here. I will not need to be quite as diligent about my visits. But yes, the television is—"

"Elaborate?"

"Yes." A brief and pinched smile of annoyance at the interruption. "Precisely, thank you. And she did not impress me as a person with an interest in movies and other such things. She seemed very focused, very active. I have not met her in person. I assume she is a bit awkward, a bit unusual."

"I think you're right, that she's not interested in any of those things. None of those devices are actually doing anything. They're all modified, controlled by a system that just blinks their LEDs."

"Oh?" Joaquin set his portfolio flat on the table and folded his hands on top of it. "Well, I am surprised."

"I don't think you are. You don't really seem surprised."

Joaquin's gaze intensified for a moment but he relaxed quickly. "I am. Why do you believe she might leave things in that state?"

"For the electricity, obviously. You pay the bills, right? I found the meter and it's running pretty fast. She wanted to give you an easy explanation for the high bills." Joaquin examined and refolded his hands as he patiently listened to what Vin was saying. "I don't think she expected you to figure it out. I mean, even if all those things were on all the time they wouldn't use all that much electricity, so she was just betting you wouldn't look into it."

"No. I see. And I suppose she was right. I did not figure it out."

"I think you did."

Joaquin flattened his hands on his leather portfolio.

"And that's really why you wanted a house sitter. Because there was no break-in next door."

A pause, then, "You checked."

"Of course."

"And you found nothing, which does not greatly surprise me. There was no police report. Many crimes go unreported to protect property values, and the neighbor in question has plans to move soon."

"Well, I also talked with the neighbor."

Again, Joaquin offered Vin the annoyed half smile, this time followed by a curt nod. "I see. That is interesting because I was told there had been a break-in. You are very industrious for a house sitter."

"I'm an entrepreneur."

Joaquin inclined his head slightly.

Vin decided to ignore Joaquin's insistence on the now discredited break-in. "I think Nerdean actually chose this house because the neighborhood is safe. There's no real crime to speak of. There aren't break-ins. Every house is alarmed except this one. You chose me for an entirely different reason. You talked to my dad. You expected me to be industrious. You wanted me to look at that rigged pile of junk and get curious about why it was there."

"But, of course, I did not choose you. It was serendipity. Your father mentioned your situation to me. I thought we might be able to help each other."

"Well, you hired me."

From down the long slope of Queen Anne Hill, the deep, prolonged groan of a marine horn sounded. Joaquin waited for it to end.

"A gut decision. I always trust my gut."

"Why didn't you just tell me what was going on?"

"It is in my nature to be circumspect, a characteristic that has often proven valuable. And, the terms of my employment also specifically state that if certain subjects arise, I must forbid any investigation of the systems in the home, including the electrical wiring. I can only discuss the conditions of my employment if I judge that avoiding the subject might create suspicion."

"I've never heard of a contract like that."

"Yes. My employment agreement is very unusual."

"You still want me to stay?"

"Oh, yes. Oh, yes."

ONE BY ONE, VIN'S DAYS in the house were flattened and lost. He bought his own wireless access point so he could get online without touching the other electronics. He bought a blender and established a diet of smoothies, until he got tired of them, followed by pizza, until he tired of it, followed by smoothies, then pizza, etc. He spent time walking about the neighborhood struggling with an aimless, incurious lassitude.

Activities meant to kill time—video games, porn, aimless Internet browsing, Twitter wars, 4Chan, whatever—were fundamentally irrelevant and therefore intensely boring. He joined in a few pranks to experience the "lulz," but there was no satisfaction in it—torturing clueless bunnies who metaphorically stuck electrodes to their lubed craniums without any notion of the potential risks. It made him feel bent. It wasn't a worthy use of his limited time in the universe.

Nerdean had obviously gone to a lot of trouble to keep her secrets hidden and, after encountering what he believed was an inflamed avarice beneath Joaquin's brightly glazed crust, Vin thought he could understand why. At Kerry Park, a small overlook with an expansive prospect that included the Space Needle, the downtown skyline, Mount Rainier and Puget Sound, he watched as wedding parties, teenagers, families and cliques of friends took in the breadth and reassuring stability of the view. He dozed in the soporific warmth of the mid-afternoon sun.

He sometimes tried to battle the sameness of the passing hours, but if he tried too hard he found himself thinking about his final months at Sigmoto, and all the mistakes that other people had made. His schedule began to shift as he woke in the wee hours and stayed awake later, poking around online or starting miscellaneous courses from the Internet schools that kept sprouting up like daisies. Bill asked about parties at the house, but Vin didn't want any encumbrance on his time. He didn't want to be involved in plans.

When this dreamlike waking life was punctuated by rare calls from family, he told them about the courses he had started. Whenever he began to relate what had gone wrong with the company, he could sense their attention wavering, at least until they could talk about themselves again. They didn't understand what he was going through. He sometimes yelled at them for their complete lack of sound structural thinking, and their incomprehension of what actually happened at Sigmoto. He didn't want to cut them off completely, but decided he had nothing meaningful to say to them. He finally accepted their diagnosis that he was depressed, but didn't feel like doing anything about it.

The puzzle of the house encroached with creeping inevitability on the regions of his boredom. While wanting to respect Nerdean's wish to remain hidden, he also began to do just a little bit of research online and, as finding information about her proved difficult, it started to feel like a game.

Nerdean had been an orphan and ward of the state. When she was sixteen she'd chosen her own name. She only had the one name, as if she imagined herself a pop icon, or she wanted a break from her past. She had earned a master's degree in physics and then a dual PhD in neurosciences and molecular and cellular physiology, all in her early twenties. She apparently didn't like photographs; he couldn't find a single one. The most substantial single document he came across was a short profile on the blog of an intellectual property lawyer. By the time she turned twenty, Nerdean had made several million dollars by selling a handful of software patents to a licensing company that the blogger indignantly described as a patent troll.

She was also listed for a time as a staff member at a lab run by a large cancer research hospital. In the few years she worked there, the lab earned some press for research on suspended animation. But after generating a lot of excitement and securing significant funding, the lab went silent. The project leader, who had done a well-received TedX, stopped giving interviews. Descriptions of the work on suspended animation were removed from the lab's web pages.

In a more recent article about digital brain interfaces, a researcher at the University of Washington was quoted saying, "We had a short but fruitful consultation on the structural subtleties of the proisocortex with the ever elusive Nerdean."

And that was it, pretty much everything he could find despite many hours of searching. As days passed and he idly pondered those few morsels, Vin created his own portrait of who Nerdean was, a model with no image.

WHEN THE DOORBELL RANG, VIN finished what he was doing, running his palm over the final feet of dark low pile carpet in the basement, then tracing his index finger over the carpet's edge. He rocked back on his heels and picked up the needle-nose pliers. It had taken him a long time to identify the sound, a recording of the Black-capped Chickadee's "Hey Sweetie" call, a single high note followed quickly by a lower note that fell off like a trailing syllable. The electronic Chickadee called again.

"What's going on, man?" When he opened the door, Bill was waving a small bag of bud. "Why'd you take so long?"

"I'm busy," Vin said. It was a warm evening and he was sweating. He pulled at his black T-shirt to unstick it from his chest.

"This place has to have AC," Bill said.

"She's here," Vin said.

"You've got a guest? Beth?"

"No, Nerdean. She's in this house, probably under it."

"Okaaay. She's under the house. Did you kill her?" Bill wiped at the hair flattened against his own forehead. He looked refreshed but his dark brown eyes were slightly glassy and maybe his pupils were a little dilated.

"No, I didn't kill her. What kind of person do you think I am?"

"Nice. We've known each other for forever but you still surprise me with the different ways you find to be offended. That was a joke. You were the one who said she was under the house."

"You know what I meant."

"How? How could I know what that means?" Bill was pushing into the foyer. "Jesus."

"This isn't a good time."

"Well, this is the time I'm here. Look at you. You're playing detective, obsessed with the missing girl."

"I'm not obsessed. You know how I get. I just started wondering why she left the house like this."

"Nerdean is a fake name, don't you think? A pseudonym? Maybe she's not a genius. She's probably a rich housewife, married and living in Magnolia or Madison Park or somewhere, with three kids. This house was just a project she got bored with."

"That doesn't make any sense."

"No, it doesn't. But it's still a lot more likely than that she's under the house."

Vin glanced outside as a brindle cat slipped from a low cluster of *Achlys Triphylla*, whose common name is "sweet after death" because when you crush the leaves they smell like vanilla. The cat fell on its side in the middle of the front walk and stared at him brassily. He shut the door, wanting to close off the cat. The door's spring-loaded weights caught and guided it firmly and slowly into place.

He said, "Talking with you is like carrying air."

"Okay. I don't know what that means either. So, what are you doing?"

Before Bill had shown up at a random time with his pointless agenda, Vin had known exactly what he was going to do. As Bill waited for an answer, Vin looked at the sharp tips of the pliers he was holding and then looked at Bill's face, Bill's eyes. It wasn't something he would ever think about, but the connections just lined up in front of him: his frustration, the tips of the pliers, Bill's eyes.

Bill said, "Have you gotten any sleep in the last twenty-four hours?"

"I don't think so."

"My friend, you're lucky I got tired of hanging out alone. By the way, you need to shave. You're doing that obsessive thing. Okay, maybe it's *almost* normal, and I get it, you found something interesting. But it just kind of looks like you might be losing it a little."

"I'm fine. I've been looking for her."

"She's a grown rich woman. She can take care of herself. And you stink, too, man. Did you know that? Let's smoke some of this. You can smoke a lot and then go to bed. You look like you need it. Then, when you wake up you can take a shower and shave and it'll be a new day."

Vin felt his head twitch involuntarily. The hand clutching the pliers was very tired. Maybe Bill was right. He walked past Bill and up the stairs to the kitchen, to the drawer where he kept a lighter.

Bill fell into one of the folding chairs. He lifted the little bag of pot and tapped a finger against it. "You have that same look you had sophomore year when you were crushing on Leana Rono and you didn't want to talk about it."

"You always say that." Vin found the red plastic lighter and flipped it at Bill. It bounced off Bill's wrist but he managed a flailing catch before it hit the floor.

Vin said, "I don't even know what Nerdean looks like. I can't find a picture of her."

"Instagram?"

"No."

"Well, I always say it because it's always true. You only have one mode with women. You're like, ah, ah, ah." Bill rocked his head and body in a parody of wide-eyed lustful panic that was kind of funny, but only because Bill was funny. "So, what do you mean, she's under the house? Do you mean, like, in a bunker?"

"No, forget it. I didn't mean anything."

"Really? It sounded like something."

"It wasn't." Vin didn't want to explain, but still, the angry way he barked at Bill surprised him. Bill made a face and raised a hand in mock defense.

"Okay. Don't mind me. I'm just here to visit a friend."

. . .

AFTER BILL LEFT, VIN'S MIND was buzzing. He slept a little but woke up stoned and ate two slices of cold pizza. He wanted to flip a crust into the garbage disposal rather than reach across the counter to lift the lid off the aluminum champagne bucket he was using for compost, but his stoned brain was stopping him. His stoned brain preferred that he follow the rules: food waste should go into the champagne bucket. He stared, trying to remember which task his other hand, the empty one, could get started on. He remembered that it should be flicking the switch that turned on the garbage disposal, but doing that wouldn't help him with the compost. He was stymied.

Then he imagined—saw in his mind's eye—one hand flicking on the disposal while the other was in it, getting shredded. He winced and felt a flood of fear and adrenaline that made his eyes water. Then a sentence appeared in huge, silver, 3-D letters inside his brain. The letters said, "It's in an appliance." Even though the letters hovered in non-space inside his brain, they cast a shadow.

He lowered himself to a squat, turned, and leaned back on the counter, the pizza crust forgotten. Slowly he folded over and lay on his side. He felt as though all of space and all of time were expanding out from where he was lying and at the epicenter of everything there stood a being that made his own existence irrelevant. He closed his eyes and tried to slow his juddering pulse. Eventually, he fell asleep.

HE DECIDED TO SEARCH INSIDE every electrical device, and began by unplugging and disassembling each of the boxes clustered around the TV, unscrewing or prying them open while sitting amid a technician's debris field of Phillips and flat-head and Torx screwdrivers, pliers, hex keys and spudgers, all of various sizes and shapes. As he worked, he set out the internals of each gutted object until neat rows of tiny screws, plastic clips, black plastic boards, and foam heat pads striped the warm floor. Any of the devices could be hiding a wireless connection, which might control a switch.

He had stopped considering whether or not Nerdean might want this done. He told himself that it was important to find her. She might be in trouble.

After the first day of pulling things apart, he'd discovered nothing of note and everything in the master bedroom was dismantled. He slept fitfully but woke at a reasonable hour feeling refreshed. He decided to find what he was looking for before spending too much time reassembling devices. He removed the panels of fuse boxes, thermostats, and external metering boxes, opened and disassembled air exchangers, air quality detectors, and curtain automation engines.

He finished at around eight, and then spent a couple of hours putting some of the equipment back together. It was a warm night and with the air exchanger in pieces the bedroom sweltered.

The next morning, tired but still enthusiastic, he brewed a pot of coffee and got back to work. He dug into the doorbell, which had a particularly maddening security plate that snapped closed on his fingertips several times in a row. He finally defeated it with a rubber mallet, leaving it permanently bruised. He used the same mallet to pop open a panel that granted entry to plumbing and electronic control for the jetted bath attached to the master bedroom. He stripped portions of the baseboard to find and pull apart the hidden speakers for the built-in audio system. To be thorough, he removed all the rest of the base-boards throughout the house.

Late in the evening of the third day of his project, he began to pay attention to a gnawing worry that he might have gone too far. There were now many pieces of many things scattered about the house. Despite a devotion to organization and systematic disassembly, he had begun to lose track of the fussy bits of devices, and even the location of some tools. He had also created a few inconvenient artifacts, such as a doorbell that remained mysteriously non-functional after reassembly. (He had killed the chickadee.)

He descended to the largest room in the basement, the only place in the house that wasn't too hot, and lay on the carpet in that dark, open space. He closed his eyes and considered the mess he'd made of the house.

This was how things had been with him since he was a kid. He could be productive, and very creative in the first flush of a project. He could imagine great things and see himself doing the nitty-gritty labor required to achieve them in vivid detail. But something always went wrong. It was as if a seam of chaos were part of the very substance of his ideas, present at the moment he conceived them. It grew within his plans, a tiny malevolent uncertainty that became a critical but unnoticed gap in logic and then spread into a network of cracks, expanding fissures of risk and negative consequence. Each of those crevices grew until they all became things in their own right, distractions that eventually overwhelmed him.

It was as if what was really wrong was something in him, as if he himself were the flaw in an otherwise functional system. He was a destructive self-reference, his life a liar's paradox of flesh and free will. Three days earlier he had had a perfectly good situation as a house sitter in a custom mansion. And now he had destroyed the house.

He rolled onto his side, but that hurt his shoulder. The concrete under the carpet was inflexible, unforgiving, and the carpet was not thick. He rolled back and threw his arm forward in exasperation. His fingertip smashed into something.

He gasped and pulled back his hand and curled up around it, sucking in breath and waiting for the pain to ease, amazed at how much a single finger could generate. As he recovered, he sat up and slowly gathered himself and then stood, a rising excitement lifting him.

He found the room's light switch—he hadn't pulled apart the light switches in the basement yet—and turned on the light. He was looking for the thing that had hurt his finger, a small thing on the floor near the wall. But there was nothing on the floor of the room. He stared at the area where his finger had hit something. He might have been misremembering the sensation. His finger could have hit the wall.

But it hadn't. He turned the light back off and waited impatiently for his eyes to adjust. When they did, the dark carpet gave away nothing. He slowly walked into the room and then squatted and placed his palms near the wall and began to move his hands over the coarse carpet. Almost immediately he bumped into an elevated square, right at the edge of the wall. He couldn't see it, but it felt as though it was raised about two inches and was roughly an inch on each side. Its sides were metallic, smooth and cool. He was sure that it wasn't there when the light was on. He pressed on it but it didn't respond. Nothing happened.

He turned the light back on and traced the carpet along the edge of the wall. No sign of the elevated square. He turned the light off again and confirmed that the square had reappeared.

He sat cross-legged beside the wall, staring at the point where the square stood two inches above everything else, invisible in the darkness, and he laughed. He fell to his side laughing and stretched out again on the dark carpet in the cool room. He had found her. He was right. He laughed and laughed and laughed.

HE STILL DIDN'T KNOW HOW to reach her. The house had only begun to whisper to him, the floor had divulged one single secret; there was more to do; he would have to listen closely to hear what the house was saying. So—start from the beginning: anything worth defending was worth defending carefully. And any single mechanism that Nerdean used might be found accidentally. What if someone happened to walk into that dark room and, despite its size and inconvenient location, happened to hit that one raised piece of floor, just stumble on it? It wasn't enough to just hide it in the dark. There would also have to be a lock. To reduce the possibility of an accidental activation, Nerdean would have to install a second trigger.

He began to work through possibilities until he felt himself following a thing that felt like truth. She had used electricity to raise the tiny bit of carpet, so the easiest answer would be a switch inside the fuse box, which was in another room in the basement. The last two fuses in the box were both very large and not labeled, which seemed odd in a house of this caliber, but not too odd. People can get sloppy toward the end of large construction projects. And there was a tiny bit of residue on the plastic beside both of the switches, which might imply that labels had been peeled away.

He didn't want to flip unlabeled fuses. Nerdean had made an effort to mislead Joaquin about how the house was using electricity. Flipping fuses might cut a critical connection and, if she was doing what he suspected, it might actually endanger her.

Of the two fuses, the top one was probably installed first. It would power equipment. The bottom one was probably installed after everything was already working. He'd been pacing as he considered the situation. He walked over to the box and before he was really sure what he was planning to do, he flipped off the bottom fuse.

He waited, frozen in the wake of what he had just done. It was possible—within the realm of possibility—that he had just killed her. But anyone could flip a fuse at any time. Would it really be his fault if her system were so poorly designed?

He walked into the large empty room where the light was off and stepped on the raised square of carpet, adrenaline making his foot shake. As he touched the square it retracted smoothly, sinking quickly until it was flush with the floor.

A moment later, there was a soft rustle from the center of the room as the edges of two pieces of carpet rubbed together. A square of floor about two-and-a-half-feet on each side rose with steady precision and light breathed up from below. Then one side swiveled higher until the panel was on edge. An open door. Vin stepped to the center of the room and looked down a long, bright, human-sized rabbit hole.

Several dull thuds sounded from upstairs, and a muffled shout. Vin had broken the doorbell and someone was battering on the door. He took a step away from the hole and stumbled back another step. He walked out of the room and looked up the stairs that led to portions of the house whose existential integrity hadn't been compromised.

Then he walked back into the room and stared down the

hole. Metal rungs lined one side of the chute. He could see the bottom, maybe fifteen feet below. What most concerned him was that the hole and the hatch that capped it were real.

Even though he had considered the possibility of something like this happening, he could not have prepared himself for its reality. A double-secret passage into the heart of Queen Anne Hill had quietly opened up in his basement. A thing that never happens had happened in his life.

CHAPTER 3

The Notebook and the Crèche

"What happened to your doorbell?"

It was late evening, the air darkening. Vin tried to answer but no words came out. Bill's face wrinkled with concern. "You actually look worse. Where were you, man? Why didn't you answer?"

"I have a lot of work to do." Bill was interrupting him again, this time at a critical step in what could be a turning point in history. In the history of the world.

Bill shouldered him aside, pushing into the house. "You might not have time to get high, but you have time." He took the short flight of stairs to the first floor in two long strides and then stopped. His head swiveled slowly left to right, absorbing the changes.

"You finally moved in."

"You have to leave. I don't have time for this."

"Really?" Bill stepped out of sight.

"Yes, really," Vin shouted. He ran up the steps, his feet almost slipping on the smooth treads. When he reached the living room he stopped.

Beyond the dominating picture window, the waters and islands of Puget Sound were dark and glittering. A distant cargo ship and a state ferry towed the white scars of their wakes through a field of liquid scree and small, colored pricks of brightness on a far shore billowed hazily under haloing mist, all of it spread out beneath the entirety of naked space, an endless hollow sky scored by the few stars resolute enough to shine through both an endless abyss and the building light of human endeavor that rose to meet it.

"You're making a mess," Bill said. "What are you doing? You're pulling this place apart."

Bill sounded as if he were talking to a puppy, a creature incapable of self-reflection. Vin flushed with embarrassment. Bill had caught him metaphorically chewing the furniture.

"I don't have to explain." Vin glanced around the room. The damage was worse than he thought it should be. He didn't remember being that violent with the baseboards.

"Well, wow, that's a strange thing to say. Of course you don't have to. I'm not the ganja squad of the Spanish Inquisition. Are you worried about something?"

"I'm in the middle of a project"—Vin was speaking quickly— "and, it's not all that important, but . . ." He didn't know how to end the sentence. He swallowed.

"Okay. No sweat. But you're acting a little bit like evil already won and the world's now a place where people just eat each other. Did you find something?"

Vin became aware of the distance between himself and Bill. Bill, watching him closely.

"You did," Bill laughed. "You did, didn't you? What is it? What did you find?"

Vin's eyes widened. He was trapped.

"C'mon, man, what . . ." but Bill's voice trailed off. Then he said, "Wow, you're freaking out." He took a step toward Vin, then slowly turned and walked to the island. "You know, okay. Maybe you don't have to tell me."

Bill glanced at Vin and moved into the kitchen, stepping close to the refrigerator, he glanced at Vin again, then he moved to the pantry door and glanced back. He said, "It's not on this floor, is it?" And then he was heading to the second floor.

Vin walked around the island to the far counter and the cheap, slotted wood block that bristled with the handles of kitchen knives. He stared at them as he heard Bill knocking around upstairs.

"What the hell?" Bill yelled down.

Vin saw his own hand resting on the counter beside the knives. He heard Bill scrambling up to the third floor. Bill was Vin's oldest friend. Vin loved him, no matter how exasperating he could be.

And Vin knew that he was not a person who would do what his own hand was telling him he might do. No matter what he imagined or saw in his mind's eye, no matter how angry his occasional ranting or how violent his dreams, no matter how often he woke from a wrenching nightmare into this world of physical laws and normal time, this world in which he drew warm air into delicate lungs and in which his blood circulated through tender extensions of veins, arteries, and branching capillaries; in the *real world* he simply could not do the kind of thing that his hand—by resting so close to a solid thicket of slim and tapering knives—was implying he might. It wasn't possible. Vin tried to see himself from outside his own form, to see how unimportant this moment really was in the long body of eternity.

Bill came banging back down the stairs. "Alright, I give up. What's the secret?"

Vin lifted his hand off the counter and ran his palm over the stubby ends of the knife handles. "I pulled everything apart because I was trying to figure out what was going on with the electricity." He turned away from the knives and walked toward Bill. "Joaquin, Nerdean's attorney, said that the house is using more electricity than it should."

"Did you check in the basement? Where I presume the fuse panels would be?"

The warmth went out of Vin, a cold wave falling through his legs and into the floor. Bill couldn't go downstairs.

"Yes."

"Okay. I'm only asking."

Bill headed into the dining room, slumped in the farthest of the folding chairs. "Tough project," he said. Vin leaned against the counter, completely uninterested in what Bill might say.

"Anyway, you want to smoke up?"

"No."

"Oh, it's going to be like that, is it? Well, what you don't know yet is that I have brought us a bonus, my lucky friend. I brought us some glass."

Bill had only mentioned meth a few times, but had never offered it before. Vin glanced over his shoulder toward the knives. He pushed off the counter and walked into the dining room, sat in the folding chair across from Bill, who dropped a small, yellowing plastic bag filled with white powder onto the table in front of him. Bill's smile was forced mischief. A weighted and dark feeling of distance spread outward from Vin's center until it surrounded him. In his current state, body exhausted, mind buzzing, he wasn't capable of really understanding where the feeling came from, but through it he could see that Bill had crossed to a place where he didn't want to follow.

"This will put some awesome between you and daylight," Bill said.

"What the hell, Bill? You can't do that."

Bill nodded and his lip curled up. "Alright. I see then. Too busy?"

"Yeah." After a pause, "If you're going to kill yourself, you should leave."

"Okay." Bill cocked his head and stared out the picture window. He said, "I don't know why I bother."

In the many years they'd known each other, they'd had two physical fights, one in elementary school and one in high school. They both knew Vin was no match for Bill, but they pretended he might be. Vin tried to calm himself. He felt breath passing through his nose, muscle lifting his gut.

"I'm still thinking a lot about Kim," he said.

"Fuck you," Bill said each word slowly. Then he stood, walked to the top of the stairs that led to the front door. "Motherfucker. Where are you going to go when they throw your ass out of here? You think of me as your backup, but now you're pissing me off too."

Vin looked away. "I don't need a backup. I have an education."

He heard Bill jump down the stairs. The front door opened and then clicked gently shut.

VIN WAS ALONE BECAUSE HE needed to be. But he didn't immediately go back to the basement. The open hatch and the chute frightened him.

He folded one of the chairs and carried it to the second floor bedroom where clothes and crumpled sheets were massed across his inflatable mattress. He pulled open the sliding door that led to a generous teak terrace and planted the chair on it, slid the door closed so bugs wouldn't go inside.

Vin had first noticed loneliness in elementary school, though he'd probably felt it earlier. All the kids had been learning the same things at the same time, learning about presidents and addition and other countries in portions determined by obscure principles formulated before his teachers were born. The system was nonsense, its lessons obvious, but each day they all repeated its lifeless rhythm. And instead of doing or reading what he wanted, he had had to go to recess or play games. Everyone else liked those things. Vin started skipping school. And then he began to realize that he knew more about many things, but the other kids knew more about topics that still confused him, like how to respond when people ask you questions, and what to wear and how to talk with each other. He thought maybe these relative differences in knowledge would even things out.

But that was a child's dream. As he grew older, he focused on learning things that had been difficult for him and he made great progress, but the other kids still didn't understand what he knew. He began to see that when you added everything up, he would always know far more. And then he saw that although different people did different things well, some few people couldn't do anything well. And it disgusted and infuriated him to finally realize that the world was going to leave a small number of people including his own best friend, Bill, permanently broken.

To other people, Bill had always seemed to have a confidence that could be trusted, but underneath, Vin could see him struggling to contain his fear—of everything—frantically trying to save his own life from everything, all day, every day. The confidence was a fragile front. In school, after only a few minutes on any topic, Bill would get antsy. He was smart, above average, but there was something missing. For a while, his adoptive parents tried to drug him into studying, but Bill was either allergic to the drugs or they put him to sleep. He fought against taking them. His parents never gave up, but Bill stopped taking what he didn't want to.

Bill had been the first person to truly admire Vin's extensive knowledge of things and to value Vin's differences, and Bill protected Vin. Vin had a temper, but he would smolder feebly, too frightened to act. Bill threw punches. When pushed, Vin might become theatrical, even reckless. He might flip a desk or call out a teacher, but he would fold in the face of real opposition. More than once, Bill stepped up to cover Vin's retreat. Bill was serious.

Bill's sister, Kim, was a year younger than the two of them. For the first years that Vin knew Bill, Kim was a weak modifier, a quiet presence whose needs created drag on their rambling play. But during the summer after Vin had finished seventh grade, Kim acquired a bright nimbus that Vin didn't understand, one that had a direct connection to the stillness that overcame him when she was near. He began to avoid her, and that awkwardness created a bond between them.

When Bill told him that Kim had a crush on him, it changed how Vin saw himself, allowed him to believe that he might be a better kind of person. Other people desired her and she desired him. The knowledge buoyed him, even when Kim started dating other people. Then, in Vin's first year of college, as he was just beginning to relax around Kim and they both knew something big was happening, Bill fell apart. He became a shredding, unpredictable cyclone of self-loathing, and he accidentally killed her.

Bill won fights by hitting first. When his opponent was down, Bill would walk away. That awed Vin—Bill's ability to seize a moment and then walk away. But Vin knew Bill didn't have the heart to press his advantage, to hurt someone more than he had to. So it was on the universe—it was the fault of reality itself—that Bill actually ended up killing someone. But it was more than a fault, it was an expression of something deeper and far more wrong that the person Bill killed was the person he loved the most, the person he was closest to.

A soft breeze picked up and the humid evening began to cool. The folding chair was uncomfortable. Vin was hungry and there was pizza in the refrigerator. He wanted to empty his mind, but he'd thought too much about things he couldn't clear away. Most of the time, he dealt with the reality of losing Kim by not thinking about her.

He moved inside to the air mattress and let his mind wander— to the bare walls around him, to the house, to Nerdean, the elusive. He pulled the sheet over himself and closed his eyes. He knew he would have to go back to the basement, would have to climb down the ladder in the pale chute and face what waited there for him. No amount of distraction would change that hatch back into a fantasy. He had trashed Nerdean's house and uncovered her secret. Nothing could undo that.

Then his eyes popped open. What if the closed hatch wasn't intended to protect a secret from being discovered by people above ground? What if it was meant to keep something that was down below from coming up?

THE LIGHT FROM THE OPEN chute had a cool yellow hue. It was near midnight as he stepped onto the first rung and looked up to see his distended shadow shifting on the ceiling like a marionette. He straightened as he dropped one foot toward a lower rung, then another.

When his eyes were almost level with the basement floor he stopped. He had placed *Life in a Medieval Castle* at the hatch's rear edge so it wouldn't be able to shut and trap him in the room below. He continued lowering himself until he could see a room expanding beneath him on three sides. He paused, but no unexpected shadows crossed the walls. He felt vulnerable on the ladder with his back to the open space. He panicked a little and pushed off the rungs early, landing off balance and crumpling to avoid twisting an ankle.

The floor of the room was white vinyl with silver and gray flecks, white acoustic tiles on the ceiling, lighting strips at regular intervals like old fluorescent tubes. Several feet to his right, arrayed side-to-side with about four feet between each, were three large caskets raised at an angle, their near ends low to the floor, far ends higher, their exteriors ivory colored and shining dimly, molded from a material that looked ceramic. A long transparent pane was centered in each casket's thick, red-seamed lid. Two caskets were empty and revealed deep, shadowed interiors, but the pane closest to him was misted, its contents obscured.

He stood, his knee twingeing, an ache that snapped into nothing as his hip aligned. The room extended several feet past the caskets. To his left, a row of computer monitors covered a long black desk. Three white office chairs with tops and sides curving inward like pieces of eggshell were tucked under the desk at regular intervals.

He stepped toward the first casket and strained to see inside, leaning over the top. When his hand touched the pane, the mist cleared. Vin recoiled, pulling his hand off the cool glass and the casket sighed as if exhaling, the pane misting over again.

In that moment the window had cleared, he had been staring into a woman's face. The spot where he'd pressed his hand still sparkled with tiny flecks of moisture. He placed the tips of his five fingers on the pane and the mist cleared again.

Her eyes were closed. She was submerged in bluish liquid

and didn't appear to be conscious. A metallic band crossed the center of her face, covering her mouth. She had a large forehead, a straight, slim nose, and a strikingly pronounced jaw. Her naked body was frighteningly thin and it was difficult to guess her age. Her face was youthful, perhaps thirty years old, though her hair—mostly floating back from her head—was completely gray.

Coin-sized discs held a number of wires to her head, body, and limbs. The wires, floating in the blue liquid, extended to nipples in the casket's walls. Her chest moved with an almost imperceptible rhythm. She was alive. Vin watched her for a long time, flattening his hand on the glass.

A soft soughing started from a far corner of the room—an air conditioner turning on. He lifted his hand from the casket and heard the brief exhalation again as the window misted to hide the woman inside.

He rubbed his palms together, feeling the moist chill of light condensation as he walked to the long desk. At its far end were several enclosed racks of computers. All of them appeared to be on but they were silent, not a single fan whirring. He turned back to the caskets. Several feet behind them rose a full wall of rectangular electronic devices, a steady green light shining on the faceplate of each.

There were three keyboards and touch pads on the desk, each paired with two monitors. Beside the last monitor was a thick, dog-eared notebook, eight inches by ten, with a cover of black paper as dense and textured as leather.

VIN WAS SURE THE WOMAN in the first casket was Nerdean and the notebook was hers. When he woke them, the monitors showed a password prompt and nothing else. He worried that if he did the wrong thing on one of the computers, he might harm her.

In a neat, spidery handwriting regularly intercut with codes, odd symbols and strange drawings, the notebook referred to the entire system—computers and caskets—as a *crèche*. It said the crèche induced a state similar to suspended animation, but that for a subject—a person in the crèche—it would feel like a lucid dream. Vin suspected that he might have missed a critical passage when he realized that Nerdean, who had clearly seen the awesome disruptive potential of safe and enduring suspended animation, was concerned about the subject's experience. Why not simply leave them unconscious?

Vin had several large and innumerable smaller questions. To start with, how did the crèche keep Nerdean alive? And when did she expect to wake up? And how could the crèche maintain both suspended animation and enough brain activity for lucid dreaming over an extended period of time? The notebook had some answers (most of which raised further questions), a great deal of unconnected or indecipherable detail, and a few terse and diary-like personal entries.

TO AVOID A SURPRISE VISIT from Joaquin, Vin called to say he'd gotten overenthusiastic about the electrical system and pulled some of the house apart but was now putting it back together. He said it wasn't a big deal, but he'd be doing it slowly to make sure it was right. When he was done, he'd arrange a walk-through so Joaquin could review things. Vin would pay expenses, of course.

When Joaquin asked if Vin had found anything interesting, Vin improvised, saying the electronics in the master bedroom drew more power than he expected, and he was still looking at communications between them. Joaquin seemed sufficiently appeased.

Bill didn't come by, and Vin called family members to say he was starting a new project. He said the new thing might be bigger than Sigmoto. He was doing a deep dive on the technology and would be out of touch for a while. He figured he'd bought himself at least a month of light contact.

The hatch on top of the chute closed automatically, and opened when approached from below. Vin spent a lot of time in the underground room with his hand on the transparent pane just watching Nerdean float in the blue solution.

The electronics behind the caskets were batteries, but the room still drew power from the local grid. Nerdean's life depended on the design of her system, so she'd built in a few redundancies.

He slept fitfully, and Nerdean appeared more than once in his dreams, naked, silent, floating in the blackness of space. One morning, he woke with a memory of her holding the notebook, its cover crawling as if it were alive. She had opened it and shown him that only a single word was written inside, but no matter how hard he tried, he couldn't read the word.

THE COMPUTERS HAD SURPRISING IDIOSYNCRASIES. For example, the connecting ports were a weird, bespoke-looking nineteen-pin plug. He wouldn't be able to automate a password attack so he started guessing. At first, he worried that a security check might lock the system after too many successive attempts, but it didn't happen and he was soon typing anything that came to mind.

Other than this apparent lack of a threshold on password guessing, the system seemed well designed. Even small details had been considered. The keyboards, for example, were exceptionally responsive and felt good to use; every cable was high quality, neatly bundled and routed through special channels; and the bevel of each battery was pleasingly snugged into its enclosing cabinet. He began to trust the design, to feel that, as long as he didn't physically break anything, the system would help him avoid dangerous mistakes. He worried less about harming Nerdean.

If he was going to find the password, the most likely path would be through clues in the notebook, the only thing he possessed that Nerdean had written. He bought a scanner and scanned every page so he could review them on his laptop.

Nerdean often used an odd mixture of letters, numbers, and mysterious symbols that confounded Vin. Many of the notes looked like specifications, with circuit diagrams or beautiful and intricate drawings of body parts, isolated organs, or small mechanical structures. Most of the drawings were annotated with numbers and short scrawls that might have been distance measurements, materials tolerances, metabolic requirements—anything really. Every so often he'd come across a gnomic expression of frustration, captured in her immaculate, miniature script.

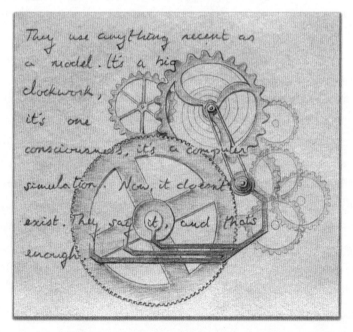

Using the scanned pages for reference, Vin typed out as much of the text as he could understand, and arranged it in a layout as close to the original as possible. It forced him to pay close attention to the details of each page. After only a handful of pages, he noticed a repetition of the word "simulation" and the abbreviation, "sim." He quickly highlighted each instance of related words, including a brief sentence at the back of the notebook, written sideways on the inside margin of a page that the book naturally opened to because the spine was broken: "Nerdean is a simulation."

Familiarizing himself with the dense complexity of her notes and the sheer scope of what she had accomplished had placed Vin in a state of sustained awe, and the brutal certainty of that sentence unsettled him. It struck Vin as an odd, accusatory note, as if Nerdean disliked herself.

One night, after much calculation and guessing, he tried the password *Nerdean is a simulation*, and then tried the same phrase without spaces and with and without capitalization, almost wincing at the message as he typed. Nothing changed. He kept trying. He tried opposite phrases and phrases with similar meanings—*NerdeanIsntHere*, *Nerdean is a Fraud*,—and then, to atone, *Nerdeanispowerful* and *Nerdeanisbrilliant*. He felt his hands begin to act automatically, flying over the keyboard and slamming the enter key. He had solved the puzzle of the house and made it to this room and now a password, a simple password lay between him and the purpose of his work, between him and understanding. He typed until all the joints of his hands ached and threads of sweat slipped across his back and arms. He typed, *Nerdeanisafake* and almost fell off the egg-shaped chair when the screen blacked out. Then he watched in euphoric disbelief as the screen drew a green command prompt.

He stared for a long time at the newly useful screen. He had crossed another threshold. When he finally willed his stiffened fingers to begin interacting with the keyboard again, he imagined a third person watching from a distance. To that person, it might seem as though very little had happened.

HE BEGAN TO TRACE HIS way through the scrolling volumes of information in innumerable files. Each casket, including the one Nerdean occupied, was heavily instrumented. He found an abundance of real-time metrics, for everything from raw material reserves, to power levels, to measures of flow and turbulence in the blue liquid (referred to as "broth"). There were checks on how responsive specific valves were and biomonitors tracking a range of indicators from heart rate, to anatomically localized muscular stress, to mental activity. There was an ongoing analysis of blood chemistry that triggered immediate changes to system functions, including adjustments to the broth. The handful of high-level summaries was all green, indicating system health.

Beyond monitoring, the documents explored an array of technical subjects, from speculation on how a subject's mind remained active while torpor was induced in the body; to descriptions of how the crèche's muscle stimulation subsystem used targeted microshocks to reduce the effects of muscular atrophy; to the various functions of the broth, including its microbial composition and nurturing of skin and hair; how the broth cycled and regenerated; how leads on the subject's neck recognized and responded to signals from her nervous system; how the whole electrical subsystem was wired; how much charge remained in the bank of batteries, and a method for estimating how long that charge might last. He found schematics that showed that huge tanks of raw materials had been buried in the hillside.

Even though the documents said a session in the crèche could be as short as twenty-four hours, he learned from the instrumentation that Nerdean had been immersed for several months. He couldn't find anything that said when she expected to revive.

As he paged through the reams of colorful graphics, seemingly limitless volumes of text, and columns of numbers, he asked himself how anyone could have conceived all of this, let alone created it and kept it secret. He found some intimation of an answer in a history of contracts and subcontracts detailing work on system components without reference to the larger project. They showed that Nerdean had been able to fully disassemble her audacious vision, break the numbingly complex whole into an elaborate hierarchy of sub-projects, and then find a way to complete those and assemble the results.

While he reviewed her documents, looking for a way to wake Nerdean, Vin's respect for her work grew, outstripping his envy until he felt a true reverence—a sensation so intense it could cause brief moments of physical pain—a fluttering ache in his chest. After two almost sleepless weeks spent learning about the crèche, he understood Nerdean to be an epoch-altering genius, apparently capable of anything she imagined. As he daydreamed through spans of near exhaustion, he found himself longing to ask her questions and hear her answers. And as for his quiet doubts (was he being a fool, seduced by things he didn't understand?), he chose to ignore them and they withered.

Fully trusting Nerdean would mean using the device. On a

crisp, late summer morning, he opened the interface that controlled the duration of an upcoming immersion, a simple text file containing two colons followed by the number 24 and the word *hours*, the default and minimum period for immersion. Once he was in the casket, the file would lock. He closed it without changing the number.

He swallowed the recommended sedative with bottled water that he found under the desk, and undressed. He climbed into one of the empty caskets and stretched out against the supporting, cushioned struts. The heavy door lowered over him and he heard bolts shoot home and lock in place with smooth precision. He struggled to calm a lurking panic, defeating it by repeatedly reminding himself that he was trusting Nerdean. He smelled ionized air as the chilled broth began to wash into the casket and cover his feet and the backs of his bare limbs.

As he wafted toward unconsciousness, a needle-like pressure stippled his skin in multiple places. The crèche had deployed its strangely lifelike bots to wriggle over him like a host of robot spiders, measuring his body and adhering to critical points. The system would not apply its breathing apparatus or fully submerge him in broth until its monitors determined that he was unconscious. There was the simultaneous pinch and snap of the initial wire leads clamping down in sixty-four places across his body, and then nothing. Until he woke as someone else.

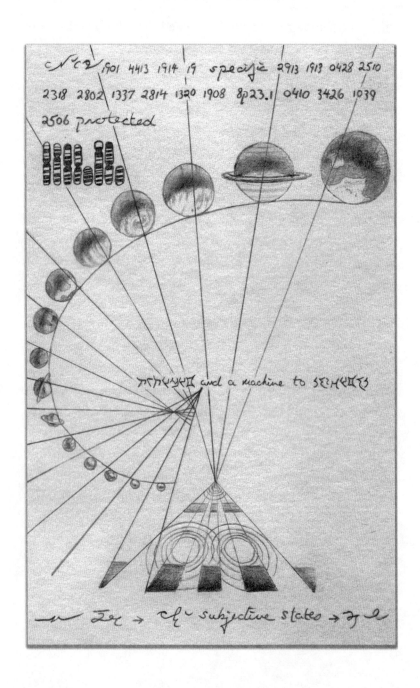

PART II

Tourism

CHAPTER 4

Ambition

His jaw and lips clamp down on a cigar and his cheeks fill with sweet, acidic smoke. The fingers of his hand are unexpected—oddly short and pale. His body folds over itself in novel ways. He's in warm water, his back, buttocks and thighs pressing against the smooth sides of a bathtub. In one hand he holds a sheaf of papers. Beyond the papers is a familiar room, leather and brass, dark and sparkling.

Vin has no memory between blacking out in the crèche and finding himself here. This must be a lucid dream. It pulls at his awareness, requiring attention the way that driving tired does. He's confused and trying to remember who he is. He says to himself, "My name is Vin Walsh." His dream responds with mysterious certainty: "I am Winston Churchill."

He can't turn, can't shift his gaze, can't affect his muscles. Before his free hand rises, he feels an impulse to move it, like being tickled by a thought. Then feels the grit of his own hair against the tip of a finger as well as the movement of that finger on his scalp.

As for the papers in his hand, it isn't him exactly who's

reading them. Unfamiliar thoughts and feelings are moving near and through him, overlapping him. He tires of holding himself separate and relaxes into them, like lowering himself into warm water. He becomes the person whose mind he seems to be inhabiting.

"Stalemate and slaughter." Winston Churchill is practicing phrases for a meeting. "In war we must recognize both opportunity and the potential for disaster. Mindless repetition leads to calamity, but in Europe today we ask our troops to endure the same horrific hours they have endured since the war began. Those who believe in this strategy call it *attrition*, and pledge themselves to its principle, that we are willing to pay more in blood than our enemy. I put it to you that this is not a way forward. We are in need of bold and surprising initiatives, of innovation, of imaginative machines and of sudden momentum on unexpected fronts. Surprise and invention will end the slaughter on the continent and win the war."

Another mouthful of sweet smoke. Words rise from the papers and become part of him.

". . . (C.) Reduction of defences at the Narrows, Chanak.

"(D.) Clear passage through minefield, advancing through Narrows, reducing forts above Narrows, and final advance to Marmora."

Vin understands that these sentences are on a telegram and that the author of the telegram, someone called Vice Admiral Carden, is supplying new and critical intelligence. But intelligence for what, and who is Carden? As he asks himself the question, he sees that Carden's face, relaxed, slim—an admirable Anglo-Saxon profile—eyes thoughtfully hooded, head bent in consideration of a problem. Carden is sharp as a hawk, his full beard and mustache swept back. He is a clear-eyed and cautious hunter, and he knows the Aegean Sea as well as anyone.

There is a strange separation between Vin and the person he is dreaming himself to be, Winston Churchill. In part, the strangeness comes from the accuracy of the dream's rendering of time. Vin can feel each second as it passes, unlike other dreams in which a year might pass with a single taste of claret. And the physical world is also vividly present—this doesn't feel like a dream house; one that might, for example, suddenly transform itself into a crypt. In fact, the dream almost feels like the waking world, but Vin sees and feels things with a fluctuating overlay of unexpected emotion and sometimes even commentary, and he cannot alter his perspective.

Without any prompting from Vin, Winston levers himself up from the bath, towels dry and dons soft underclothes and striped woolen trousers. He sips his watered spirits, savoring the scent of char, peat and alcohol and the weight of the glass.

Winston is thinking that today's meeting will be a turning point. Once again, he will be that young man that his Clemmie married. He shrugs into a starched shirt and then Vin follows the intricate motions of his body as he assembles the public image of Winston Churchill, His Majesty's First Lord of the Admiralty, the hero whose foresight saved the Great Fleet at the start of this conflict, and who is now poised to save the world. Which top hat will best protect the realm?

OUTSIDE, CHILL AIR SWEEPS AWAY the comfort of his warm home. Churchill is in London, where sunlight is always measured, especially in mid-January. The scent of rot and tannins chases away the windborne ghosts of river swells. The world of air has degrees of clarity and its sudden changes can communicate every fact worth knowing; a bright winter morning carries the crisp weight of truth.

Deference from the gloved driver (Thomas is his name), eyes averted as he opens the car door. A smart, horse-drawn hansom rattles past in the road beyond. Winston returns to practicing sentences.

"To capture the great city of Constantinople, I propose a surprise as historic as the gambit of the Trojan Horse. This is a strategy to break the nerve of the Turk in a single stroke, to retire his armies from the board, reopen the Black Sea to shipments of Russian grain, and bring the neutral states to our side of the conflict in anticipation of carving up the Ottoman Empire. And all of this can be accomplished almost solely with naval power, without diverting a single battalion from the deadlock in France."

The ground war in France is a butchery that feeds on the virtue of soldiers. There has to be a choice other than that slaughter. (And if not, then what is the purpose of empire?)

From Vin's perspective, the Winston in his dream has a design problem. That's the right way to conceptualize it. The tools and processes of war need updating. In the hypnotic way that thoughts can glow in dreams, Vin can see that however crushing and horrible war itself might be, the Empire still needs it. Therefore, new approaches are essential. Vin finds this perspective fascinating. It requires the kind of systems thinking that he, personally, excels at.

But other issues linger. Winston has an acute, unarticulated feeling in his lower gut, a concern—or perhaps a fear—that is almost threatening to consume him, and somewhere between that feeling and the chaos of ideas that Vin encounters in his mind there flickers an image, a decorated Colonel in a neatly pressed uniform who is sitting with his back against a stone, a slate of medals shining on his dress jacket; his head and the top of the stone are missing.

AS THE CAR PULLS TO a stop outside Number 10, Winston is pleased to see the lanky profile of Arthur Balfour. Balfour, who would never appear to be waiting for anyone or anything, is simply taking air, but he and Winston speak briefly and enter together. For Winston, Balfour's remoteness is a calming intoxicant. There were years when Balfour was a mentor and champion of Winston's career.

"Beware a fetishistic pleasure in the exercise of power beyond one's comprehension," Balfour had once said to him. "The most frightening thing in the world is a man who from the depths of congenital, benighted ignorance cheerfully decides the fate of life on earth." But it is Balfour's pretense of airy disinterest that is his true gift and greatest lesson.

As the cabinet members find their seats, the First Sea Lord, Jackie Fisher, greets Winston and Balfour with a masculine warmth that lifts Winston's spirits. With his cropped ivory mane, Jackie is fearsome and blunt, Arthur's dispositional antipode. He is as explosive as the muzzle-loading cannon that ruled the waves when his career began and he is Winston's bulwark against naval professionals who distrust their First Lord's youth and inexperience. Together, Jackie and Winston speak for the Empire's Navy with a single voice. Winston's.

THE MEETING BEGINS WITH TALK of Russia. Vin can follow the sense of what is said, but the details waver in proportion to his willingness to relax into the dream of being Winston Churchill. If he pays attention to himself—to being Vin—he loses the sense of the discussion and even accents become difficult to follow. If he forgets himself and listens as if he is Winston Churchill, he has no problem understanding.

For the first time in the dream, Vin is glad he can't affect Winston's body. The men in the room are sedately discussing topics that entangle millions or tens of millions of lives. There are moments, such as when they detail the casualties of the last six months, when he wants the dream to stop. He wants to groan or stand up and shout in appalled disbelief, but he can't. Everyone at the table is similarly unmoving.

As they debate deployments for new volunteers, new men to go to the continent and chew barbed wire, there is a moment when Vin realizes that Winston is amused and is no longer tracking the discussion. Lord Kitchener and Lord French are sitting across the table, though not beside each other. Winston expects the two of them to oppose each other on most issues. French's drooping mustache quivers over his heavy jaw, whereas Kitchener's is waxed to curve up at its ends in a surrogate smile. These two men regularly disagree and Winston imagines a dramatic conflict between their mustaches. He sees the mustaches standing huge and faceless at either end of the table, brandishing sabers made of gray whiskers: *moulinet, parry-riposte, counter parry-riposte, touché, salute, en garde, point thrust, inquartata, touché*, etc. Lord French, the frowning optimist, wins on points; his rakish mustache with its hair saber bends in a courtly and well-groomed salute.

With well-calibrated *sangfroid*, French is saying, "This situation clearly explains France's invitation to the Japanese to field a European army."

His comment draws an audible huff of annoyance from Kitchener, whose mustache trembles with frustration. Kitchener views the invitation to Japan as a vote against his own leadership. Although some might not wish to see an army of yellow men in Europe, Winston has no objection. Ultimately, as Balfour has said, the thing in war is to win.

The topic changes. At last, Winston stands before the wall map and sets forth his case for action in the Dardanelles, their only real choice beyond fighting in the trenches. He begins by describing risks, the mines at sea and forts on the heights. He lists the rewards of success and painstakingly reviews his and Lord Carden's plan to neutralize each risk. He concludes by repeating his central point. "From twelve thousand yards, the big guns of a Lord Nelson–class battleship are three times more likely to strike their targets than an equivalently sized howitzer, and one hit disables the target. Our naval guns are so accurate and our naval gunnery so precise that not only will we hit the forts from safe ranges, but we shall hit, in succession, each and every emplacement. By acting quickly, before the enemy fully comprehends his peril, we will win clear passage to Constantinople."

Winston has been gauging the room while he speaks and believes he may have won over Lloyd George, but Lord Kitchener and Lord Asquith are unreadable. He introduces his *coup de grace*. "Only yesterday," he says, "Admiral Fisher provided new information that, to my mind, decides the matter. Jackie?"

Fisher makes a small nod, then fires off a rapid series of assertions, ending, "As you *know*, the *Queen Elizabeth* is our first *super* dreadnought, and is our *fastest* large ship. She is *irresistible!* Rigged with an *unprecedented battery* of *fifteen-inch guns* with an *effective range* of over *twenty thousand yards*. Moving with *celerity* to join the *fleet*, she may be *leading* in the bombardment at its *outset*. Rather than *test* her new guns with *meaningless* target

practice, we shall *limber them up* by *ending* these *Turkish forts!*"
His open palm slams down on the resonant cabinet table.

The other men in the room are chuckling and casting sidelong
glances at each other. Winston is agitated. Fisher's energetic
performance seemed overly deliberate, even by his flamboyant
standards. Within the room, however, Winston glows with satisfaction.

A quiet overtakes the assembled warlords. If it were possible, then using naval power alone to change the game would
be an unqualified win, and participation by the *Queen Elizabeth*
is a new fact. The Empire's heroes display their conspicuous
approval. There is agreeable muttering and a few palms even
thump the tabletop as reserve tips toward acceptance and acceptance falls to guarded enthusiasm. Vin feels an inward thrill of
triumph.

CHAPTER 5

The Other Resident

Vin was himself again, lying in the crèche. The dream of being Winston Churchill was over and he understood the meaning of the device as he remembered a passage from Nerdean's notebook.

> Why create a machine to render a virtual reality when each of us has one already? With a perfect knowledge of its operator and her desires.

The dream experience had unlocked something in him. In a single day, he had gained a whole life as the kind of man he always knew he could be. He remembered the feel and smell of it, the embrace of the supple leather chair, the sweet cigar smoke in his throat and the complexity of the claret chasing it, and the stimulation—the electric, thought-broadening, gut-loosening, muscle-freeing intensity of all that power.

Feeling light, unburdened, he put a shaky hand on the edge of the open casket. He might jump to the ceiling in a single motion. Could it be that every home in the city (in the country? in the world?) contained a secret like this?

Nerdean had called it lucid dreaming, but Vin knew a man named Jackie Fisher now, remembered arguing with him into early morning hours, debating the logistics of an amphibious attack on U-boat pens at Zeebrugge, Jackie endlessly certain of his contradictory assertions, his blue eyes flaming, spit flying from his thick lips.

Equally surprising, Vin knew what *Zeebrugge* was, and *where* it was. He rocked out of the crèche and logged-in to the middle computer system and typed the strange place name into a search form. A map of the Belgian port filled the screen. It was where he expected it to be.

He pulled on his fallen jeans and dragged his T-shirt on over his damp hair, then sat again and searched for the term "dardanelles strait 1915." He read a Wikipedia article titled "Naval Operations in the Dardanelles Campaign" with a sliding sense of déjà vu.

Over the next few hours, he read many articles. The people in his dream—Jackie Fisher, Vice Admiral Carden, and the others—were all real. After that meeting, Fisher had renounced Churchill's plan and resigned from the government. The swift attack using only naval power had become a ten-month land campaign on the Gallipoli Peninsula that caused close to four hundred thousand casualties. Vin's eyes passed over the number

multiple times before digesting its sense. He had a faint recollection of watching an old World War I movie named *Gallipoli*,
about incompetence and carnage.

When he was too tired to read more, he leaned back in the
eggshell chair. Nerdean's machine did more than induce lucid
dreaming. It must have both invigorated his imagination and
returned endless buried memories—details from the movie,
maybe comments captured from school lessons that he could
never have recalled on his own, passages of books he'd read and
forgotten, knowledge he would never have suspected that he
still possessed. It had used all of that to shape a dream that was
a fulfillment of Vin's deepest ambitions. To influence the fate of
hundreds of millions. To help move the world forward.

And everything had felt real. The shine on the table that the
warlords circled, the subtleties of gestures and postures that
were readable the way the bodies of living people are. Those
details must have come from Vin's imagination, but they were
perfectly integrated with the facts from his memories.

His dream explained why Nerdean had researched subjec-
tive experience during suspended animation and it also clarified
the full scope of her project, which was even more daring and
impressive than he could have guessed. The crèche had connected disparate circuits in his mind, generating new cognitive
capabilities that were able to build a seamless combination
of eidetic recall and creative virtuosity. It had allowed him to
imagine a new reality. Nerdean had built a device that induced
creative genius. She might have even used the ideas behind the
machine to enhance her own abilities, in order to build the full
device. If Vin was right—and he was sure that he was—then
the crèche was an almost unfathomable revelation, and so much
more than he had hoped for.

. . .

HE WANTED TURTLE SOUP BUT didn't have any idea where he might get it. He had left a pizza in the refrigerator though, in case he was hungry after twenty-four hours in the crèche. He carried the box to the card table, flipped it open and eased into one of the folding chairs. The chair felt too light, flimsy and stiff against his skin, almost unreal compared to the soft warmth of the furniture in his dream.

He'd brought the notebook upstairs. He wanted to look for evidence of his new theories about the crèche, but found it difficult to concentrate. He ate the pizza slowly, a cold length of crust drooping over his fingers as he flipped through the notebook's pages.

Midday light filled the open and empty room like nourishment, the distant water silvered under a gray-white sky, and pain came and went in his throat and chest. He kept feeling a sickening sense of *accountability*, his mind imagining casualties from that campaign in the Dardanelles that he had been arguing for.

He needed sleep. He dropped a half-eaten slice back into the box and walked to the stairs, but then realized he'd lost the thread of what he was doing. He went back to retrieve the pizza box and began to climb the stairs. Halfway up, his toe brushed a soft and living thing that flicked against his ankle.

He jerked backward, throwing the pizza box up and almost toppling over, only grabbing the railing at the last second and pulling against it to save himself. A fluffy thing with embedded needles had swept through his legs. Holding the railing, he pulled himself close to the wall and closed his eyes as he bent to sit on the low carpet of the staircase.

When his pulse slowed, he blinked and saw a pair of eyes staring up at him. They were round and green and around them was a cream-colored, fur-covered face: a cat was crouching near the bottom step.

He tried to say "Hello," but his mouth didn't move and the word didn't sound. He tried again, saying it softly, then, "Who are you?"

The cat's eyes narrowed. There might have been movement at its ears.

"Who are you?" he said again, and then, "Who could you be?"

Its gaze shifted so it was no longer staring. It moved a front paw forward and its shoulders relaxed.

"What are you doing here?" he asked, and the cat yawned.

"Come here," he said. The cat stood quickly and ran up the stairs toward his extended hand, pushed into him as he pet it. Yellowish, medium-length fur, white at the ends of its paws and around its muzzle. The touch of it, its warmth and interest in him were profoundly comforting. He bent forward and continued to stroke as it leaned toward his hand and shin.

A measure of pain that he hadn't realized he was feeling drained away and the drenching strangeness of the day faded a bit. He saw the pizza box at the bottom of the stairs and felt as if he had just landed inside himself.

He didn't want to think about Winston Churchill anymore. He stood and the cat stared up at his face. "Let's go," he told it, and walked slowly to the second floor. The cat followed.

He fell on his air mattress and folded the sheet over himself. A tuft of cat hair rose and floated off the bed toward the door. "Cat," he called, and the cat ran over, jumped on the bed and meowed. Its voice was creaky, both demanding and fragile. Vin patted a spot beside him and fell asleep.

. . .

HE WOKE HUNGRY AND THIRSTY in the early morning, opening
his eyes to see the cat watching him from halfway across the
bed. He remembered being Winston Churchill, but the very
specific feeling of inhabiting someone else's body was already
fading and he could think of no way to preserve it. After a
moment of blankness, he wondered what it would be like to be
inside a cat's body, a cat's mind, its *umwelt*. Would he feel the tail
rising and falling? Would he be able to follow a cat's thoughts?
Would there be memories? History? The cat returned his gaze.
Vin wondered where the cat had come from.

He rolled to the side of the bed. The cat called out loudly. It
hopped off the air mattress and hurried toward the stairs, belly
swaying. He heard soft pulling noises—its claws catching on
carpet as it descended toward the lower floor. Vin showered,
shaved and dressed. He heard the cat meowing downstairs.

In the kitchen, near the sink, there was an empty aluminum
bowl with a smear of dried cat food. An identical bowl was half
filled with water. A few cat hairs floated in it.

He went to the basement and then hurried down the chute,
dropping the final few feet into the office. The lights had come
on, as they always did. The air conditioner's hushed whisper was
the only sound. A chill shook him as he placed a hand on the
transparent pane of the first casket. The mist cleared. Nerdean
was still there. She had not gone out and adopted a cat while
he was in the other crèche. Where did the cat come from?

Upstairs, he checked the notebook again, flipping through in
search of a thing he wouldn't have been able to describe—and
then stopped, having found it. While the page included lines
of incomprehensible notation, a beautiful pencil drawing of

a medium-haired cat consumed most of it. The drawing was annotated with measurements and underneath was the large, handwritten name, "Sophie." Vin didn't remember seeing the drawing, but an intuition, like a stranger in his mind, had pulled him toward the notebook.

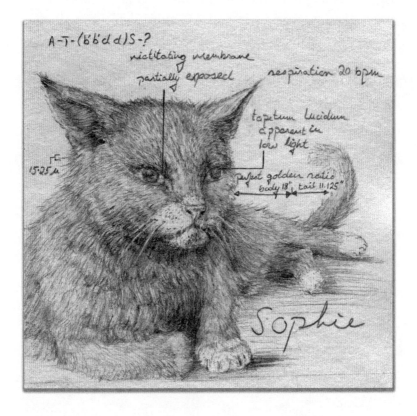

HE FOUND CAT FOOD UNDER the sink and fed the cat and changed her water. Joaquin hadn't mentioned a cat. Vin didn't remember "Sophie" at all. He watched her eat as if she were a ceramic lie.

He was rubbing his chin with the back of his hand as he stepped into the living room and saw a wooden cat platform in front of the picture window. It was covered with brown carpet and topped by a cushion. That hadn't been there either.

He pulled on a windbreaker and left Nerdean's house, the door's mechanism catching in the last inches to guide it shut. The day was clear and cool. He climbed the concrete stairs to the overlook at Marshall Park, a small grassy area on the west side of Queen Anne Hill. Wind brushed against him as he sat on a wooden bench and watched the shadows of the massive grain silos below, watched sunlight like chrome dust on the wrinkling water.

After many rings, Bill answered his phone.

"What the hell, man?" Bill's voice was scratchy with sleep.

"Hey. It's Vin."

"Yeah, I know. The phone tells me who it is. Yours does too. That's what the big name is when the phone starts ringing."

"Something's wrong."

There was quiet.

"There's something wrong, Bill."

"Well, you woke me up, so, yeah."

"No. There's a cat. In Nerdean's house. There's a cat in here. This morning."

"What?"

"A cat. In Nerdean's house."

"A stranger cat? Did it get in a fight with Sophie?"

"What?"

"The cats. What happened?"

Vin didn't answer. Bill said, "Are you going to apologize for the last time we talked?"

"You know Sophie?"

"Are you joking, man? What's going on with you? Did you forget that you told me not to blow weed smoke at her?"

"I don't remember that."

"What's going on? Are you stoned right now? Look man, are you going to apologize or what?"

"About Kim?"

"Yeah, you fucker."

"I'm sorry."

"Okay, apology accepted. I know how you feel about me and drugs. But you don't really understand it. I'm not an addict. I can stop if I want to, like I did before."

"Alright."

"Alright? Don't just *alright* me." A heavy breath. "Shit. Okay, now, you remember the cat's name? That's been dealt with? So, what's going on over there?"

"Bill, I gotta go."

"What?"

"I'm going to get some coffee."

"Well, what are you doing later?"

"I don't know."

"Well, why the hell did you call me then, dammit?"

"I called . . . I called to apologize."

WHILE HE WAITED FOR JOAQUIN to arrive, Vin watched a Bruce Lee video on his laptop. Though the entertainment and martial arts icon spoke with a theatricality that should have seemed like artifice, a confection spun out of condescending B-movie send-ups, he seemed completely genuine. The video was low resolution, a black-and-white close-up of Bruce Lee's long head against a dark background. He rarely blinked as he spoke and his hands gracefully shaped and emphasized his points, which sounded simple but which he invested with gravity. In an era when every gesture of even passing interest spawned an endless lineage of copies and minor variations, Bruce Lee's words sounded clichéd, but he struck Vin as authentic, his commitment to what he was saying created a mesmerizing sincerity. He was talking about the way water changes its form as it fills a vessel and he ended the video with an instruction to "be water."

Such an absence of boundaries seemed irrational, but it was apparently what Bruce Lee believed in, and he was an avatar of human aspiration, a man who had tamed violence and could contain or express it with primal purity. Vin paused the video to respond to the Chickadee's "Hey Sweetie" call, the doorbell having somehow fixed itself.

After a greeting, as they walked room-by-room through the mostly recovered house, it became clear that Joaquin was uninterested in the damage. He nodded a few times but didn't question Vin until they reached the master bedroom.

"And, you took each of these apart?" Joaquin pointed at the individual electronics that glowed and blinked around the TV, his index finger moving in precise increments to clearly indicate one after another.

"Yes." Vin was noticing that the ends of the tassels on Joaquin's walnut-colored leather loafers were brushed with a light blue accent color. "Of course, I don't know what all the internals should look like. I just referenced the electronics inside with what I could find on the Internet, and they all look genuine. But they were shut down. They weren't really drawing the power you'd expect, given the activity portrayed by their"—Vin nodded toward the boxes—"front, blinking lights."

"So, they have been altered?"

"Yes, but not shorted, like I originally said. Their electronics are just bypassed. The exterior lights are controlled independently. That little one there is the master controller, and it runs them all in patterns. So they'll look authentic, I guess."

Joaquin's leather portfolio was clutched in his right hand. He wore a lightweight, neatly fitted, dark-gray suit jacket, almost navy. The perfectly fitted collar of his white silk shirt was starched but didn't dig into his neck. His tie was an embroidered paisley swirl of powder blue on a slightly darker blue background.

He half smiled. "So you still do not know what the electrical power is actually being used for?"

"Not yet."

Joaquin gave him a searching, skeptical look. His voice remained friendly though. "I see. Well, that is too bad." A note of sympathy from a favorite cousin.

"I'm working on it." Vin had a clear feeling of letting Joaquin down.

As they walked downstairs, Joaquin said, "Do not worry about damage to the house. I appreciate that you are conscientious. But in the future, as you explore, you do not need to be concerned about putting things right. Do not spend your time restoring things. Your other activities will be a better use of your time. I will make sure that all of the other details are addressed at the proper time, and that the house is returned to its original condition on a schedule that will satisfy Nerdean."

In the dining room, Vin asked, "How did you meet Nerdean?"

"That is the sort of personal question that my employment contract forbids me from answering."

"It's in your contract, huh?"

"Yes."

"She doesn't like people to know much about her, does she?"

"Again."

"Okay. Look, I don't know if I can stay much longer."

"Oh?"

"Yeah, I'm just not sleeping well here."

"I see that you have not purchased any furniture. Would it help if I ordered a bed? Or, you could sleep in the master bedroom. Although I would understand your decision to leave, I am happy with our arrangement and would willingly support you further by making things more comfortable, if that would help."

"Okay, but, why do you really want me here? Really?"

"Really? For all the reasons we have discussed, that relate to your efforts to investigate the home's electrical mysteries. And, of course, to provide some companionship for Sophie."

"The cat." Vin's face tightened and his vision blurred then cleared. He had been trying to decide how to ask about the cat. "I found a cat box, and things."

Joaquin blinked. He had turned slightly away, but now he turned back and watched Vin thoughtfully, saying, "Yes?"

"And, so, you were feeding the cat before I moved in?"

"As I've said. Yes."

They exchanged a few words about Sophie. Vin couldn't read Joaquin well enough to know whether he might have recently brought the cat and was lying for some reason, or whether the conversation was making Joaquin wonder about Vin's reliability. Joaquin showed a bit of irritation as he walked through some obvious steps for cleaning Sophie's litter box.

"Alright, I get all that," Vin said, frustrated by feeling that he shouldn't ask what he really wanted to know.

"Then I do not understand. What are you asking?"

"I mean—I'm asking if what I'm doing here is, well, if I'm taking care of both the house, and the cat?"

"Yes. Feeding Sophie, playing with her, cleaning her litter box. Yes."

THE NEXT MORNING, VIN PLACED an extra helping of dry food near the dish with Sophie's fresh canned food. He changed her water and put down an additional bowl of fresh water as well. He was wearing a white bathrobe that he had bought the night before. He checked his email and voicemail. No one had an urgent need to talk with him.

He descended to Nerdean's office, naked except for the robe. When he arrived, he logged-in and checked the status of the second crèche. All of its systems appeared to be operating flawlessly. He spent over an hour looking at the raw data generated by his last immersion. Very little made sense to him, but what did—temperature maps, heart rate, blood chemistry, vasodilation, brain activity—all remained well within the expected ranges that he found in the documents and online.

He stepped to the first crèche and placed his hand on the transparent pane, watched Nerdean floating in the blue liquid. Small bubbles sometimes escaped from her mouth. They rose in the broth and broke into smaller and smaller bubbles as they looped toward a recycling port above her head. All of the questions he had for her were useless while she was on the other side of the casket's door, unseeing and unhearing.

Yesterday, he had noticed with surprise that Nerdean's hair color seemed to have changed. It was not the steel gray he remembered, but a very faded auburn, and it was the same color from its roots to its ends. He wasn't sure what to make of the change. He didn't believe he was misremembering. He didn't see how that could be possible. But he also wasn't sure when the change might have happened. Maybe something about the light in the room and the faintly blue liquid had made the faded auburn look like it was gray. Or maybe the crèche dyed your hair. Maybe it offered other subtle cosmetic services as well.

But he had to face another possibility. His experience in the crèche may have damaged him. It had been an intense, hallucinatory dream. Maybe stimulating creative genius—possibly growing new neural pathways—had also cost him some clusters of recent memories? To put it in Bill's vernacular, maybe the crèche had fried his brain, just a little.

In retrospect, it seemed ludicrous to have lain in the casket and allowed automation to clamp wires to his skin and snake a tube down his throat, to have trusted his life to a system that submerged him entirely in a mysterious blue liquid. He could only understand his decision as something like a temporary break, a nearly insane choice enabled by the stress of losing his business and all the strangeness that had followed, by the days of looking for the underground room and then trying to understand its contents, by how he had been affected by the bizarre contents of the room, and by his awe at what Nerdean had created. He'd always wanted to invent things that could change the world. Nerdean had made something he wouldn't have dared to imagine, and she'd kept it hidden. In the end, he'd used the device because he had to know what it meant.

And he had survived, which changed everything. The very last risk was that his mind might have been slightly altered. But even if it had been, if the experience had cost him the memory that he was house-sitting a cat or if it had unraveled his recollection of a hair color, it had been worth it. And he felt good. He wanted another mind-blowing experience.

And this time he knew what to expect. He wouldn't become disoriented. Maybe he'd be able to control the dream, return to the moment of Winston's triumph and then, guided by his knowledge of history, reshape world events. He might even figure out how to succeed in the Dardanelles, where even Winston Churchill had failed. And then, maybe, if he could imagine a better world in his dream, could he help create one in reality? Maybe a vision of a better world was what Nerdean had been working on all along. In any case, she clearly believed the device was safe.

Vin stroked the transparent pane. He'd bought a notebook that looked as much like hers as he could find, and had written a complete description of everything he had done. If he didn't survive a second immersion, then when someone else found the room, they'd find his own story next to hers, a testament to how deeply he understood her achievement and how deeply it had moved him.

He lifted his hand from the glass and with the expected, soft sigh, the mist returned and she was hidden again. He pulled off his robe, hung it on one of the eggshell chairs and entered the second crèche, the one beside her that he thought of now as his own. Once he was settled in, the automation activated and the door above him swung closed.

CHAPTER 6

ANGER

Vin had been expecting to dream of being Winston Churchill again. Instead, he becomes aware of himself this time in a bar called Owlsville, observing the world from the body of a man named Bucky Wright. Bucky is twenty years old, the oldest son of a mill worker, and is finally away from the shit after two years of being in it. It takes Vin a moment to realize that "the shit" means combat in the Pacific, and that Bucky expects to go back. Vin wonders why Bucky is on leave, but the question evokes a sensation like a thick callous scraping against seared skin and Vin quickly lets go of it.

Matt Deaumont, a thirty-year-old high school teacher who is 4F because of a heart arrhythmia, sits across the table from Bucky, who is picking at a cracked pad of skin between his thumb and index finger and watching tiny points of blood dilate into being before swiping them away.

"Bucky, you have to tell somebody what's going on." Matt leans forward, his beer forgotten. His hands, both palms down on the surface of the table, are large and soft. Matt is too sensitive, too concerned about every damn person.

Bucky shakes his head, says, "I don't have words."

Matt says, "When you go back, you'll be carrying our prayers with you."

"I might not go back." Bucky says it like a question.

"What's that?"

"I don't want to, and I don't know if they want me."

Matt sits back. "How do you mean?"

Inside Bucky, a smoldering pressure crowds at Vin, pushing and burning. Bucky lifts his head. "Look, let's walk."

With the prospect of being outside and moving, the pressure slackens. In some ways, Bucky's mind is more habitable than Winston's had been. Winston's had been barbed at every turn, swept by sudden flurries of jagged associations. Bucky's is a quiet forest at night, with a predator hidden in the trees.

Matt is a little afraid. Bucky surges out of his chair, a large young man whose uncoiling limbs are strung with active, ropy muscles that are still thickening toward their full weight.

"Where do you want to go?" Matt asks, his brown eyes squinting up.

"Just out. Just move around."

"Alright. How about we walk down the trail to the bluff?"

IT'S EARLY AFTERNOON, THE SUNLIGHT soaked through by shadows that are falling from high gray clouds. There's a damp and spicy smell of cedar and fir, and a cool breeze with a trace of sea salt. Bucky looks up at the sky. He wants to remember how all this feels.

He pulls his cigarettes from a jacket pocket and puts one between his lips, then folds the pack away. All the cigarettes you'd ever want here, and so much of nothing happening.

He can't bring himself to light a match though. He can't see far enough into the trees to know whether anyone is watching. He knows he's safe here, but even in daylight a match is bright and sudden and draws attention.

Matt comes out, denim jacket draped over one shoulder, fingers hooked under the wooly collar. He notices Bucky has a cigarette in his mouth and digs in his jacket for his fancy Elgin lighter. He knocks it open and strikes a spark, holds it for Bucky.

"I'm going to leave my coat in the truck," he says, the coat dangling from his hooked fingers like the skin of a man. Matt's about a foot shorter than Bucky, solidly built and always neatly put together. Bucky knows it was a big disappointment to Matt to be rejected. Matt's the kind of guy who looks like he belongs in the army. Those guys aren't special though. Bucky's seen enough of their insides.

The trail leads straight to the coast, then bends and winds along the bluff's edge. Bucky hears Matt's truck door squeak and bang shut.

Then there's a thing happening when they start walking. They're both trying to get up in front a little, trying to get their shoulder to be the lead shoulder. That's how it seems to Bucky. Finally, he lets out a laugh. Who the hell cares, he thinks, and lets Matt lead.

It's a few minutes before Matt starts talking. Soft sound of their feet in the dirt. "You know, your dad asked me to talk to you." Matt seems a little on defense. Maybe because Bucky laughed at him.

Truth be told though, Bucky's a little surprised. If his dad had something to say, why didn't he talk to Bucky himself, man-to-man? Matt adds, "I kind of feel responsible to do that. Not just because he asked, but from respect, too."

So, first Matt's taking the lead on the trail, and then he has a message from Bucky's dad, and now he's feeling responsible. This is all really something. Bucky isn't sure where all of this is coming from.

"I want to do my part here," Matt says. "You're doing yours. And I can see that sometimes even just talking might be important. Do you know what I'm saying?"

Bucky grunts. He doesn't care much for what Matt Deaumont has to say.

The trail is ample. It's nice to step through the old forest in the quiet and tell himself not to worry.

Matt says, "You seem jumpy."

"That's a joke," Bucky says. He notices birds looping from tree to tree. A gull screeches. It feels like home. He wants to think about how safe he is. He even tells himself it's a good thing he has some company.

Observing Bucky's internal conversation, Vin can't help but try and influence it. "You're really alright," he tries to tell Bucky, but it doesn't seem to have any effect.

The trail comes out near the bluff and they stop walking. It's a bit windy but neither of them is uncomfortable. Low scrub and yellow grass shelve down in broken degrees toward a rocky shore and then the white, foamy edge of the ocean.

Bucky pulls out his cigarettes again, shakes one loose and offers the pack to Matt, who pulls one out. Matt finds his lighter, lights himself, then holds the flame for Bucky. Smell of naptha while the wind folds the flame over.

"Guy I know," says Bucky, "told me a story about the invasion of Virginia. You ever hear about that one?" He flicks the butt of his cigarette, sprinkling ash.

Matt shakes his head. Bucky can tell Matt will listen to whatever he has to say, so he decides to give the very long version. It's a rambling story about how in the early days of the United States, an Egyptian architect by the name of Bin Howzit rowed with a bloodthirsty army across the ocean to conquer the thirteen colonies. Both sides ended up talking it through though and the war was put off, probably forever, because they all had a lot of work to do. Matt listens patiently to the whole crazy thing so Bucky adds some details like descriptions of old houses in Virginia, the yellow fences and turkeys hiding behind cherry trees, just to draw it out. Finally, he gets sick of hearing himself talk.

They smoke for a while, watching the water. It might be the best Bucky has felt since he got back. He flicks away his cigarette butt and starts walking again.

Catching up, Matt says, "Somebody told you that?"

"I know I sound like a cracked egg."

"Bin Howzit sounds like a name from the funny papers."

"Guess so."

Matt says, "It must be nice to be home." Testing whether he understood why Bucky told that story.

"Guess so," Bucky says, but low. Matt can barely hear it.

"We're with you, Bucky. And we'll be with you when you go back."

"You know, why don't you tell me again why my dad asked you to talk to me?"

"I don't know. I don't think it was a good idea. I mean, I'm glad to, but he should talk to you himself."

After a while their pace slows, both of them thinking about how far they're willing to go and when they should turn back.

Matt asks, "So, why'd you hit him?"

Bucky stops, shakes his head. He scratches the back of his neck and gets another cigarette. As he waits for Matt to get the lighter, he says, "He was just standing there, Matt."

Matt, cupping the flame. "Berry's a kid. Your baby brother. He looks up to you."

"He's a baby alright."

"It's just . . ." Matt is having a hard time saying something. He shifts his weight and then shifts it back almost like he's waiting to pee. Bucky doesn't care.

The gray ocean moves, it's cold, it should be lifeless but it isn't. It goes on and on. Bucky shivers. His body wants to run away from that. But he doesn't run anymore when his body tells him to. That's not what a man does.

"He was happy to see you," Matt says.

Bucky looks at the dry grass, almost waist high, just off the trail. "Yeah." Even if he could say some things, he wouldn't need Matt Deaumont to hear them.

His kid brother, Berry, had walked up with that cocky grin. He was going to enlist, Bucky could see it in his eyes, and he wanted to brag about it. Bucky was just trying to talk quietly with Maureen, but Berry looked like he knew it all—like he knew what Bucky really wanted with Maureen.

"I bet the Japs are scared of you," Berry said, finding something stupid right off the bat. Berry always put himself right in it. Their dad would tell him to watch his digits, like it was only a matter of time before Berry lost a finger.

"Everybody's scared of me," Bucky had told his brother. "Everybody with any sense." Which made Maureen look worried.

Berry said, "Tell her how many you killed."

Some people count but Bucky doesn't, and he could see that the stupidity of the question, the babyish-ness of it, got to Maureen. Then Matt Deaumont walked by. Calm, safe, thoughtful Matt Deaumont, who Bucky's mother said all the girls were noticing now that he was one of the few men left in town. Matt Deaumont, who his dad said helped fix the pickup. Maureen was like a lost puppy looking at an open door.

So Bucky hauled off and hit Berry, and pretty hard, because he meant it. Then kicked him a couple of times. That had been too much. He knew right away. He didn't mean to hurt Berry, just shut him up.

When the dust settled and everyone was gone home, Matt Deaumont came over. He said it was probably tough to take time out from what was happening on the islands. Like "the islands" was a place and he knew where it was. He told Bucky he admired him, asked if he wanted to get a beer and talk.

Why not? Bucky thought. He was going to have to kill time here somehow. "Why do you think you're safe with me, Matt?" Bucky asks now, in a friendly way.

Matt looks at Bucky, looks away, and then looks back at him again. "What makes you say something like that?"

"Nothing, I guess. Only, I spent most of the last year and a half now trying to kill guys."

Matt doesn't say anything. Bucky says, "There are a lot of different ways to do it, and once you put your mind to it you get more ideas. That's not a thing that you think about here though, is it?"

Matt shakes his head *no*. Maybe he's having second thoughts about helping Bucky out.

"No. Because you don't have to. You just think that you can show up and talk to people. You're just here, with my girl and my family. And I'm out there, doing that." Bucky's smoking a cigarette and watching the ocean.

"You're wrong. I just want to say, I wanted to talk to you like a friend, a brother."

"Oh, like, if we had the same dad."

Matt shakes his head and folds his arms across his chest.

"I didn't even know you that much, did I, before I left? So why are you talking to me now? Is that a right you get when you steal a guy's girl?"

"Bucky, I'm not after Maureen. She's waiting for you."

"Well, last night, I couldn't talk to her. And I saw her looking at you. Saw the way she looked."

"I don't know anything about that. I've hardly said two words to her in the whole year."

"Which two words were those?"

"You've got it wrong."

"Must have been a pretty good two words. Maybe you can teach them to me?"

"You've got it wrong. I admire you. I would never touch her."

Matt's eyes are soft because he's asking for something. His big ears stick out like a hog's. You shoot a hog. Or you knock it with a sledgehammer if you're planning to eat the brains. Grab its bristly ankles and twist around while another guy ropes. A hog smells sweet and earthy until it shits itself. The other guy throws the rope over the hanging bar and you both haul away and pull the body up. Some guys use a winch. You get a sharp knife and cut its throat, firm and fast. The blood slings out, crackles when it hits the bucket, then hisses, then gurgles. You drain the hog.

Matt says, "Bucky, you don't need to take everything on yourself. There's no end to it."

Bucky would feel ashamed if he wasn't so tired of that. He turns back to the trail, so it's him who sees the thing first, high up in the sky and coming around a point to the north, carried by wind and dropping slowly.

"What's that?" he says, pointing.

Matt shades his eyes and squints. It's a gray thing, round, and a triangle of ropes below it extend to a thick point, like a basket. "I don't know." A moment later, "Well, it's a balloon."

"Yeah. Sure as hell."

It's far enough away so it's difficult to gauge its size. It's big though, maybe thirty or forty feet across at its center. They can guess where it will probably come down—about four hundred yards north, maybe a hundred yards inland from the trail.

Bucky pulls out another cigarette and asks Matt for a light. Matt hands him the Elgin. After lighting up, Bucky takes a drag and says, "Let's go," then flicks away the lit cigarette and starts running up the trail.

He is tired of conversation and walking and really wants to move. Four hundred yards isn't far. He sprints and opens up a distance between himself and Matt. When he gets to a good place to turn off the trail, the balloon has dropped out of sight.

He jumps into the thistly scrub and runs as fast as the uneven ground allows. He jumps small depressions in a rising bank and gets thirty or forty more yards before a wall of brush slows him. He bulls in, cutting his hands on thorny stalks, nearly skewering an eye. It doesn't matter.

At a clearing near where the balloon came down he stops and waits. He hears Matt thrashing away, more cautious in the brush than he was.

The balloon crashed on a stony stretch where the grass is thin. It's collapsing down and is half-folded over on itself. A bubble of gas is trying to raise the center, the unsteady wind pushing around the whole thing. It looks like an octopus with floundering arms trying to crawl away from the water. Trying to evolve maybe.

A particularly thick tangle of rope stretches toward the water and ends in a jumble of twine around silvery cylinders, a few broken open. Heavy, yellowing bags are mixed in.

Matt walks up to Bucky's side. "Do you know what it is?" Matt asks.

"Looks like a bomb to me."

"How's that?"

"Japs send them. They fly at high altitude. Can cross the ocean and come down over here to blow up."

"Well, that's a hell of a trick." Matt is catching his breath. "Why wouldn't it just be a weather balloon? Or something simple?"

"You want to know for sure, maybe you should walk over and take a look."

Vin can see that Bucky believes he knows what the balloon is. At the start of his medical leave, he had a conversation with a pilot who was also headed home. While the pilot was stacking a tower of scrambled eggs on his plate, Bucky told him where home was.

"Well don't get too comfortable over there," the pilot said. He told Bucky the Japs were sending balloon bombs into the jet stream to cross the ocean. Bucky thought it was a stupid idea and that the pilot was probably crazy. But he guessed what the balloon was as soon as he saw it. Something about the way it looked was Japanese, the way they made things.

Vin is frustrated. He wants to have some influence on the dream, to change something.

Matt jumps down from the big rock and walks to the massed debris at the end of the lines. The ropes shift and tug and the balloon struggles, trying to get a little farther inland, to someplace where it might make sense to blow up. Bucky edges down the rock and walks over.

Matt says, "That does look like a bomb." Bucky can hear

the fascination in his voice. As wind blows across the balloon's ropes, it lifts a fine powder from the broken cylinders.

Bucky is flicking the flint wheel of the Elgin, watching the flame spark out of the corner of his eye.

"I guess the war found us, didn't it?" Matt says, his voice warm, excited. And Vin sees what Bucky is thinking, and why his thumb is playing with the flint wheel. This is a dream, Vin thinks. Anyway, maybe this guy, Matt, deserves it. Maybe he's a dangerous person who just seems like a nice guy. He could be. In a dream, Vin can create whatever truth he wants.

Okay, Vin thinks. I'm going to try this. "Throw it," he thinks, adding weight to a thought Bucky already has. "Throw it. Throw it."

And just like that, Bucky does. Just like Vin imagined. He almost casually pitches the lit Elgin underhand toward the massive pile of grounded explosives. The lighter arcs up and past Matt. And Vin thinks, oh no.

Then he thinks, maybe the wind will put out the lighter, but he sees the flame land in the perfect center of the pile of parchment bags. It may be that another moment passes in the beautiful sunlight of a warm afternoon on the Pacific coast. Maybe not.

VIN'S EYES ARE OPEN. OR maybe they're Bucky's eyes. And there are thousands of stars above him, looking down. He can't hear anything. Bucky has had an experience like this twice before over the last year and a half. Shock that left him numb and deaf. This time though, he can't move his legs and his arms are heavy and wet and he doesn't want to try to move them. His eyes hurt terribly. There's pain all over. The small, squirrel-like breaths that he's able to take are very difficult.

And Bucky thinks, this is the moment. This is the moment I've seen other guys go through, where all the love, all of the effort comes to nothing and the eye of the world passes over you without even noticing that you exist, just before the world snuffs you out.

PART III

What Could Have Been

CHAPTER 7

Meeting Again

Light glowed from strips on the ceiling of Nerdean's office. Vin forced a weak cough over a scratchiness at the back of his throat. He shifted his weight, feeling the moist warmth of the casket's soft walls after the cycle of revival—when the crèche coaxes its subject back into the real world. He raised himself far enough to grab the lip of the casket, then pulled upright.

His groan reminded him to listen for the air conditioner whispering in the background. It had come on before the lid opened, to manage humidity and air composition as liquids from the casket evaporated. When he left the crèche, the lid would close and the device would initiate the cycle of rejuvenation, sterilizing its interior, running self-diagnoses and replenishing consumables.

He stretched, relishing the tension in his healthy muscles, the absence of pain. His body worked, his limbs were useful. Moments ago, he had been lying on stony, uneven ground, unable to move his head. He stepped out of the casket and backed against it, hungry to feel it pressing into healthy skin.

He stood and retrieved his robe, its soft cloth raising goose pimples as he pulled it on and walked to the chute. He was tired and reluctant to climb the ladder but didn't want to stay in the office with the ghosts from his dream. After the ladder, he went to the second floor where Sophie was sleeping on the inflatable bed.

HE WOKE WITH A NEED to get as far away from the house as he could. He fed Sophie because she insisted and then almost ran out the front door. Something about going up and away from the house, getting above it, made him feel better as he climbed the stairs to Marshall Park. He sat on a wooden bench at the overlook but couldn't think clearly.

He understood why he might dream about being a man like Winston Churchill, but why have such a vivid dream about being Bucky Wright, a walking casualty? No part of Vin wanted that.

He wanted to be in a crowd. He hurried to Queen Anne Avenue, all the way down Denny, and then walked along First into Belltown. He went all the way to the Pike Place Market, where he slipped into the slow scuffle of tourists. Eventually he crossed the street and ordered a slice of pizza at a quiet store facing the market.

While eating, he idly unlocked his phone and opened his contacts. In the B's, his list jumped from Tom Biny to Blue Highway Games, which was wrong. It took him a moment to realize that it was wrong because "Bill" was missing. He typed "Bi" into search and only "Tom Biny" came up. Bill didn't. He stared at the phone, closed the list and opened it again, but Bill still wasn't there. He power-cycled, eating and watching the colorful craft market across the street as his phone turned off and then came back on. Bill still wasn't in his contacts.

He tapped out Bill's seven-digit number. "Stanley, been-there-done-that-not-interested," said an unfamiliar man's voice after the second ring.

"What?" Vin said, "is Bill there?"

"Nope. Stanley's here. Only Stanley. Wrong number."

Vin said, "Thanks," hung up, and tried again. Stanley said, "Never call again, please," and hung up. Vin tapped out the number again, this time with the area code, though he shouldn't need it, but the call went straight to voice mail: "Stanley knows who you are, but not why you're calling."

After the short tone, Vin said, "My friend had this number, I think, yesterday. I'm worried that something might have happened to him. Did you just get this number, today, or yesterday?" He left his own number and hung up.

He called customer service and asked if there were any circumstances that would lead his mobile service provider to remove a contact from his phone. He felt uncomfortable asking, as if he were addled and paranoid. He was told that the service provider could not access or change his personal contacts. Vin ate and pondered. Could he have been so distracted by the crèche that he'd accidentally deleted Bill's info and was misremembering Bill's number?

He wandered out of the pizza place and over to the small but busy park at the north end of the market where a totem pole overlooked Puget Sound. Beefy bike police in blue and black were chatting and surveying the unraveled souls who nodded off on benches between tourists and office workers. Vin found a seat as far from the police as possible. A guy wrapped in a heavy wool blanket, his face a blizzard of frayed black hair, ambled past trailing a cloud of stink.

"Hey," a muscular policeman called at the guy, then pounded quickly toward him. The blanketed guy turned and stared numbly. Though he hadn't done anything wrong, Vin got to his feet and hurried across the street. He headed north on Western Avenue.

• • •

HE FELT LIKE A BURGLAR as he let himself back into Nerdean's. It wasn't his house. He didn't belong there and its strangeness wasn't his strangeness. When he came up the stairs, a woman was sitting in the vast dining room backed by the wide picture window.

A sway of light umber skin, bare neck and shoulders above a black dress with an orange floral print. She was looking at the back of her hand. He had come in quietly and was frozen and silent as she turned her gaze to the picture window. When she turned toward him a thousand points of cold rose out of his legs, skimmed along his spine, robbed him of breath and lifted the individual hairs at the nape of his neck and the back of his scalp.

She stood up and said, "Hi! So, where do you want to go first?" Then, "Vin, are you okay?"

For a moment, breathing was difficult. He both did and did not recognize her. She was older than she got to be, but definitely was who she was. And her eyes—she was relaxed, even tentative, but her eyes were bright with a vulnerability he had forgotten. She smiled, concerned, and waited for him to respond.

"Kim?" was all he could say.

She shook her head, waiting for the greeting she'd imagined. "What's going on? Vin?"

Time shifted, the river of time. If time was a river, Vin had stepped out of it. He had crossed it and was on the side where everything was catawampus and events could occur in any direction, the side where people who had died could step out of a slice of sunlight and ask if you were okay.

Her confidence broke. "Do you still want to go?" she asked.

The deafening, skittering chill rushed through him again. He took a half step closer to her, drawn by an urge to see her breathe.

"Vin?" she repeated with a note of panic. He saw tiny

movements around her mouth, at the base of her throat. Was that her pulse flickering beneath her skin or was it his own pulse pounding into his eyes?

"I'm sorry," he said, and wasn't himself enough to prevent the next question that came to mind. "Can I touch you?"

"What? No," she half laughed—a lost fragment of a remembered musical phrase—and straightened from her twist of self-doubt as she took a step back, "not like this. You weirdo. What's gotten into you?"

There are ways to distinguish events that can be happening from events that can't. For example, if you share a room with a person who stands and talks, then—almost by definition— that person is not dead.

He said, "You're here."

"Did you forget? We have a date." He could see her struggling to be chipper, also not an attribute of the dead.

After Kim's death, Vin had had terribly sad conversations with her that he only vaguely remembered. But they'd both admitted wrenching things. That had been fine. You could talk to a dead person, and listen to one. But no one should hear the voice of a dead person.

He said, "A date?"

"Yes. You said you didn't know how to furnish the house. I said we should go look together. Do you remember?" She was concerned. Was she thinking that *he* had been resurrected?

"Kim?"

"Yes?"

"I'm, uhm—sit down."

His legs gave way but he was near a chair and managed to shift into it. When he hit, it nearly tipped. It was a flimsy chair and needed to be replaced.

"I'll get some water," she said.

When she pushed a plastic glass at him, he said, "New furniture would be good."

"Yeah." She squatted beside him. "You remember? You wanted me to come here." She touched the back of her hand to his forehead. Checking for fever. Her hand was cool. She smelled of lavender hair product and perspiration.

He put the glass to his lips but didn't drink. He stared at her. "Thanks." He rested the glass on his leg. Their faces were close and she was alive.

"Should you lie down?" Her breath was warm.

He leaned back. A tin of mints was wedged into the pocket of her bag (black fabric, white floral print). Maybe the same mints she used to like, flecked with hot-pepper oil. The summer after his first year away, when she had just graduated from high school, they were standing in the entryway of her family's house. He had come to see her for the first time—her, and not Bill—and had asked her out. She had been wearing green sweats and one of those beanie hats that hid her hair and emphasized the bones of her broad face. She told him she was busy, and as he recovered she'd said she would be busy on every night he asked about, but she had been smiling and had one of those mints on her tongue and he wondered whether she was teasing and how she would respond if he asked again and then he realized they were alone in her family's house. He saw that she was aware of it too, the awareness filling the air between them.

In a hurt, clumsy way, he had said, "Well, okay. I've got to go." And as she nodded, years ago, her uncertain smile had blossomed into the broader, more confident smile that he was familiar with. He had thought about that smile for years after, and wondered whether she might have been sheltering a second, softer smile within the one she'd showed him. He had wondered if it might have been the empty house rather than his presence that had given her pause.

Her hand touched his, pulling him to the present. "What's going on?"

He saw that the current trajectory of their interaction would lead to an emergency room visit, where he would have to explain that she was dead. (And a whisper in the closet of his darkest fears suggested that if they left the house, Kim would melt back to memory.) He needed to explain her impossibility to her, but also had to acknowledge that she seemed to believe she wasn't dead. He had to get past his denial of a sensual truth: she was here, despite the fierce opposition of his intellect.

He said, "I have something to show you."

Within the dynamic field of irresistible existence, one outrageous truth deserves another. He would show her Nerdean's office, even though the idea of descending with her into that pale tract of technological voodoo was heart-stopping. After all, the device down there must have been the thing responsible for restarting her heart.

SHE STOOD BESIDE HIM IN the dark room as his foot fumbled and then found the square of raised carpet and pressed down. There was the soft sound of carpet against carpet and then light spilled up from below.

Kim's voice came low from the back of her throat. "What is that?"

"That's what I want to show you. Down there."

She took a step forward and flinched back and then leaned toward it. "What is it?"

"We have to go down. I can't explain without showing you. Follow me. It's safe. I promise."

"I'm not going down there. What is it?"

"A thing, a machine with racks of servers and—Nerdean, the woman who owns this house, made it all. It's a kind of dream inducer. I don't know what else it does." He waited for her to understand how important that sentence was but she didn't respond in any way so he said, "She's down there, in it."

"She's down that hole, in a machine?"

"It's her laboratory down there. I think she's experimenting on herself."

"Hey," Kim called down, "*Hey.*"

"No, no. She's sleeping."

"She's *sleeping* down there, *in a machine?*"

"Yes. It's an incredibly complex system—bio-stimulation, neural response management, a mind-body interface, torpor induction, broad-spectrum synthetic nutrients, maybe skin and hair rejuvenation. I don't know. I think it might augment creativity. I think she might be trying to make herself smarter. I don't understand it all. I need help understanding."

Kim watched him closely as he talked. She took a step away from the chute. "You want *my* help?"

Vin nodded and started down. When he got all the way down to the floor of the office, he called up, "Come down." His voice sounded flat under the acoustic tiles.

"Vin, please—step away from the ladder."

He retreated to the chairs, near the desk.

"Are you far away?"

"Yes." He heard the faint sound of her moving, positioning herself on the ladder.

"Will this door shut on me?"

"It opens automatically when you come up."

Another pause and then the rasp of her feet against metal. She descended slowly. At the bottom she stepped off the ladder and stood leaning forward, braced like an explorer.

She turned in a slow half circle, taking in the strangeness of the room, the eggshell chairs, the stacks of servers, the wall of batteries, and then fixing her gaze on the three caskets. Her eyes widened as she took in their shape, reading hints of the room's purpose in the lighting strips and the transparent panes. When she looked at him, he saw fascination beneath her surprise, curiosity and courage overcoming her fear, but she was still immune to her own miraculous strangeness.

SHE SAT IN THE EGGSHELL chair closest to the chute, leaning away from its curved back. From the farthest chair, he told her as methodically as possible how he had found the chute and what had happened between his first conversation with Joaquin and his dream of being Bucky. She seemed fascinated by the sheer strangeness of their situation, as he was.

He tried not to stare as much as he wanted to, not to show that he was rattling inside like chimes in a wind tunnel. When he mentioned Bill, she put up a hand and stopped him, lowered it after a moment and shook her head and asked him to keep going. When he slipped in the fact that she had been dead, she blinked, asked a minor clarifying question—"This whole time?"—but let him continue.

When he got to, "You appeared here," she interrupted with, "You invited me . . . ," but stopped as she looked around the room. She couldn't argue a small point about a past event while their surroundings were conspiring to twist the present into knots.

He put a hand on the desktop, felt its chill. "You see why I don't know what's going on?"

"Can I see the notebook?"

Both notebooks, his and Nerdean's, were near his hand. He pushed them forward, then stood, lifted them and walked them to her. "You only need one of these. The other is everything I just told you. In case anything happens to me."

"What do you think would happen?"

"I don't know. Anything. I mean, you're here."

She flinched and then reached out and picked up Nerdean's notebook and opened it and scanned the first pages. "You don't know what's going on, or whether this is safe, whatever it is, but you went in? Twice?"

"Yes."

"That must be why you didn't answer yesterday when I came by. But, didn't you say there was someone else in there?"

"Nerdean.".

"The woman who owns this house? And you said she was sleeping?"

"Yeah."

"Why is it empty now?"

It was true. The first casket was empty and clean, like the others.

They searched. Vin called Joaquin but he didn't answer and Vin didn't know what to say on a message so he hung up. Having moved nothing, dropped nothing and picked up nothing—as mysteriously as Kim had appeared—Nerdean had disappeared, leaving no hint at all that she had been in the casket.

KIM LEANED AGAINST THE ISLAND as he picked up Sophie's food dish and began to rinse it in the sink, his index finger burrowing into the remainder of Sophie's previous meal, a dried brown gunk. It calmed him to focus closely on what he was doing, even as he was mildly repulsed by a mental image of the cultivation of small animals, caged hens swelling like fat bacteria in a large damp petri dish of a factory before being rousted by numbed workers who shackled their feet so they'd hang upside down as they were dragged through a paralyzing electric bath, their throats cut, blood drained, bodies plucked, shredded and ground, passed on a belt through an oven, pressed and canned, the cans stacked on a pallet and shipped from one country to another, one state to another, to a central warehouse and then all the way to a local grocery; and from there in his car to this house where he would peel open the sealed band of metal and scoop out a gelatinous pâté, a cream of chicken bodies, mash and stir it on a ceramic plate like this one so that Sophie—a cat who had appeared out of nowhere and therefore had only a dubious claim on existence—could nourish herself on a small portion of it and leave the rest to dry into this cadaverous glue he was now rinsing into the garbage disposal. Shreds of nausea laced through him as he consoled himself with the recollection that the cat food had also only recently appeared. It was also only half real.

He set the scrubbed dish in the dishwasher and got a clean one from a shelf above, another from a set of five he didn't remember having before Sophie showed up. He opened a new can and scooped out its contents, mashed them and set the dish near Sophie's water. Sophie ate ravenously, as if the food in her stomach had disappeared when he came out of the crèche. She purred as she ate and he petted her cheek, noticing that she had dark spots at the ends of her paws. He remembered her paws being white.

Kim was leaning against the island, prepared to leave, her purse on the floor beside her.

He straightened and took a step toward the counter. "I don't know what's happening. I'm glad you're here."

She nodded. She was watching Sophie gulp her food, her arms crossed.

"Can you stay here tonight," he asked, "with me? It's a big house." He wasn't sure he wanted her to stay though. If there were something wrong with him, he might be better off alone.

She touched his arm. "No. I'm going to leave." She held up the notebook. "Are you okay if I take this?"

"I didn't know you—" he said quickly, but her head tilted. Something about how he was saying it bothered her. He started again. "Where would you take it?" he asked.

She took a breath as the things that they didn't know about each other waited for her response. "Maybe, to the secret lab under my apartment?" she said. "We didn't get a notebook with ours."

"You'll bring it back?"

"Yes."

"Please don't show it to anyone."

"I won't." She folded open the front cover and slowly fanned through the pages. "Do you want to come with me?"

It was easier to look at Sophie than at Kim. "I can't," he said.

"Why?"

She had worn that dress to join him shopping. He said, "It wasn't the day you were expecting, was it?"

She laughed, "No."

"Whatever this is, I'm going to stay and try to figure it out."

"Okay, I understand." She picked up her purse and pulled the strap over her shoulder. "But, do you think that might be a mistake? To stay here? I mean, I don't understand what's happening.

I definitely need some time to process—all this. But, just a little while ago, you told me that I was dead, and you also said that there's a woman who's skeletally thin and who's missing, and you think that she's probably in this house, hiding."

Vin had to say it sooner or later. "I—I can accept that I've been wrong about some things. But, Kim, I do not now, and never have believed in ghosts."

"I can't tell you how relieved I am to hear you say that."

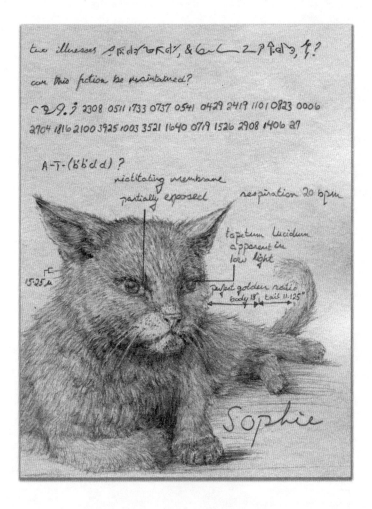

CHAPTER 8

Romance

Vin jerked upright, pulling sheets over his sweaty ribs, the room strobing red and blue in the darkness. Sophie jumped onto the end of the bed and he pulled back. She was in on it, whatever was happening.

He waited, tried to calm himself. He revisited old memories of Kim. They had gone to the lighthouse at Discovery Park . . . But the memories were disorienting. His thoughts were rippling, unstable. He unbent his sore limbs and slid his legs over the side of the air mattress, his eyes adjusting, pulsing colors gone.

Sophie watched. He knew it was unfair but he didn't trust her. He walked out of the room, pausing to be frightened of the hallway, his heartbeat surging then backing off. He descended stair by stair to the kitchen. He wasn't thirsty but was sticky with sweat so he filled a glass with cold water.

He couldn't stay in the house alone but didn't want to leave. Kim was in his contact list. He called and she picked up on the first ring.

"Hi. Surprise, I'm still alive," she said. "Are you?"

"I can't sleep," he said. "It's too much, and I'm wondering where Nerdean went. I dropped off for a while but dreamed I was at a dinner party with Henry James. He was my friend."

"The writer?"

A soft clattering and loud hissing sound started. The neighbor's sprinklers turning on, their noise crowding through a window that was cracked open.

"Yes. I have this clear picture of him in my mind, from the years before the war. It's like I really knew him. In the same way I know you or anyone. And by 'war,' I mean World War One."

"Have you looked up things you remember about Churchill?"

He turned on the tap again, letting the water run for a moment and then putting a hand into it. "Some. I can't explain but it feels real. Not like a dream. Almost as if I shouldn't be asking whether I have a decent grip on reality, but whether reality has a decent grip on me."

"Oh, no. No, that's not what you should be asking."

He held his breath, then turned off the water and drank from his glass.

She asked, "Why don't you tell someone? Maybe you could have that thing analyzed?"

"But—have you looked at it, the notebook?" As he drained the water his head seemed to be clearing.

"I was looking when you called."

"And?"

"And it's"—she took a long breath—"alright, it's amazing. You were right, of course. Of course you were. And, I understand what you're saying. It's just completely fucking amazing. I don't *get* a lot of it, but what I do understand is . . . it's just . . . part of it is like ravings though. She wrote, 'I am Marguerite de

La Roque.' Marguerite de La Roque was a real person. I looked her up. So, what does that even mean?"

"It must have been a dream like I had."

"But you don't believe you *are* Winston Churchill. And then, right away, she's talking about unified phenomenal experience and cranial alpha wave patterns, and—I recognized some of the terms and I looked some of it up, and, it's all real. At first she's a lunatic and then it's, like, she's a genius."

"She wanted to keep the device secret. She hid it all. Maybe there's a good reason."

He walked to the island that separated the kitchen from the dining area and lifted the top of the old pizza box. There were only strands of stale cheese.

"I'll come over," Kim said, and he heard the fascination and anxiety that were typical of her and that he had forgotten.

SHE ARRIVED IN BAGGY SWEATS wearing a dark beanie as if it were mid-winter, the kind she used to wear in high school. "You were kind of goth, weren't you?" he said as she walked in. "Before? I mean, your eyes, the makeup . . ."

She laughed as she looked at him steadily. "You said that already."

They were both uncomfortable with difficult questions, so when they carried chairs to the deck outside the darkened picture window and sat in the warm, loitering air they started by talking about Bill and the pharmaceutical sales rep that he had dated in his senior year of high school. He had disappeared with her for days at a time. Then, after he dropped out, she disappeared.

As she sat completely still, leaning slightly forward, her mouth partially open, Vin began to tell her about the road trip that he and Bill had taken after Vin got his bachelor's degree. Just six months before that, Bill had been living on the street. But he had been trying to stay sober and Vin wanted to support him so he suggested they do something big together. They spent a couple of days meandering around eastern Washington in a Datsun B210 that Bill had fixed up. The car was a mess but it ran great. Then Bill gave it to Vin. Bill said if he kept it, he'd probably trade it for drugs. He said he wanted to get his GED and find work as a mechanic. Then he dropped out of touch again and his mobile number got disconnected.

"How did I die?" she asked abruptly.

There was no scale on which to measure the strangeness of the conversation, no way to know whether he'd gone too far. So he told her about the Thanksgiving dinner when Bill had called out of the blue and asked Vin to lend him ten thousand dollars. Vin was home from college for the first time. Bill called just before they carved the turkey. He was wasted. Vin had to say no to the money three times, and then Bill stopped talking. To get a response out of him, Vin finally said okay, but Bill hung up.

"Bill told me the rest of the story on our road trip. He had memorized it by repeating it so many times for the police. Are you sure you want to hear?"

"Yes. I want to hear." Vin could see how he must sound, could see her trying to believe him.

Bill had called him the next night, but Vin didn't want to go through it all again so he didn't answer, so Bill called Kim and told her he needed a ride home. But when Kim arrived, Bill asked her to join the party—Bill, plus three dudes and a chick on a moldy couch with their eyes rolling back in their heads. Bill said one of the guys was a good friend and they were going to go into business together.

Kim insisted he leave. He finally said he would if she helped him finish some lines. He rolled up a five-dollar bill that had a crimson stain on it and teased her into it. Bill said she sucked up the first one "like a demon," to show she wasn't scared.

Kim's face wrinkled up. "What's wrong?" Vin asked.

"Nothing. Just, that sounds like me."

But the coke had been cut with almond powder and Kim started to go into anaphylactic shock. Bill had told Vin that he wasn't too worried at first. He'd thought about her allergy a lot and knew the list of things to do. He called 911. An operator picked up, but then things got confusing. He was high, and people were yelling and he couldn't hear the operator. Kim fell and crashed into things, clawed at her throat. Bill lost the phone while he was trying to keep her from hurting herself. There was foam on her teeth and lips and she was struggling and jerking. He got her close to the floor but she was suffocating and thrashing, trying to breathe. She hit her forehead on the coffee table. There was blood in her hair and on his hands.

Someone shouted about her heart and a locked pair of hands came down on her chest and made a terrible crunching sound so he took over and he was trying to give her corpse CPR when the EMTs arrived. They surrounded her, moved him away. Later, he remembered the EpiPen in her purse. Using it was the first thing on the list of things to do.

Kim was still staring out at the water. Vin stopped and she looked at him and said, "Shit."

Her eyebrows went up a little. She was waiting for him to go on. He told her that he and Bill couldn't stand to spend time with each other after that. Bill disappeared for a couple of years. The next time they really got together was for the road trip.

Kim had begun crying, quietly. Vin waited. After a while,

he got up and went into the house, got them each a glass of water. There was no alcohol. He waited inside to give her a bit of time, though not too long. He didn't want her to think he was avoiding the situation.

He handed her a tissue and then a few moments later, the glass of water.

"How is Bill?" he asked.

She paled. She took a drink of water then leaned forward and set the glass on the deck. Vin sat back down.

"Is he okay?"

She shook her head. "He's gone."

It took awhile for her to be able to tell him how Bill died. It was almost the same story, but in her version, which she said Vin had told her, Vin had answered the second phone call, and Bill had asked him for a ride home. But when Vin got there, a man named Lincoln said he wanted to see Vin's money. Bill got into a fight with Lincoln. At this point, Kim stopped and they waited. Then she said, "He put the gun up to Bill." She touched her chest, above her heart. "Here. And you said that while they were looking at each other, Bill smiled, and then Lincoln pulled the trigger."

"I don't understand," Vin said, breaking their silence at last, much later, after the moon had slipped through the mottled dark all the way to the edge of the lights that were spreading upward in the south.

Kim seemed to come out of a trance. "What happened to the car?" she asked. "The Datsun."

"I sold it. I was making money that summer. I wanted a new car. I'm not proud of that. I was in graduate school for about a year before he started texting me again, usually just one word, like, 'Hi'. Or he'd leave a voice message that was just, 'Hey man,' and then I wouldn't hear from him for weeks. It felt like he was killing himself."

"But you said you weren't seeing him. So, why do you say that?"

"When I asked about pot, he always came over. I just think he's doing more drugs than he lets on."

"Are you doing them with him?"

Vin understood that from a certain perspective, it might seem as though he was using Bill to maintain his own habit. He said, "Well, yeah. But I don't think it's like that. We don't *do drugs*. We might smoke a joint."

She was looking out at the water and the sky again. "How can you be making all this up?"

"In the last couple of years, you know, he came over a lot when things were bad for me. Building the business was hard. I usually couldn't hang out, but he came over in a good mood and he was funny, and it made me feel better. He was holding down a job. At a grocery store, and then a garage, one of those oil change places."

"But?"

"I don't think he ever felt good after you died. Your parents threw him out."

She whispered, "Did he have any kids?"

"No."

And the half moon, factotum of secrets, slipped behind distant, hazy lights.

THEY WENT INSIDE AND SAT at the table, neither of them ready for whatever would come next. Vin found some blue corn chips and bean dip and they nibbled at them until he said, "So, I killed him."

"Did you?" The question and her vehemence surprised him.

"What I mean is, when I went into the crèche, Bill was alive. But, something about what I did . . ."

"Just, just stop with this whole thing, please. This *crèche* story—"

"You saw the notebook, the machines."

Her jaw clenched. She shut her eyes and opened them. "I'm sorry," she said. "You're right. I just, I don't know what to think. When you said you killed him—you know, I've thought a lot about that. How things might have happened differently if you didn't go there. If it hadn't been you. Did you start the fight with Lincoln? You were the one who always got into trouble. And he would have stuck up for you."

She bent forward in her chair, her arms folded around her waist. He leaned toward her. "No, I wasn't there," he said. "I wouldn't do anything to hurt him." He took a breath and felt that something that had burrowed into him a long time ago was wriggling free. "But if I had *to choose*,"—he said—"if I *had to*, I would have *chosen* you."

"What?"

"If only one of the two of you could live. I think, I might have let Bill go."

"That's not—. Don't. Don't ever say that."

"But why? If it's real. And what if I made this happen? Somehow, with that machine?"

Kim sat back and looked away from him. "What does it say when you log in? Does it say you can change things?"

"No. It has system information and construction details. The files describe how things happen. They show how to monitor the crèche, but the notebook is the only thing that talks about what it does."

"So, you have lucid dreams when you go in, and they uncover memories. Then you dream a world that includes your memories. Don't you think there might be a side effect? That it might alter your memory?"

"And when I come out it only feels as though things have changed? Because I have different memories."

"Yes."

"I did think that might be happening, in a small way. But, I would notice a big change. There would be too much that was different. It doesn't seem possible. Right now, I feel like I can't trust anything I remember. But I know this is real, here and now. And I know it is because you're here. We're both experiencing it."

"I hope there are other ways for you to know this is real," she said. They were close, both leaning on their knees, thinking about how to respond to the device, the house, the awful eeriness of it.

Vin said, "I was alone in the house before. If I went in again now, it wouldn't be the same."

"What?" She sat up. "No. What are you saying? No. You're experimenting with your *brain*."

"You're here. This can't change," he said. She sat back in her chair. "We're in this," he said. "We can't back down. To find out what's happening, we have to go forward."

"That is—just—the risk. This—" Kim put a hand to her forehead. "Don't. Oh, god. Nothing changes when you go in *except you*. What's real doesn't matter if you don't see it or believe it. Do you really believe that the only reason you can't bring Bill back to life is that I'm here?"

"Of course that's not what I'm thinking. But I want to know what the crèche is doing. I'll write down the details, what's here and how it works. When I come out, I'll see it in my own handwriting. And I would *have to believe* what you say. We could learn what's happening."

"But what is there to learn? You know what's happening. I'm here, *right now*."

"I can almost see him."

"See, that's it. You're trying to make reality fit your guilt. A machine won't fix that."

"Do you have the notebook?" he asked.

After a pause, Kim stood, walked to the glass door beside the picture window, where she'd left her bag. She got the notebook and put it at the end of the table, her hand pressing down on it.

"You didn't write this?"

"How could I?"

She shook her head, her mouth half-open, a look of disbelief. "I don't know. You're getting a PhD in mad science and this is your doctorate? You tell me."

"No. I didn't write it."

There was an orange sticky on the cover with his name, *Vin*. Questions were scribbled on it—"Where are things stored?" "How does breathing work?" It was her handwriting, tall up and down strokes. He'd forgotten her handwriting.

"What about you?" he asked. "Do you have kids?"

"I don't know what to think of you."

"I could show you Bill's emails. But they're gone. And his messages to me. They're gone."

She said, "You don't remember?" He looked confused. "Me," she said. "Not as a kid."

"What should I remember?"

She looked at the notebook then pushed it toward him.

"I'll change this," he said.

"I don't think you will."

But he could see that she wouldn't fight him.

HE LAY IN THE CRÈCHE thinking about lucid dreaming as the system whirred to life. Wikipedia described a lucid dreamer's "awareness of the capacity to make decisions," but Vin hadn't made any decisions. The one possible exception was urging Bucky to throw the lighter and Bucky might have done that anyway. This time, he wanted to focus on making decisions and taking action.

As for everything else, his world had changed in dreamlike ways. He had tried to see through Kim's Kim-ness into what was really happening, but the person he had been talking with had an individual particularity that was so precisely like Kim that she reminded him of many things he had lost when she died. The person was very intensely Kim. Element Kim.

And he couldn't think of her alive without seeing Bill's shadow stretching out behind her. The thing that would always bring Bill back from a bender was Kim asking him to stop. Vin had a brother and sister who were much older, but his blood siblings only paid attention to him when they were embarrassed by him. They were faded still images compared to Bill and Kim.

Bill and Kim had always been patient with him, and with his temper. Over time, he'd figured out how to avoid the bigger tantrums, how to avoid breaking things and scaring people, but his family remembered and would recite a litany of incidents they maintained by consensus. His howling meltdown when the Cinerama reopened and they wouldn't refund him for the box of Mike and Ike that had all the candies fused together. The time he flipped a desk, shouted over and over that his biology teacher was a sock puppet, and stabbed himself in the thigh with a pencil. Their voices and laughter ignored his reasons and exaggerated the humiliating details, blurring away the real Vin until all that was left was the thing they believed or wanted him to be. Bill and Kim remembered, but they also listened to his explanations. They heard him when he told them he knew what was happening but couldn't help himself, and when he promised to change. Element Vin. Element Kim. Element Bill.

CHAPTER 9

Frustration

Select. Mount. Press. Strong. Right hand. Select. Mount. Press. Strong. Right hand. Select. Mount. Press. Strong. Right hand. Select. Mount. Press. Strong. Right hand . . . Anxiety crawls just below the surface of his skin, across his back and down his limbs. He willfully deadens his body, ignoring it so he can concentrate on his work.

His right hand is crammed with small plastic nozzles. His right thumb and the portion of his palm near it roll a single nozzle toward his fingertips. His thumb and index finger mount the nozzle on the end of a short hose held in position by the fingers of his left hand. He presses a plastic lever, propelling a tiny jet of water through the end of the nozzle, watches the water spray, and decides whether the jet of water is good—strong—or if it is bad. If the jet of water is strong, the nozzle gets tucked into his right hand and the cycle starts again.

Select. Mount. Press. Strong . . . no, this one showed a split stream. He quickly tosses it aside and selects another.

In this dream, Vin hasn't seen much yet, just the space around his hands: a huge bin full of tiny plastic nozzles on his right that he dips into to fill his hand, and the bin on his left where he occasionally deposits tested nozzles. As he becomes more aware, Vin feels a terrible discomfort around his waist. He has been testing nozzles for a very long time. He is bored, but he cannot change what he is doing.

He's inspecting the nozzles because it's his job. He's wearing goggles. Bits of moisture gather on them so he must sometimes wipe them on the loose sleeve of his green uniform.

The person Vin inhabits, a man named Gao Cheng, looks up from the small space where his hands diligently manipulate the flow of nozzles. Like a river of iron shavings in the presence of a sun-sized magnet, his attention immediately and unshakably fixes on a woman working on the line across from his, at a station four places ahead of his—Li Yehao. Gao himself spins through the void, orbiting her cosmic presence.

He looks back at his hands, which have continued testing nozzles while he was away. Vin realizes that the pain at Gao's waist is a furious erection, one that no matter how he shifts his weight continues to press with iron intensity against the limits of his restraining jeans. At that very moment, Gao shifts in his wheeled chair, pushing his rump backward as far as he can and flattening and straightening his lower back to decrease the pressure from the fabric at his crotch.

Select. Mount. Press. Strong. Right hand. His right hand is full of nozzles. Any more and he risks dropping one and slowing himself by bending to pick it up. He stretches and empties his hand over the lip of the large bin he is filling with pieces that have passed inspection.

Vin feels the shivering tension in Gao's body even while his eyes are relaxed and staring at his hands. Vin wants the hands to stop moving. As thoughts shape themselves in his mind, Gao quickly flattens them to nothing or starves them of attention so they fade like smoke. In his mind there is a background hum of frustrated interest like a current of buzzing gnats, but Gao's attention is as implacable as a moving sculpture, and he defies Vin's explorations with single-minded, clockwork motions that also radiate an oily fear. Vin can't figure out how to influence this dream, so he thinks about the person he is dreaming himself to be.

For Gao, who is almost twenty, this job is a temporary solution to the problem of earning money, and a starting point for his ambitions. He will not put his future at risk by doing things that will slow down his work—standing, for example, or talking more than necessary, or thinking about odd things. At the same time he is riven by a fear so strong as to be almost disabling. It has many tributaries: fear of exposing himself as a failure; fear of hunger; fear of discovering himself to be a weak man; fear of the choking pain in his throat and chest when he has to talk with influential people; fear of the way his body shakes and trembles when women look at him or notice him in any way; and, most particularly, a fear of his inexplicable, durable and lawless erections. His lanterns of shame.

If he works diligently he will not need to stand up, and so will not risk exposing his mutinous part. He hunches tightly over his work and focuses his mind. His shift has five more hours.

Select. Mount. Press. Strong. Right hand. Select. Mount. Press. Strong. Right hand.

Miss Li's breath must be scented. Gao's father used to talk about his mother's breath, of how it smelled of ginger and green onion, like good soup. "Fragrant breath," his father told him, "is a gift you will appreciate when you marry." The thought of marrying nearly blinds him for a moment. His hands continue despite it.

Miss Li's cheeks are round, and beneath them her face straightens into the lines that eventually curve around her pointed jaw. Some people probably don't think she's as pretty as other women in the factory. Her jeans fit loosely, her legs are thin but strong, and she has a sweet and capable air that has captivated Gao since he first noticed her, two weeks ago. She smiled at him and he was able to trust that she meant it because he had the impression that she was a genuine kind of person, a person who wouldn't try to fool anyone.

Since then, she has noticed him watching her. She sometimes glances over her shoulder, and has looked directly at him. When their gazes have met they have both been jolted into breaking the connection. So far, they haven't spoken.

This line of thinking makes his jeans so uncomfortable, so painful, that he gasps. He has to shift in his chair and stealthily pull at the denim, allowing himself just a momentary distraction before resuming his work. Select. Mount. Press. Strong. Right hand. Select. Mount. Press. A bad one. Toss away.

Vin is trying to make Gao stand up. He slowly becomes aware that Gao believes that his jeans will tighten and the pain at his crotch will be worse if he stands. In frustration, Vin eventually relents, and relaxes into the rhythm of the work.

Gao is remembering the lean muscle on Miss Li's arms and contemplating the hint of her breasts implied by the swelling of her blouse. She wears the blouse of the green uniform most often, but twice he has seen her wearing a white blouse with a crease under each arm.

Select. Mount. Press. Strong. Right hand. Select. Mount. Press. Strong. Right hand. Select. Mount. Press. Strong. Right hand.

It's difficult to imagine what the next step on his path at work will be. How can he advance quickly enough to become more attractive to a woman as desirable as Miss Li? An echo of loneliness wrinkles through his chest, collapsing his ambition. The only path that would allow him to speak with Miss Li regularly is to become a boss. Without that, which could take years, he simply does not know how to overcome his fear of talking with her.

Vin, who wants to stand and walk over to Miss Li's station and say hello and be done with it, feels the acute pain of this paralyzing combination of fear and urgent infatuation. But Gao simply will not consider Vin's direct scenario, so Vin looks for a tool to draw the young man's attention, and in the scrum of Gao's thoughts he finds a name, Mr. Zhang. The name pops up, like a cork that had been held underwater. Vin focuses himself on one single thought, repeating and repeating it: "Look at Mr. Zhang."

And then, Gao almost does, he almost glances toward the spot on the factory floor where he believes that the tall, thin, powerful and handsome Mr. Zhang is likely to be walking past a row of workers, his stiff, switching step making his neatly groomed head bob up and down.

Mr. Zhang is the B Group Quality Monitor, and directs all the bosses. Gao has considered working his way into a job like that before, but it is almost unthinkable. Though Gao doesn't know the actual numbers, he is certain Mr. Zhang must earn enough money to be attractive to any woman in the factory, maybe even to some of the higher ups. If Gao had that job, Miss Li would notice him. But how could he ever manage it?

Vin hears the question, feels the fissure of doubt. He responds instinctively and immediately, as if he were responding to a deep concern of his own, with an emphatic *yes*. "Yes, you can do it!

Certainly you can!" At which point Gao lifts his head and looks over at Mr. Zhang. Did Vin make that happen?

Gao's erection had subsided but now when he looks back at his hands, his chest is lightened by hope and the erection returns full strength. With Gao so uncomfortable and desperate for relief, Vin recognizes an opportunity to experiment with influencing his behavior.

Vin thinks about shifting in his seat to relieve the pain, imagining the precise motion very clearly, and is stunned by a sudden movement as Gao does just that, exactly as Vin imagined. Vin thinks about pulling at his jeans again to entrain another moment of relief. Gao doesn't do it. Vin concentrates on pulling out at the waist of his jeans, vividly imagining the freeing sensation, even if it only lasts for a short time. Gao pulls at the waistband of his jeans. As he does, he has a fleeting thought that the movement is only a short interruption and the relief is very welcome. Vin imagines it again and Gao immediately repeats the movement. Vin has made something happen.

SELECT. MOUNT. PRESS. STRONG. RIGHT hand.

Over the next few hours, Vin finds that Gao will complete small actions that Vin suggests, but Vin has to imagine the act physically—think it in images and sensations—and it has to be something that Gao considers relevant to his own concerns. After the erection has subsided, Vin manages to convince him to stand and to stretch his lower back. As he does, he looks about the factory.

Gao's station is a part of a tan steel structure that stretches the full, impressive width of the factory floor. It supports a central column powering a line of fluorescent lights. On either side of it are heavy steel desks notched with stations like his. To his right, row on row of these structures—tan metal columns supporting central lighting and winged on either side by ranks of individual workstations—stretch into the far and very dim distance, fading eventually from sight in a haze of light created by the endless rows of low fluorescent tubes that mixes with a yellower, clearer light pouring in from high windows. There is no visible end to the ranks of desks and workers. They simply fade away.

Lining both sides of every row are workers in factory-issued green jackets. As the rows recede into the distance, people are identifiable by the small spot of color on their heads—either the yellow of the official bandana or the black smudge of loose hair. Occasionally a worker will stand and swivel about, replenishing a stock of pieces, checking a reference or handing something off. Along every few rows, a quality monitor paces back and forth.

Gao stretches his arms upward and swivels left and right at the waist. On his left, the scene is just as it is on his right, but there is a distant wall, a faintly visible end beyond the rows of workers.

Gao won't extend his break for long. He won't avoid his work. He feels lucky to have a job and his anxiety started to accumulate as soon as he stood. He sits back down and bends over his nozzles again. A few moments later, a buzzer and a bell both sound. Final break of the day.

Today is payday. Gao likes to be paid in cash. He empties his last handful of inspected nozzles into their bin, and opens his right hand over the bin of un-inspected nozzles. His palms have pink dents from holding the little plastic pieces, and are pruned and shiny from the water.

Gao is slow coming out of his station. If he's being honest with himself, his erections and fantasies are the only excitement he has on a workday, but they keep him tense, too, which he believes makes him more tired late in the day.

"Problems with the plumbing?" Guo Hua says. He's another wide-faced country bumpkin, like Gao. They usually stick together but Guo Hua seems fed up with something recently and has been a little mean.

"Yeah, Gao. Good work," says Peng Jun, filing out right behind Guo Hua and nodding as he passes Gao. Gao is confused. What are they talking about? Then he notices the stain on his crotch. His spunk. Leaking out. Shit. Of course, it's happened before. He should have known. He quickly turns to face his desk so no one else can see it, and he considers his options.

He still has to walk to the pay line to retrieve his envelope. He should be making deposits like most people, but having that money in the company account makes people more free with it. Gao likes to see what he's spending. It helps him save and every little bit counts.

There's no way to hide the stain on his jeans. He'll just have to ignore it and walk over there as if he's already a boss.

He's just about to step into the file of workers heading out—is imagining doing it—when he sees Miss Li standing four feet away from him, looking at him. If she sees his pants, she'll know what kind of person he is. She'll know what he spends all those work hours thinking about. She'll connect it with the times that she's noticed him watching her. Then, he will die.

She half smiles. Workers are still walking out, creating a temporary distraction that he can use to avoid looking at her, but now that he's seen her, she's waiting for him to say something. He notices that when he looks toward her and her smile broadens, she has a small extra wrinkle under each eye. The observation lances through him. That really is her and not the imaginary her he has been dreaming about. She can't see him like this.

Despite Gao's lust, shame, and dedication to his work, Vin has been better prepared for this dream than he was for the others. As Gao powered through the day, setting his steely will against his own inclinations and slowly cutting through the minutes that led to this crisis, Vin has paid close attention to his own thoughts and feelings, and how they were affected by the dream.

But try as he might, he can't reset even small segments of time. He can't go backward and do things over. He can't will the erection away. In fact, he hasn't been able to change anything in the physical world, not the number of nozzles in Gao's hands or the display on the factory clocks. He hasn't been able to raise Gao's body into a moment of levitation above the factory floor, make a wall of the factory transparent, or turn even one of the nozzles into a feather. None of it has worked. But he has influenced Gao's actions. Now, while Gao is aflame with panic, ashen with fear, Vin tries again.

"Run," he thinks out loud, inside Gao's head. "Run away from her."

"No," comes the clear response. Gao is answering Vin's thought. Gao hears him and is talking with him. Vin has succeeded in affecting the dream again. "This is my chance," Gao is thinking. "I can't run. She was brave enough to come here to talk with me. I have to be brave too."

"No," Vin says, feeling the thrill of real influence and improvising a relevant argument to change Gao's mind, so Vin will be certain that he has had an effect. "You must hide from her." Vin speaks to Gao's experience. "She will hate you if she sees what you've done."

Vin creates a mental image of the front of Gao's jeans and the stain where his erection had pressed against them. The truth is, Vin doesn't think the stain is all that impressive. Gao's two friends Peng Jun and Guo Hua must have noticed it because they've had similar problems. But now Vin imagines the stain as very dark and very large—a big wet spot, as if Gao had emptied a bowl of semen into his underwear. Vin imagines trying to explain to Miss Li, and in his image of it, he emphasizes the horror of that moment. She would stare in shock as she took a step away from Gao. Then she would fall into the distance and be gone forever.

"Run," Vin thinks loudly. "Protect yourself. Avoid the shame."

It all happens in less than a moment. Gao ducks his head so he is looking down and can no longer see Miss Li's hopeful face, then he steps quickly into the passing line of workers and walks as fast as he can away from her.

THERE IS A DEADNESS TO the air, to the sounds of voices around him. The slight chill on the breeze carries a rasping premonition of endings, of winter. Running away from Miss Li, humiliating her when she made such a brave gesture—Gao is hollowed out, and Vin with him. After such an act, there can be no consolation. Vin can barely maintain a firm enough mood to keep himself coherent and avoid dissolving in Gao's morose feelings.

Gao is remembering when he found the dead body of Xiao Hui, the dog who was his best friend, lying under leaves on a day just like this. Xiao Hui's throat was torn, and one leg chewed. A tough, smart, black-and-gray terrier with wiry hair. Whatever killed him had passed very close to the back of Gao's house. But Gao didn't know what was happening, and he didn't help Xiao Hui.

Now as Gao waits in line, the gray sky piles itself on the back of his bent neck. Peng Jun came over to smoke a cigarette with him but Gao couldn't speak, couldn't say anything to him, couldn't even look at him. Peng Jun eventually punched his shoulder softly and left. Work breaks are too precious to spend them feeling bad. Gao only has a few more minutes to gather his pay, and then he should hurry over to the team meeting for the final part of Mr. Zhang's summary of how the day has gone so far.

The gold envelope is pushed toward him. Gao makes his mark on the sheet, lifts the envelope and steps away from the line. The envelope is so small and light, filled with only paper. Everything he wants is all around him, but all of it is inaccessible to him. At this moment, everything he owns is in the palm of his hand. He pulls the lip of the envelope out and unfolds it.

He looks up and sees massive clouds thundering in the silent distance. He sees so much air. Only a few years ago, everything that Gao felt in the world—even the mild chill on the wind—carried promise. He would never have imagined his life narrowing to such a sharp point so quickly, his choices flattening so completely, leaving his future to be wholly determined by such a tiny mutiny. And all in pursuit of this, these paper bills in a paper envelope. Taken together, this was the shape and limit of his future.

Vin has stopped trying to affect Gao, or change his actions. Gao pulls the short pile of colorful bills from the envelope, leaving a few coins within. He lets the envelope drop to the black asphalt and takes a step away from it. The bills in his hands are wrinkled, faded, green, purple, brown and red. He fans them out. This is his life.

In a single, swift movement he lowers his hands and then throws the money up at the sky, flinging the small pile of bills and watching it scatter on a gusting wind. The money flutters as the breeze strengthens, and then the bills begin to drop, twisting slowly toward the paved ground. He walks away from them.

GAO WALKS ALL THE WAY to the distant dormitory room that he shares with five other men, all of whom are at work. He curls up on his thin mattress and faces the wall. For the rest of the dream, Vin counts the moments ticking past. The dream has become very painful, and terribly boring.

Vin tries to get Gao out of bed. He tries to imagine elaborate conversations with Miss Li in which they both recognize that they're destined to be with each other. He visualizes walking to the mess area and trying to find her during the evening meal. Some of the ideas he has, he repeats over and over: Maybe Miss Li will try again tomorrow; maybe she'll forgive Gao, especially if he apologizes. Nothing, no matter how extravagant or quotidian, draws a response from Gao. Gao, convinced that he has humiliated Miss Li when she was most vulnerable and has missed his only appointment with fate, has descended beyond depths from which mere imaginings might recover him.

Gao now knows he is the kind of person who behaves callously toward others and is too frightened to be brave. He imagines the consequences of his actions. Devastated by the loss of face, Miss Li will quit her own job and move back to her country village. Her parents won't welcome her. Things will go badly.

No, Vin insists, from his place inside Gao's thoughts, that's ridiculous. Go back to your station now and you'll see her at hers. She might even smile at you.

But Gao can't allow himself a hope so intoxicating. He is not going to complete the last part of his shift. The world is merciless and his supervisor will note his absence. Miss Li is crushed. Gao is nearly penniless and soon will be unemployed and homeless. Nothing will ever be good again.

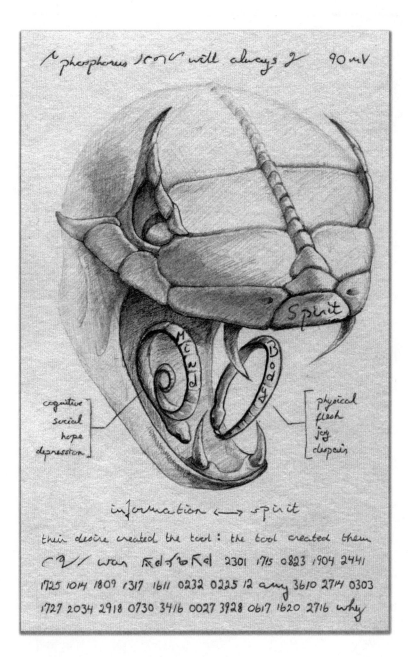

PART IV

Real Life

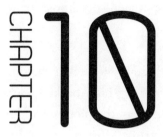

Passing Through

When the dream was over, Kim stood while Vin climbed out of the crèche. He moved slowly. He still felt like he was Gao Cheng, as if the two of them were a double image. He was still struggling with frustrated desire for Li Yehao. The lively pressure of Kim's hands and the feel of the robe on his skin had an unreal quality, a perfect familiarity that dissolved his ability to speak.

The light in the office was smeary and yellowish. Kim said, "Let's go upstairs. I made us breakfast."

He looked up into the chute and remembered Xiao Hui as a wire-haired puppy, remembered the lead soldiers Winston Churchill had spent hours of his childhood arranging in painted ranks for his father to notice, and the white edge of a ripple of blue water rolling onto a sand beach in the Philippines. Loneliness shivered through the memories.

"I'm okay," he said, as he began to climb. "But it was difficult. Very lucid. It's already almost impossible to remember how real it feels. I did make things happen though. But only in certain ways. I did something cruel."

Kim was climbing behind him. "It was a dream."

He waited in the dark bedroom. When she was out of the chute, she said, "I watched you almost the whole time. Nothing happened."

THERE WAS A LARGE FORMAL table standing lengthwise in the dining room, circled by high-backed, carved wooden chairs. Mid-morning light from the picture window caught the table's varnish in bright strips. Most of the table was stained dark, a slightly greenish color that muted the wood grain. A four-inch decorative inlay highlighted the grain around the edges. A seam in the middle suggested insertable leaves.

"I like the table," he said.

"So do I," Kim said as she went into the kitchen. "I'll get breakfast."

He pulled a chair out and sat, placing both palms on the table's smooth surface. Kim stopped moving. She said, "That's not what you meant, is it?"

"No."

Kim was in jeans and a loose yellow blouse that accentuated movement. She had an oven mitt on and was lifting a plate of eggs. She set it on the island and watched him.

"You don't remember the table, do you?"

"No, I don't."

"What do you remember?"

"A small card table. A folding table. Cheap. With cheap folding chairs. It was here when I moved in."

"The room was empty when you moved in. You told me you got that from Craigslist."

"That didn't happen."

"No, you don't remember it. It's only me telling you that it was different, right? Like I said it would be."

Vin nodded, acknowledging that she had anticipated this risk.

"What do we do?" Kim said, unnerved. "I have to ask you things now. Okay? So, what is your name?"

"What?"

She raised her hands, palms up.

"Vin Walsh," he said.

"Okay. And, who am I?"

"Kim . . . Kimberly Badgerman."

"And my brother, what is my brother's name?"

"Is he alive?" Vin jumped to his feet, almost losing his balance as he pushed back the chair. "Did I do it?"

Kim held his gaze.

"He's dead," Vin said. He sat. "His name was Bill. He was shot by a man named Lincoln." Vin looked across the table at an empty wooden chair.

"I bought this?" he asked.

"Yes."

"Kim. This may sound crazy, I know—and maybe it's offensive to say—but I don't understand what, well, what evidence do I have that you're not doing all this?"

"What—are you saying to me?"

"I mean, could you be replacing . . ." Vin heard how absurd the sentence would be if it were completed and stopped talking.

"Am I making all of this up? Is that what you're asking? Whether this is me? Whether I'm gaslighting you?"

Vin froze, unable to acknowledge the question.

"Well, first, according to you, I'm dead. I mean, I think that would be a strange thing to do to you. And, I made us eggs."

They didn't talk as Kim brought the platter and pulled four slices from a toaster he didn't own and carried them over with silverware he didn't recognize. Using a long black plastic spoon that hadn't been in the house before he went into the crèche, Kim put portions of eggs on unfamiliar white plates and offered one of them to him.

"The crèche is stealing your memories," she said as he reached for the plate.

"You don't know what's happening."

Oregano and cheddar in the eggs, the way he liked it. But he had no appetite and the smell was making him dizzy. "It's not stealing memories. I have different memories," he said at last. "But, you're right. I can't go in again."

"And what about her?" Kim asked.

"Who?"

"That woman. The one in the other crèche."

SHE WAS IN THE THIRD casket, not the first, floating naked in the blue solution, and it wasn't the same woman. This woman was short and heavyset, square-cheeked, her bobbed hair a slate and clunch-colored marl.

Vin's hand was on the transparent pane when a segment of the lighting strip that bordered it began to flash yellow. Then a strip around the edge of the lid blinked green. Vin lifted his hand and the pane misted over. The crèche made a gurgling sound.

"She's waking up," Kim whispered.

"The cycle of revival," Vin said.

"I'm glad she's still alive."

The way she said it jolted Vin. "How long has she been here?"

"Since you found this place."

"But . . ." Vin had something to ask, but wasn't sure what. He found the notebooks on the desk, picked up Nerdean's and opened it, flipping through the pages one at a time. They all looked exactly as he remembered them, but because so much of the text was in Nerdean's unreadable code, he couldn't tell whether or not it had changed.

"Did I tell you if I knew her name?" he asked.

"That's Nerdean. That's what you said."

"No, I don't think it is."

They tracked what was happening as the lights changed—yellow, green, yellow, blue, and then green again—accompanied by gargling and draining sounds and an occasional monotone whistling.

Kim said, "You should get your clothes on. But bring back the robe. I'll stay with her."

THOUGH THE FULL CYCLE OF revival required more than an hour, it passed quickly. At the end, a segment on the indicator strips around both the transparent pane and the edge of the lid turned green. The segments of light kept pace with each other as they made a full circle around the casket. There were a series of crisp clicks and then the lid lifted, paused, and smoothly turned on one side as it swung open.

The woman lying within was on foam that they watched deflate and retract into the crèche's interior, like an anemone retreating into its shell. Her eyes twitched under their lids and then opened and she drew in a long, tranquil breath. As she became aware of Vin and Kim, a flash of fear crossed her face. She opened her mouth but made a wheezing noise and shuddered into a spasm of soft coughing. Kim took a step forward, holding out the robe, but Vin reached to touch her arm and hold her back.

The coughing lasted a long time and the woman beat on her knee in frustration. When it subsided, she straightened, stretched against the bed of the casket and wiped her mouth with her wrist.

"Hi." Her voice was a croak, worn, ragged like a fraying shirt. "Thanks for the help." Kim glanced her disappointment at Vin. The woman said, "I don't know you, do I?"

Kim shook her head.

"Have you been in one of these?" the woman asked, and Kim shook her head again. The woman said, "But, you must own this house, huh?"

"Yes," Kim said, as the woman coughed.

"No," said Vin, when she'd stopped. "I'm house-sitting."

"House-sitting. Okay, I see. You found this room?"

Kim and Vin both said, "Yes."

"Then, this must be strange for you."

"It is," Kim said.

"Yeah. And, well, me too." Her voice was loosening up. "And I'm not good with strangers. Maybe it's not a good idea for us to talk right now. You don't mind, do you, if I stay in here? That would be okay, right? We could turn this back on, when it gets ready to go again. I'll just take another little nap. A short one. You wouldn't mind, would you? Do you know how to turn it on?"

Kim held the robe up toward her. "You don't want to come out?"

The woman looked past the robe. "You have to go over to the computer . . ." She gestured at one of the monitors. "Over there. It won't cycle again unless you press the—you know how it works, don't you? Just turn it on, and I'll be on my way. I mean, I'll take a quick nap. How about if we just do the minimum here, okay?"

Kim didn't move and Vin didn't say anything.

The woman took a long breath. "Okay. So. You probably want to talk, then. Is that it? Questions? Answers?"

Kim nodded and the woman put her hands on the lip of the

casket and strained to pull herself up. Vin stepped to her side and reached to support one of her arms. Her lip rose as she glanced at him, annoyed, but he helped her take a first, shaky step. Her arm was soft, fleshy but strong. Her skin had both an antiseptic smell and a faint whiff of sulfur.

Vin helped her find the sleeves of the robe. When she had it on she held her arms in close, shoulders hunched, and rubbed her palms against the soft fabric.

"Thanks," she said. "I always prefer an empty room, though. You know. Nothing against you. I don't know you two. I just don't like having anyone here when I come out. You never know who—like, who the two of you—might be."

"The two of us?" Kim said.

"Forget it. And there's no one else, though, in . . . ?" She nodded toward the other two crèches and wiped curls of liquid off her forehead, pushed back her dripping hair.

"No," said Kim.

"Safe upstairs?"

"Yes," said Kim.

The woman walked toward the ladder. She put both hands on a rung.

"This damn ladder," she said, leaning back and looking up, then half turning toward them. "It's damn hard to get up after a long shot. I once came out and there was a body here. Must not have had the strength to climb. Or, maybe he was at the top and fell and broke something. But he'd been there for a long time. Months maybe. Skin gone to pieces. Maybe he bled out. Maybe. Or starved."

HER NAME WAS MONA AND when she began to fall asleep on her feet they showed her to Vin's room. She barely made it to the inflatable mattress before falling and lapsing into a hissing slumber.

Vin took the blanket and one of the pillows from the master bedroom and lay them down on the floor in the dining area. Then he and Kim sat at the table and he told her what had happened to him in the crèche while they ate. After cleaning up, Vin lay on the floor while Kim surfed the web. Daylight leaked away.

He woke once when Kim grunted in frustration and stood up from the table, then woke again as she set a pillow down and stretched out on the floor beside him.

IN THE THINNING DARK OF early morning, Vin saw Kim standing at the end of the table near Mona, who was eating pizza. As he closed his eyes again he heard Kim talking quietly, trying not to disturb him. Kim was thoughtful, cautious. Mona's voice, though worn and hoarse, was slightly higher in pitch. She sounded casual, a little aggressive.

"You know," Mona said at a normal volume, not concerned about waking him, "you got one of the nice ones here. Sophie's here."

He heard a chair scrape the floor and imagined Kim sitting and adjusting it. She said to Mona, "You were in there for a long time."

"It's not really like that. But, yeah, it has been a long time."

"And, are you okay? I mean, outside of it? Do you need to adjust?"

"I don't know what you're asking."

"I don't mean anything, but you still look a little tired. And shaky."

"Are you saying I'm an addict?" There was an edge to the question.

"Umm, I'm not—well, is that what you think?"

"No." When Mona spoke again the edge was gone. "I mean, I guess that things you do can be addictive. But if you'd just always prefer to do it and it doesn't matter whether or not you do, then, what does the word mean, in that case?"

"Maybe, that it's hurting you, and you should stop?"

Mona laughed, a soft snort. "Okay. Maybe. Fine." After a moment, she asked, "How far have you gotten?"

"I'm sorry?"

"In the puzzle. How far have you gotten in the puzzle?" Maybe she sounded nervous.

"I don't think we've gotten very far."

"Do you have any soda?"

"No. Just water."

"I got some," said Mona. "But you have the notebook, right?"

"Yes."

"But, you don't know what it says?"

Kim was still keeping her volume low. "It sounds like you don't either."

"But you haven't used it, the crèche?"

Kim must have shaken her head because Mona said, "But he has?"

Vin rolled onto his back and said loudly, "Yes, I have."

"How long?" asked Mona.

"I've had three. One-day dreams." Vin sat up, shook off the blanket and stood. "The one-day minimum, three times."

"Dreams, huh?"

Vin walked to the chair beside Kim and sat down.

"The dreams feel strange," he said. "But it's when I wake up. I'm not sure my memory is right."

"He says a cat appeared," Kim added. "Out of nowhere."

"She did," Vin said. "Sophie. You said her name. But also . . ." he glanced over at Kim and then stopped talking.

"Oh, I see," Mona said oddly, as if humoring him. "Sophie wasn't here when you started?"

"No."

"Okay." Mona set the pizza crust down and leaned back in her chair.

"And," Vin said, "this table, it wasn't here. I mean, are you following? The *table* didn't exist. Now it does. Do you know anything about that? Does that make any sense?"

"Yeah, it does."

Vin put his fingertips on the table's edge, feeling the neatly cut and smoothed lines of the wood. "Okay. Then this table could just appear here after I wake up from the crèche, out of nowhere? Is that what you're saying?"

"It was always here," Kim said. "His memories have been affected."

Mona looked toward the window. A few lights were steaming out of the cloudy morning distance.

"You two know each other?" she asked, not looking at them.

"Yes," said Vin.

"So, let me ask you—it was Vin, right? You knew, Kim, before you went into the crèche?"

"Yeah," Vin said. He squeezed his lips together, then said, "But she was dead before I started."

"Oh? She was— Oh, jeez. You poor babies."

"Can you tell us what's happening?" Kim asked.

"How can my dreams change things? I don't understand how it works." Vin placed his hands on the table, palms facing up. "What I remember," he moved one palm, "and what's in the world," he moved the other, "are different. I don't know what's going on."

Mona said, "'Nerdean-is-a-fake,' huh? That's the password you're using? You haven't found the other one?"

"That's the only one," Vin said. "Wait, there's another one?"

"Yeah. Did you try, 'Nerdean-is-real?'"

"No," Vin said, lowering his eyes, his shoulders falling forward. "Of course. No, I didn't think of it."

"Okay, then, after I'm gone. Wait until I go, and then, why don't you give that one a try?" Mona's voice was low and even, her gaze sloping like a gently descending road. "What year is this?" she asked. "What month?"

"What'll it do?" asked Kim.

"You're just going to have to try it. You wouldn't believe me if I told you. I tried it really early on, on my own. Guessed there might be more than one. Just on a lark. No one told me how to do any of this shit. I just figured it out. And it worked. It totally fucking worked. And now everything is hosed up."

"But, *what is it?*" Kim's voice wavered as she leaned over the table.

"I don't know a goddam thing. I could tell you what I know, but, it wouldn't sound—it's not believable. Use the password."

"Kim was dead," Vin said, "and her brother Bill was alive. And then I came out and Kim was alive but Bill was dead. We're not anywhere close to believable anymore."

Mona tilted her head a bit to the right and her jaw came forward. "I see. And did those two deaths—the brother's and Kim's—happen at about the same time, in a turn sort of thing, one or the other?"

"Yes," Vin said.

"That's how I think it works. Yeah. Most often."

"How what works?" asked Vin.

"First, you have to know that when you go into the crèche,

that you're not dreaming. You do know that, right? You know it in your gut."

Vin shook his head very slowly.

"Yes, you do. You do know it. Just like I did. You can tell. The edges aren't rubbed off like they are in regular dreams, everything has weight, everything has a smell. When you figure out how things work, it feels matter-of-fact, like it does when you're awake. It feels normal, right?" Vin nodded and Mona continued. "Yeah, you just haven't believed it could be real. You're probably too smart to believe that. Not like me. I'm not as smart as you. But we both know that it's as real in there as it is out here. And when you come out, you remember things that you couldn't know, never learned. And some things from inside the minds of the people you're with." Mona paused. "I mean, do you know what"—one of her hands gripped the side of the table—"do you know what the best, safest way for a woman to kill a powerful husband was in the city of Kota Gelanggi?"

"No," said Vin.

"You didn't even know there was a city with that name, did you?"

"No."

"Neither did I. No one told me. I never read anything about it. But I've lived there."

"What are you two talking about?" asked Kim.

"What I'm saying—I'm saying there is no safe way to kill your husband in the city of Kota Gelanggi. Yeah, and there are . . . *penalties* for a woman whose husband dies suddenly, or suspiciously. But that's not the worst. Not even close."

Kim stood abruptly, walked to a wall and turned on the room's lights, washing away the thinning gloom of the under-developed day.

"I'm sorry," Mona said, sitting back, "but it's all real. What you do in the crèche really happens. Believe me, I know what's real. I lost my family. I lost my two kids to that thing." Vin's hand covered his mouth. "So I know," Mona said. "I've been trying to get back to them."

"You're saying that Vin's memory of my brother is real?"

"Yes. Different things happen in different worlds."

"Kim?" Vin asked. "Are you hearing this?"

"Yes."

"The crèche is"—Mona appeared to reconsider—"look, I could go back in. You could both leave the house. Your life might go back to normal."

"No," Vin said.

MONA BEGAN TALKING IN A swerving, disorganized way about her inability to understand what was happening to her. Eventually she took a deep breath, paused, and said, "I never really thought about time, but that's where this thing starts. To us, to you and me, there's a path we follow. We do one thing and then another and so on, moving forward. But it doesn't really work that way. Everything that happens exists at the same time. And not just the past and future, but every past and every future, every one that's possible. Everything that could possibly happen is real and is happening right now."

Vin said, "You're talking about alternate universes. Or one very complicated one."

"Yes, and—"

Vin interrupted. "Infinite worlds, and every possibility exists. That machine—nothing could ever do what you're saying."

Kim said, "Don't cut her off."

"Well, then you know," said Mona.

Kim had been sitting at the end of the table. Now she rose and walked a few feet, her sneakers making a soft *scrik* sound on the hardwood. She stood beside Vin, who was staring at the floor, his shoulders bunching up, and put a hand on his back.

Mona said, "You did things in the crèche, didn't you, when you thought it was a dream? You figured out how to influence people, make them act, and you did things?"

"Yes."

"Well, but, think it through," Mona said. "Think it all through. Something terrible happened, right?"

And Vin remembered the brutal scissoring of time cutting on and off while Bucky Wright lay slashed and bleeding on the firm earth. If what Mona said was true—and it felt true—then Bucky's family, and Matt's, would be waiting for them to come home from their talk.

"Think it through," Mona said again, recalling him. "Yes, the crèche sends you to other worlds, and what you do is real. But, *everything* that *can* happen *does* happen somewhere, so *you* don't make a difference. Nothing you do makes a difference. All that changes is *you*. What *you are*. The crèche isn't about doing something. It's about being something, and living with yourself."

"But, I killed them both."

Kim said, "You didn't kill anyone."

"Yeah, he did," Mona said. "Sure, we all do. We're all a part of things that are larger than us, that don't even consider life and death at all. I mean, it's a privilege to even think like that, about whether or not to kill. We get to do that because we're limited, because we have our own perspective, our minds. But we're a part of a thing so large that the question doesn't even exist if we don't put it there. So you decide to go hiking with a friend. You stand together near the edge of a cliff and look out at a beautiful view. There are worlds where one of you or both of you fell and died. You were the one who decided to go hiking. You killed yourself and your friend."

"That's wrong," Kim said.

"I agree, but it's how things are. Everything happens, it doesn't matter whether it's meaningful or not. Look, I made mistakes too. I live with them. They matter to me. But what you find out when you use the other password is that we just live inside all of this, all of these possibilities, like air. You can't stop these things."

"Kim is alive now."

"And you can't see the worlds where she's not anymore. When you make choices they matter to you, they matter to her. But they really don't matter because every possibility happens. Look, that's all I know."

Kim said, "What is the crèche?"

"I've read everything about it backward and forward. You get to a point where you have to. When you try that other password you'll find documents that say that consciousness, your—your feeling of things—is a basic part of reality. The crèche makes your consciousness go to another world."

"How can that be?" Kim asked. "I saw his body. He stayed in there."

"No, it's about your *consciousness*. The crèche can't move your body."

"How does it decide where you go?" Vin asked.

"At first, I thought that was random. But I've done it enough. I think there are patterns. It connects with something and you go to certain situations almost as if your feelings aimed you. I think that's why they call it a 'shot.' Because it's aimed. Sometimes the aim seems obvious, sometimes it's not."

"I don't just go anywhere. I'm always inside people's heads," Vin said.

"Yeah. The crèche turns your consciousness into probability. Probability doesn't exist in a single world. A person in another world somehow notices you, their consciousness connects to you, so then you are in the place you were noticed. That's where you go. It can happen, I think, when the person you go to is sort of looking for things they wouldn't normally see, when they're open, so, a moment of crisis, a really emotional experience, for example. You become a part of their experience."

"I don't believe it," Vin said with a faint stroke of anger.

"Well, don't believe it then. I don't care. But you felt it, didn't you? And I just explained that feeling, didn't I?"

If he accepted what she was saying, then Matt Deaumont and Bucky Wright were dead. Gao Cheng was lying in the dark torturing himself because Vin wanted to make him do something, and the euphoria of the Empire's war council as they chose to attack the Dardanelles, the elation and certainty that Winston Churchill felt, that and the carnage it led to, all of it was real.

"But what about the changes," Kim said, "when he wakes up?"

"The changes. I'm sorry, but those are real too. That's a thing that no one expects. I've never met anyone who understood at the beginning—"

"You keep talking about other people," Vin interrupted. "Who? Who are they?"

"They're people, like us. People who go into the crèche."

"But, where are they, then? They're not in this house," Kim said.

"It's because of the way it works. To move you, it changes the state of your consciousness, so you have a probability of being in many places, like how an electron works. But it has to do the same thing to get you back, which means the machine, the crèche, has to let go of you, because your consciousness isn't in one world anymore. And, because there are infinite worlds, you never get back to the one you started in." As Vin processed the words, Kim's hand pressed deeper into his shoulder. Mona continued, "Sometimes the differences between worlds are small, things you'd never notice, sometimes they're huge. In some worlds, other people have tried the crèche, so there are people in the house, or the caskets. You do this enough, you meet people, but I've never seen you two before."

"We're in other worlds," Kim said, like she'd known it all along.

Mona said, "But, it's hard to say what's *you* exactly, isn't it? If there are different versions on infinite worlds."

Vin's head hurt, as if a murder of crows were shouting into an angry day. "That's not possible."

Mona rewarded him with an exaggerated look of surprise. "Possible? You know all about that now, do you?"

"Wait a minute," Kim said, "You go in—"

"Think about it like a box of chocolates," Mona said, "or chocolate covered cherries, with one of those slotted plastic things to hold them in place. Every candy is the same but slightly different. You open the box, spill them all out, then put them back in. The candies are your consciousness, the plastic slots are the bodies in different worlds. None of the candies go back in the same slot they started in."

"But what about his memories?" Kim said. "His memories are in his brain. That can't just change. They're part of his physical brain."

"She's right," Vin said. "Kim's mind and her memories, and her body for that matter, they've always all traveled through time with her. Everything has stayed together. There's never a chance of a mismatch."

"Yeah, but that's not how it works, though. That makes it sound like memories are a thing that you can take with you or leave behind, but they're not. Memories are a kind of interaction between all the things you are in a particular moment. Every time you remember something, you're really creating a new experience. That experience depends on what happened to you in the past, but there's nothing unique about that. Everything depends on what happened in the past. Memories aren't really different. Because each memory is a new experience, there's no way it can be a mismatch with what you are now, in the way you're thinking. The fact that you're in a new world probably does change your memories, but there's no way for you to know how. I mean, it's a kind of mystery, right? If you go that deep, you always find a mystery."

"Not with technology," Vin said. "That's just lazy thinking."

"Okay, how about this then." Mona's jaw jutted again and her eyes narrowed. "I'm not just saying if there was a crèche it might work this way. I'm asking myself, what the hell is going on with this thing? What I told you is as close as I can come. I'm sharing it with you because you asked. And by the way, lots of things people make, they don't know exactly how they'll work."

After a moment, Kim said, "We did ask."

"You believe I wasn't born in this world," Vin said.

"Well, the idea of *world* almost doesn't make sense. But, to answer what you're asking, then no, you weren't. And I wasn't either. But this world could be pretty much identical to where we were born. I mean, maybe exactly the same except one cherry blossom ten or ten thousand years ago, or one moment in a different galaxy a billion years ago. On the other hand, maybe most things here are different except for things about you. I do think that the more shots that I do, the bigger the changes are when I come back."

"I'm not hallucinating," Vin said.

"I don't know about that."

"You're not," said Kim.

Mona said, "I've left notes after really bad shots, to warn other people, but there are still infinite worlds without the notes, so. But the good news is that you usually seem to come back to a place close to the one you left."

"But"—Vin was trying to fit his experience into what Mona had said—"why would the designers, why would Nerdean, construct a system with so many terrible flaws? How can it all be so fucked up?"

Mona shook her head. "It's *tech*. I don't know."

"And so, *you're* saying that,"—at the curdling sound of Kim's voice, Vin twisted in his chair; Kim's face was tense with a dawning realization—"that this Vin isn't *my Vin*. You're saying *my Vin* went into that thing, and that he's never coming back. And this is someone *else*."

"I think some people might see it that way," Mona said. "But you don't have to see it that way. You could also think of it just like, Vin made a decision, and it changed him."

"But, you're saying I wasn't born in this world."

"That body was. Maybe you've had some different experiences than the person born with it, but you're close enough to fool the crèche, and for the crèche to fit you into that body."

"Musical chairs," Kim said.

"Yeah." Mona nodded. "With bodies. Look, I need to get back in there."

THEY COULDN'T CHANGE HER MIND. At one point, upset and clearly feeling badgered by people she'd only just met, she rounded on Vin, asking him why he had gone in the last time, after he knew there were risks. The two of them were alone. Kim didn't want to have anything more to do with the crèche, so she hadn't come down to Nerdean's office.

"I was trying to find Bill. I wanted him to come back, like Kim did."

"See, that's what happens," she said. "That's why everybody goes in. To get back what they lose. But maybe nobody ever does that. Maybe you can't."

"Why are you going back in?" Vin asked her.

"I lost my two kids. If it's possible to find them and I don't try, then what am I? Why am I alive?"

Before she got in, as she was standing naked, heavy and sallow, a kind of weariness radiating from her as if her concerns could dissolve worries about vulnerability or self-consciousness, she said, "Listen, I want to tell you one more thing. Give me back the robe. I'm cold."

He lifted it off the chair where she had dropped it and handed it to her. She put it on, and ran a hand through her short, tangled hair. "You should know something, about me."

She sat near him and put a hand on his knee for a moment, then lifted it and leaned back in the chair. "I found this place, maybe four years ago, my time. I think. I don't know. Maybe a little over a year ago your time. Time on a shot isn't always the same. Anyway, none of that matters. It was all in a galaxy far away. So I went into the crèche. My husband and I had been fighting, and I wanted to dream. I wasn't smart, like you. I took a long shot right away, a week. Some things happened. You know what kind of things can happen. When I came out after that first time, I didn't know what was real. And then, my husband didn't believe what happened to me, when I told him. I couldn't really believe it either, so I don't blame him. But he wanted me to take medicine.

I guess I believed I might be going crazy, but I also felt like, after what I had seen, I felt like nothing at all was real. You know? That all this was an illusion. So I set my house on fire. And, I killed—I lost my two kids. The fire did it. They burnt all up."

She stopped talking. She stared at him for an uncomfortably long time, as if he might say something that would explain what had happened to her.

"I'm going to go into the crèche again," she said. "And I'm going to find them. I am. But, what I want to tell you, is to warn you, I guess. I don't know who will come out of it the next time this body wakes up. There was a very long time when I wasn't a good person. If I come out like that . . . The thing is, I'm not sure that you're safe with me. Even now. As I am. I mean, me right now. And I guess the truth is, whoever comes out of there next time, you might not be safe."

"What should I do?"

"Well, that's the question, isn't it? On the one hand, nothing matters, because everything that could be done is done. On the other hand, everything matters, everything we do. Because it matters to you, doesn't it?"

She didn't wait for an answer. She stood, stepped forward so her back was to him and dropped the robe onto the floor of the office.

"Joaquin's in this world, isn't he?" she asked, not turning to face him.

"Yes, I guess so," Vin said.

She started climbing carefully into the third casket. When she was in, as the LED lights on the casket started blinking she said, "Vin, don't let Joaquin know what's down here." A whirr as the door began to lower. "Don't let him know," she said again, "and maybe things will be okay."

. . .

A WEEK LATER, JOAQUIN SAT on the other side of the big table, facing Vin and Kim. He was not quite as put together—his hair not as perfectly set, lock on lock, his clothes not as immaculately formed—as Vin remembered. He seemed sad, and Vin noted that the table didn't surprise him. But then, Joaquin and Kim were from this world. Vin was the interloper.

"So you haven't found anything?" Joaquin asked a second time. Vin had told Kim that Mona warned them about Joaquin, and now Kim was sitting with her arms folded, giving Joaquin a bit of a stink-eye, though she wasn't openly hostile.

Vin wanted to be done with Joaquin, who now scared him a little. He wanted more time alone with Kim.

"That's right," Vin said. "I think there might be an electrical short somewhere. Inside the walls."

"I see. And I wonder, have you found any written material, any records anywhere in the house? Anything at all? Any notes or diagrams that might have been forgotten or left behind, accidentally? Or on purpose?"

"No," Vin said, shaking his head as if he were reviewing everything that happened over the last few months. "No. I would have mentioned anything like that. Just empty."

Joaquin placed his hand on the leather portfolio that lay on the table in front of him. "This is, um, an interesting place in our relationship then."

"How so?"

"Well, at this point in your custodial responsibilities, I have been authorized, or rather required"—a house alarm began clanging loudly outside and Joaquin took a deep breath—"I am required to offer you a choice."

Vin glanced at Kim but she was watching Joaquin.

"What choice?"

"I'm required, by my contract, to inform you that the home—this house—is soon going to be changing hands." Kim made a small noise of concern, a soft gasp. "If we do not hear from Nerdean within a month, I am required to sell the home. That would mean that you would have up to two more weeks of residency. This requirement becomes effective if a very specific additional condition is not met."

"Okay."

"The additional condition," the alarm was still going and Joaquin shifted nervously in his seat, "is that the house will be sold if you choose not to accept it as a gift."

Kim's arms dropped to her sides and she leaned forward. "What?"

"What?" Vin asked at almost the same moment. As Joaquin smiled stiffly in response, Vin said, "Can you explain?"

The house alarm stopped and the sudden quiet lifted Joaquin's voice. "Of course, I understand it's a surprise. Nerdean didn't want anyone house-sitting. I've told you that. But she did contemplate the possibility, within my employment contract. The contract is very complex but incredibly well written, marvelously consistent. It is *sui generis*, a work of art. A thing of beauty that forks with natural inevitability like the limbs of a tree, each new path defining distinct possibilities, each splitting further into new contingencies until in aggregate they form a catalog of every foreseeable possibility within a specific district of the law. It is a document I am grateful to have a relationship with. If there were a museum for contracts, then this contract, this incomparable document, would be its prized possession. I have been so hoping to meet her." He cleared his throat. "I have even considered breaking the terms so that I could ask a colleague to sue me, if only to test her magnificent contract in court, where its full power might begin to be admired." He laughed weakly. "I'm sorry. I've devoted my life to these things. The simple truth, which I'm sure Nerdean must have anticipated, is that I will abide by the spirit and letter of the contract if only out of respect for the intelligence that created it.

"But, and I didn't tell you all of this earlier—in a situation in which I believed that the, um, privacy, of the home might potentially be compromised, such as with the possibility of a break-in, then I had the latitude to arrange to employ a house sitter, to protect the house and, of course, to provide companionship for Sophie. In my judgment, employing a house sitter seemed like the correct thing to do. And, Vin, when your father told me about your situation with your company, I thought you would be an excellent choice. An intelligent, resourceful young man. As you know, I hoped you might learn something about the unusual utility bills, and the odd electronics upstairs, which— they do appear somewhat suspicious. Am I not correct?"

"Yes," Vin said, "that whole setup is really strange. Like Nerdean was trying to hide something."

"Yes, that's what I thought as well, and so I hoped you would tell me if you discovered anything of relevance." He was almost pleading.

"You couldn't just hire someone to look at the house?" Vin asked, though he knew the answer.

"No, as I have said, that was forbidden." Joaquin leaned back, put both of his hands in his lap and nodded slowly in an exaggerated way. "But, you see, I believe Nerdean also anticipated the possibility that I might use the clause that allows for house-sitting as a ruse, if you will, to bring in a gifted and curious individual to inspect the home." He nodded at Vin. "And so I did. So I did. Her remedy, in such a case, was to essentially fire me by having the house change ownership. When your father first told me of your situation, I felt the risk would be warranted. I had faith in you. But . . . And, we find ourselves here. She is a very determined person, Nerdean. And, perhaps, spiteful."

So Nerdean had used Joaquin and that contract to emboss her will onto the present. Vin was thinking through the implications of owning the house, and didn't respond to Joaquin's wistful bitterness. No matter what Nerdean intended or Mona had said, Vin now wanted to tell Joaquin about the crèche.

"So," Joaquin continued, "the present state of affairs is that you will have two days to make a decision: whether you will accept the gift or not. If you accept, the paperwork is already prepared. We'll make a legal transfer. There's a condition that requires that you not resell the house for a minimum of ten years, and asks that you never resell it at all. The condition is in the contract, but once you have the title, it becomes merely an emphatic request. Though you will need to agree—verbally, in my presence—before receiving the title. And, of course, I must tell you that I'm sure Nerdean hoped you would never sell it. She may yet return, though you would be under no obligation to her. If you decide to reject the gift, then you must move out within two weeks and I will place the house on the market in thirty days."

"Before I make a decision"—he turned to Kim and paused midsentence. Her face was set, worried.

"Yes?" asked Joaquin.

Kim was staring, trying to tell him something. He lost the thought he had been pursuing, said, "I'm not sure, I need to think about it."

Joaquin seemed to be waiting for something more definitive, so Vin added, "It's been a real pleasure living here."

"Is that what's giving you pause? Gratitude?"

"Yes," Vin said. "I think. I'm just surprised. And I'm trying to process it, I guess."

AFTER JOAQUIN LEFT, KIM SEEMED panicked. She started talking when the door clicked shut.

"He's going to give you the house?"

"The contract says he has to, but I think I should tell him about the crèche."

"But if you tell him, he might not give you the house."

"You want him to give me the house?"

"Of course I do. It's beautiful. And didn't Mona tell you not to trust him? Not to tell him? That he might be dangerous?"

"I don't know whether we can trust Mona."

They had walked to the dining table. "We could live here," Kim said.

"What do you mean?" Vin couldn't bring himself to repeat the word *we*.

"This house is big and empty," she said. "It's a little spooky, but it's incredible."

"What did you mean though?"

"I don't know. I don't know."

"Okay."

"I'm not trying to push anything. But, if things did work out . . . This decision is important. And, Vin, I need to tell you, I'm"—she stopped herself, but for Vin the moment had the sudden feel of clarifying logic, as if all of the puzzles of daily living had been swept away on a wave of certainty.

"I've been thinking about it," Kim started again. "I see what

Mona meant when she said that the thing down there is just like a decision. You are the person I know. You smell the same, you look the same, you talk the same. We remember our childhoods together."

Vin accepted the house and didn't tell Joaquin about the crèche.

IN THIS WORLD, KIM AND Vin had been dating for two months. She already knew things about him and she treated him with the familiarity of a childhood friend. In the bedroom, she moved as if ignoring the effect of the crèche, and he was both thrilled and distanced by the assumed intimacy, the collision between dream and memory. The full effect was both awkward and erotic, their desire reconnecting them, their bodies familiar and strange.

In the first weeks, Kim talked more freely about her life after Bill died. After barely graduating from high school, she'd started waitressing and she'd saved money obsessively. "I started thinking about what I really wanted and getting rid of every part of me that wouldn't help with that."

She was frightened of falling into the kind of poverty that she assumed led her biological parents to give her and Bill up, and she was frightened of becoming what her adoptive mother had said of Bill after he died, "a nothing, nobody." Those words spoken by their mother, a blunt articulation of something that Kim had suspected her parents of feeling, had dug a trench through that moment in Kim's life.

She knew it wasn't quite fair to blame her parents for not saving Bill, but she decided to keep her distance from them. Reading insulated her from the requirements of survival and she specialized in the kind of thick, translated novels that excite academics. In her sole concession to pharmacology, she sometimes downed sleeping pills to avoid the hours after work. After two arid years on her own, she enrolled at a community college in Communications and Digital Arts.

"One thing I did right was to walk, a whole lot. I didn't want to talk to anyone, but I remembered those jazzy, rambling walks you and Bill did around the city when we were kids. I loved that so much."

She told him that skydiving had been a turning point. She knew when she learned about tandem dives—two people harnessed together rejecting the fable of stability—that she would use a jump to say goodbye to her brother. The stranger who mentioned it in an offhand way became her only friend for three months, and two tandem and three static line jumps.

It took years of inching forward at community college before she accepted the utility of student loans and transferred to Western Washington University.

"But I've already told you all of this," she said.

For Vin, Kim possessed a glow of germinal irreality that set her apart from the strictly factual world. Her existence demonstrated an incoherence in space and time, a contradiction in the structure of the universe. And he had been changed by his experiences in the crèche, his mind darkened by the shadows of the events and longings he had encountered there. There were moments when he observed himself like a third person, enjoying his time with Kim in a way that he wouldn't have understood before he went into the crèche, almost as if it were a food they shared.

When she finally did say, "I'm pregnant," he didn't have the courage to tell her what he was really thinking—"the body that I'm in fathered your child, but I didn't." And anyway, she already knew that. She had brought it up during their conversation with Mona. And it really didn't matter, did it? The child would be his. No matter who had fathered it, he would be its father.

CHAPTER 11

Settling Down

Their new home rested on a foundation of mystery, its security reliant on a willingness to dampen their curiosity and accept that what lay below them shouldn't play a further role in who they became.

Since Mona had told them that the worlds in the crèche were real, Vin had been thinking about how his hosts had felt his presence. Had he been a voice in their heads, a current of desire, an inclination, an obsessive focus? And how much of him was exposed? The ideas made him feel porous, as if influences with undetectable agendas might transit through him and change him, as if awareness might be a colloidal presence, shifting in interactions with a boundless expanse of mind.

"I don't think we can use it anymore," Kim said one evening, interrupting his reverie. "We shouldn't even log in. I want our lives to mean things that make sense. And that thing isn't right. I don't want to think about it any more than we have to, to take care of Mona."

"No," Vin agreed, realizing that his experience with the crèche and the reality of having Kim in his life had made him a different person. He felt indebted to Nerdean, and strengthened his commitment to maintaining her secret. Rather than start a company, he found a good job as a software developer, one that allowed him to work almost entirely from home. The people he knew all seemed unchanged from the people he remembered and he didn't notice anything different about the world itself, but that didn't quite make sense. He assumed there must be differences he hadn't discovered or couldn't detect.

He tried to enjoy planning a future with Kim, but a persistent feeling of looseness in the linkage between events baffled him. How could he fully embrace this life when he was not entirely sure how it came to be? There were stretches when it felt like time was passing so quickly that it became a blur, a roar in his ears, and others—often at night—when he lay in the sleepless and broken reality of a passionate desire just to see an hour end, and in the whiplash between those two he wondered what he had landed in, and what he truly was.

After her internship, Kim took a job as an event planner at a small game company. She captured how he felt one evening after a late dinner. "It's like I'm a skipping stone," she said. "I'm completely there, and then I lift off and skip to the next thing so fast it feels as though nothing happened. Big changes happen, are happening, but I only make a choice and then move."

They converted the basement into an apartment with a separate entrance. He negotiated time to remodel before starting his job so he and Kim could do sensitive work themselves. The plumbing and electricity were already in place.

They put walkie-talkies in the apartment and their master bedroom, and stocked the apartment with canned and boxed food. Vin never told Kim that Mona had warned him about herself. When he suggested adding a second deadbolt to lock the apartment door from the outside, a one-inch cylinder with a hardened steel core that couldn't be unlocked from inside, Kim didn't comment.

They agreed to visit the apartment two times each month, together, but Kim only went a couple of times and the visits became his responsibility. He started adding an occasional, unscheduled visit. Concerned that Mona might be getting thinner, he took a few pictures to create a visual baseline. Within a few months, he had settled into a routine of making one short visit each week.

KIM WAS DETERMINED AND SURE of herself as the challenges at her work increased and Vin watched her build the foundation of her career. She traveled and worked late and on weekends but they managed a few overnights in the mountains, in Eastern Washington, and Las Vegas. They were married during Kim's eighth month in a small ceremony attended mostly by family.

Vin fell in love with the complexity of her pregnancy, her needs, her vague grumpiness and the imprecise mutinies of her body. He was delighted by moments of contentment that arrived like unexpected weather when she relied on the bond that still surprised him and leaned close so he could comb his fingers through her hair.

No matter how cool their room was, Kim sometimes threw off the covers. One night, after shifting about for an hour or more, she lay on her back, propped on extra pillows, with her arms around the top and bottom of her belly.

She didn't usually talk when she woke, but she asked, "Are you awake?" He moved a hand to her side in response. She said, "I've been thinking about . . . What if it isn't possible for Bucky to throw that lighter unless you're inside him? Then the worlds where he kills Matt aren't created unless you're there."

He felt the stillness of the room seeping into his body, filling him and defining his borders. "From what I felt," he said, "it was possible for him to throw it."

"But we don't really know, because you were there."

He bent his legs and shifted to relieve pressure on his shoulder, then turned away from her and lay on his back.

"I'm sorry," she said. "You probably think about that sometimes."

"It's a good question," he said. "Whether it would have been possible for him, emotionally, without me there." They stared at the geometric plane of the darkened ceiling.

"Are we doing the right thing," she asked, "for her?" They knew their child would be a girl.

"Yes."

"I can't fix what's happening in the world. Why am I making a new life?" The hard edges of the digital clock shone and the modest electronic beads on the room's devices each insisted on its individual presence, a combined blue light misting the hour.

"My belly is a big curl." She rolled toward him. "She's already turned me into a question mark. My whole body is asking what her life will be. She's turned me into punctuation." She was playing with the complaint.

"She's asking what all our lives will be," he said.

"I already see mothers and children differently. I've already changed. New babies have opaque eyes, like animals, like birds or fish."

"She won't be an infant like that," Vin said, uneasiness flowering. "You'll see her differently."

She waited, then sighed, her open hand snaking between his

arm and torso, her voice warm. "You always try to answer, but we're not a question."

ONE TRUTH HE DIDN'T EXAMINE was that Kim's pregnancy was distancing him from his experience in the crèche. Shortly before their daughter, Trina, was born, Vin realized it had been weeks since he'd dreamed of inhabiting other people.

The delivery seemed difficult to Vin but the doctor told him it had gone smoothly. After, Kim told him that she was uncomfortable housing a desperate stranger in something like a prison in their basement. Mona always appeared to be peacefully sleeping. They had put a tablet, books, notebooks, and pens in the apartment, but nothing got used. They never encountered her but she sometimes changed caskets.

Vin took Kim's concern seriously but didn't want to exaggerate the problem, so he didn't tell her when he bought a .38 caliber handgun and stowed it with a small stack of cash in the bedroom safe under the title to the house, Kim's adoption records, and their living wills. And, working from home, it was easy to discretely visit a firing range. It wasn't that he didn't want her to know, it was that he was preparing for a possibility so remote it wasn't worth discussing.

TRINA HAD WISPY CHESTNUT HAIR and steel-gray eyes, a wide face and plump baby cheeks that looked happy and vaguely middle-aged. As soon as she came home, Kim started to strategize about how they'd talk to her about drugs and addiction. Vin wanted to look at their new creature, this coagulation of living systems thickened by mutual interdependence in a way that invited future expansion, that offered forage for bacteria, and that promised to be friendly to autonomic function, to the transformation of proteins, the binding of oxygen in organic matter and the irresistible catalysis of affection. He wanted to put the conversation off.

While Kim's ability to rigorously assess a situation and make quick decisions awed Vin, that brilliance also made her creative with her fear. She faulted her parents for being distant and said she wanted to be close to her daughter, but in the early months, Vin felt she was often cool toward Trina. He saw it when she blinked in response to the same floods of affection that he felt. She held back, as if she feared unintentional currents would submerge her or pull her into error.

A standing person can face in any direction, but the first step Trina took was toward Kim. Kim and Trina were on a lumpy blanket in the big room, Kim cross-legged and glancing through a magazine, Trina squirming on all fours like a felted sea creature. Sophie was stretched out on a plank of sunlight, just beyond Trina's reach. Vin sat at the dining table, tapping on his laptop. Time blurred and sharpened and Trina was standing, her legs bowed but suddenly stalwart and a puzzled look on her face as if Kim had asked her to describe the purpose of a flint-lock. Kim straightened to breathless attention. Trina's foot twitched up and then wound forward, her arms stretching. She grinned at Kim. Her foot jerked down and she pitched toward the ground. Kim scooped her up before she hit.

"What are you thinking?" Kim asked, hefting Trina to her shoulder as she stood and carried her laughing to the big window.

BEFORE TRINA TURNED TWO, VIN got a windfall from the sale of Sigmoto. The new CEO had done a decent job—not great, but decent—and one of the technology behemoths snapped the company up, killed the product, and moved staff to other projects.

Then Kim got pregnant again, but in her ninth week she fell into a depression, calling in sick for a week and a half, dragging out of bed at eleven, and saying little beyond what was necessary. Even Trina didn't move her, and then she miscarried. She felt responsible, tormented by the possibility that her depression had triggered the loss. Her new gynecologist told them Trina's birth had defied the odds; Kim had always been more likely to miscarry. Surgery might help.

They were angry with the doctor who had delivered Trina and hadn't told them about the risks. Kim was still struggling, forcing herself out of bed early and into each wobbly day, forcing herself to exercise, reminding herself to smile at work even though it felt mechanical. Vin worried about her backsliding but the opposite happened. Weeks after the miscarriage, Kim began to recover her old self and she rediscovered skydiving.

One evening as she was cutting celery, Vin asked what had helped her through it. She shook her head, her strong fingers pausing the knife midstroke, mouth half-open, dark eyes unfocused.

"I jump to feel the rush," she said. "It sort of connects me with how big everything is. I think, before, I could feel that kind of thing in a quiet way too. I didn't need to jump. I could look at the world and think about things. But, with this sadness, nothing seemed to matter except what my body was doing, almost without me. It was like I didn't have my own body anymore. And I lost that feeling. But I was able to stay in things, and I did. And then I started to feel that I did need to be here, and it started getting better again."

Kim liked to skydive in new locations, often when she was

traveling for work. Vin sent pictures of himself and Trina making *V* signs to celebrate her courage. Kim said she kissed them for luck. She bought a helmet-mounted camera so they could watch her. Moments after she left the plane, there would be a minute when the sky was so large, the horizon so distant that the falling was invisible. Except for the constant rush of wind, everything seemed still.

AS SOON AS THE PHONE started playing Vin's custom tone—the first fourteen seconds from the "Floe" movement of Philip Glass's *Glassworks*—Trina yelled, "Tell a phone," from her high chair. Kim straightened from where she'd been leaning against the island counter, stepped over to Trina—who recently turned three—and kissed the top of her head. "That's right," Trina said proudly.

Vin killed the flame under the morning's tofu scramble and answered. Than Nguyen was calling to discuss a large software check-in that Vin had finished the night before. It was the kind of thing they could have covered in the regular morning call, but Than was being extra careful because Vin was working on a public interface. It only took a minute for Vin to reassure him.

Kim was leaning against the island, tapping at her phone. "I really have to go, now," she said, glancing up as though she were repeating herself. "They want me to look at the end-caps that got delivered to the office. I need to sign off before the shippers come. And I'm out of town on Monday. I've got to go to Chicago."

"Okay. But, no breakfast?"

Vin was wearing a loose short-sleeved T-shirt. Kim was in her work uniform—a navy jacket and slacks with a maroon silk blouse—an outfit that would have been inconceivable to the Kim he knew in high school. She'd recently been asked to review two production contracts in addition to her marketing responsibilities. "People wear lots of hats," she had explained to him, happily. He would have hired her at Sigmoto.

She tapped out the last fragments of a message and straightened, lifting a hand at him. "I don't have time anymore. I was really in a hurry."

"Oh. That was Than again. You know. He's trying to go the extra mile, even though I've already done it."

"Yeah, sure. You don't have to justify your"—she looked down and took a breath—"I'm not trying to make a big deal out of it. I just don't have any time anymore."

"Well, the food was done, you could have served yourself." Vin moved the frying pan to a trivet.

Kim said. "Okay. You didn't tell me. I'm not angry."

"Okay."

"Or upset. Right sweetie?" Trina was trying to fold a big chunk of apple into her mouth. She pulled it out and said, "No, Mom."

"You should cut the apple smaller than that," Vin said.

"She's okay. It's not a problem." Kim turned to Trina. "Aren't you?"

Trina nodded.

"I just know how she likes it," Vin said, "and usually, it's smaller pieces than that."

"Okay," exasperation drove Kim's voice higher. "You just do what you want. You always know what's right." She stopped, took a breath, and then asked Trina, "Do you like the apple, sweetie?"

Trina nodded.

Kim said, "Okay. See? She likes it. I've got to go."

She was looking at the screen of her phone again as she hopped down the stairs to the entryway.

"Alright," Vin said, "love you." He heard the door open. "Thanks," he yelled quickly.

"What? Why?" Kim called back.

"For cutting Trina's food when I was on the phone," he yelled, but the door had clicked shut behind her.

Trina would get picked up for daycare just after nine, and he would retrieve her at three. It was Friday, and they were planning to host a barbecue after work, their first attempt at hosting in years. Clouds had rolled in and it was looking like it'd be a cool day for August—seventy degrees, or maybe high-sixties by dinner, though it wasn't supposed to rain.

He said to Trina, "Daddy's going to be on the call."

Frowning, she shifted her head back and forth in an exaggerated gesture of indifference. "I'm going to be quiet."

"Thank you, Loop." Her pet name was their code word for a circle, a perfect shape.

"You're welcome." She was coloring a mouse that had grown too large for its house and now towered above it and she seemed intent on using each of her thirty-two crayons. Vin imagined she was searching for the difference between complexity and sophistication.

The morning call was routine. Afterward, Trina surprised him by asking why he had phone calls.

"It's work," he said. "You know, so I can make a living."

"Why do you make a living? Momma makes a living."

"Yes." He wasn't sure what she was asking.

"Why don't you ask her to bring what she made to our house?" Trina concentrated on coloring the air around the mouse dark green. "Then she could show you how to make it."

. . .

WITH TRINA AT DAYCARE, VIN brooded, batting away a growing sense that the life he was enjoying was limiting him and
he should be trying for more. Raising a child well was one of
the most important tasks that individuals could set themselves
to, but the world beyond his home was still rife with the lethal
problems that his parents' generation had allowed to fester. He
felt he was losing his balance.

He wished he could call Bill and get high. He'd been thinking
about Bill a lot recently. Dead, but only in a limited sense. The
person he knew was still alive in another universe, or many
others. And who was wearing the body that Vin had been born
with? Had that person been surprised to see Bill? He tried to
distract himself from spiraling into metaphysical confusion. He
answered a few emails, but got little real work done.

He'd uncovered a bug in a server operating system. For his
use case, it crippled performance on an object he needed. He
had half a mind to submit a patch, just to keep moving, but if
he wasn't seeing the whole picture—and he probably wasn't—
that could be a massive waste of time. More to the point, his
company allowed contributions to external projects only after
endless discussion and negotiation. Better to wait for a response
from support.

In this sort of situation, he would usually work on tests and
designs for the next sprint, but today he decided to visit Nerdean's office. He wanted relief from the aching, dragging sense
of sameness that was unexpectedly grating through his limbs
and chest.

The crèche was a wild and dangerous secret, an endless
opportunity to imagine alternate futures, and even though

nothing could eject him from his protective orbit around Trina, he wished there were a way to release just a scent of its power into his day-to-day routine. He stepped outside and followed the curving walk of circular concrete pads to the apartment's yellow steel door.

Mona was a lesson in the risks of the device, and flashbacks from his own shots could still hit him without warning, an almost paralyzing sense that everything, even the air embracing him, might suddenly thin and be stripped away. To hide the panic, he would pretend to be deep in thought. He pitied Mona and wanted to sustain her privacy and shelter, but didn't feel capable of explaining all of that to Kim.

He unlocked the door's second deadbolt and then the knob, but the door wouldn't open. The top deadbolt was locked from the inside. He'd never found it locked before.

A phone app could unlock both deadbolts. Though his phone's manufacturer assured customers that the phone's radiation was too weak to do harm, Vin kept his phone beside his computer, where he'd left it. He couldn't see past the curtained half windows. He knocked loudly and waited, then knocked again.

He went to the master bedroom where the walkie-talkie was charging, and pressed the button that would sound a tone on the basement handset. He waited, and then pressed the button to speak. "Mona? If you're there, this is Vin. Would you like to talk?" He tried twice but received no answer.

The point of the top deadbolt was for Mona to signal that she wanted to be left alone. She might be in the shower or sleeping after a long shot. He decided to give her space and look for an interesting design problem to work on.

. . .

THE EVENING TURNED OUT TO be warmer than expected and when people began arriving for the barbecue the house felt stuffy to him, its bright spaces dimmed, its rooms stilled and sullen. On the plus side, he'd put the best gas grill he could find on the first floor deck and would be able to cook while feeling as though he was levitating over Puget Sound. His mood was improving and he liked almost everyone they'd invited.

He didn't tell Kim that Mona was moving about. The less they discussed Mona, the less likely Kim was to insist they do something about her. He poked the long tip of a steel thermometer into a grayed chunk of pork that was cooking on the hot side of the grill and left it in for a moment, watching the needle on the radial dial tick upward.

"So?" John Grassler, a senior developer on Vin's team, was standing beside the grill. He waved a large hand over the rising heat, drew in a deep breath through his nose, and made a smacking noise. John was in his midfifties, heavy, bearded and bald, with sometimes veiny pink cheeks and a resonant laugh that spread comfortingly through enclosed spaces.

"Maybe another minute and a half for that one," said Vin.

"And thusly do we stalk our desires," said John.

"Do we?"

"Aye, with mighty grill and spicy sauce."

"Verily," said Vin, "and we lucky few will have all the desires we can eat in just a few more minutes."

Through the sliding doors, Vin could see that the table inside was already packed with food and Kim was setting down a large bowl of corn on the cob. They'd decided not to grill it to make more room for the meat. Trina was near the sectional, showing a new drawing to one of Kim's co-workers, Hanna Dawkins—a young black woman with a beautiful, dimpled smile and an alert reserve. She was in her second year at the company and, to hear Kim tell it, might be running the place in a decade.

Kim had also invited her boss, Laughlin, whom she described admiringly as a "take-charge kind of guy." Vin had invited John Grassler and two younger programmers, Brant Spence and Corey Nahabedian. Corey, Brant and Hanna had formed a little clique on the sectional with Trina. Kim and Laughlin were in the kitchen at the other end of the room, just out of sight.

Everyone turned toward a pounding at the front door, an insistent hammering with the fleshy part of a fist. "What's that?" Vin said. Kim was coming out of the kitchen and crossing toward the entry. She said something over her shoulder, presumably to Laughlin. There were more blows at the door, then muffled shouts.

As John said, "what's their problem?" Vin handed him the tongs and the thermometer, saying, "Can you keep an eye . . ." John quickly set his beer on the edge of the grill to manage the handoff, and then Vin was in motion.

Kim stood in the wedge of space between the threshold and the partially opened door. Vin couldn't see who was on the other side but heard a man's voice, threatening and indistinct, crackling through a catalog of curses. Just as Vin reached the entry, the man yelled in a deep, hoarse voice, "I know it's in here. I've been in here."

Kim paled and leaned back. Vin pulled on the door and she let go, letting it swing open so Vin could see their visitor. The man outside took a half step backward.

He might have been in his late thirties, with a narrow face, high forehead and short dark hair. He was wearing an army service uniform, a black jacket with yellow piping and gold buttons, white shirt, black tie, blue slacks. The uniform was loose, shiny with stains and rumpled by hard wear. His tan face was mottled by the pink of high temper, his eyes red-rimmed and glassy as if he hadn't slept for a while. A holstered weapon was strapped to his belt.

"Can I help you?" Vin asked as he shot Kim a look that was his best attempt at asking her to call the police without actually saying it. She, of course, had no idea that he was requesting anything.

"What's going on, Kimmy?" Laughlin asked as he arrived behind Vin, his presence announced a moment before by the spicy scent of pot.

"You," the man said loudly, staring at Vin, "I know you."

"I don't think we've met." Vin could feel his blood pressure rise, feel the sudden arrival of the floating sensation that could lift him into real anger.

"You were in the war cabinet," the man said, and Vin went cold, shut down. He was able to whisper, "What do you mean?" but it appeared as though no one around him heard it.

"Are you drunk?" Laughlin demanded from behind them.

"Only a few," the man said.

"What are you doing?" Laughlin, who was larger than Vin and built like a boxer, was leaning on Vin's shoulder, trying to step in front of him.

"Someone drove my car here," said the man, "and someone's driving me here."

"Why? How would someone drive *you*?" asked Laughlin, his voice reasonable and engaged as he finally pushed between Vin and Kim and onto the concrete pad in front of the door, forcing the man to take another step backward.

Laughlin's mildly positioned question seemed to disarm the man. His brows came together and he suddenly looked confused. He mumbled something, a long phrase Vin couldn't hear.

"Well, you need help," Laughlin said in response.

"Yes," said the man. "Please."

"Come down here," Laughlin said gently, and led the man to the concrete stairs beyond the path. "You can sit on the wall here. Can we call somebody?"

The man walked down a few stairs and then sat on the stone wall.

"Who should I call?" asked Laughlin, pulling his phone from the front of his jeans.

"Don't call anyone *I* know," the man said loudly, his anger turning to fear.

Kim stepped outside and Vin followed. The other four guests had filled the small foyer. Vin, seeing them, turned and went back into the entry. He took Trina out of Hanna's arms and said quietly to the others, "We should give them space."

He carried Trina up the stairs and into the dining room and called 911 while she sat on his forearm and leaned against his chest, her arms around his neck. Soon she'd be too big for him to carry like this.

John Grassler had gone outside, closer to where Kim and Laughlin were talking with the man. The rest watched quietly from the foyer.

Vin told the 911 operator that a man who appeared to be wearing a gun had pounded on their door and sounded aggressive and altered. Trina was starting to squirm so Vin carried her to the sofa and sat down as he talked to the operator.

"Why is everyone over there?" Trina asked. "Who is that?"

"We don't know him," Vin said after he finished the call. "He's just a man who came to our house."

"Why?"

"Loop, you know that sometimes there's no answer to that question."

A few minutes later, Kim came up the stairs. "Everyone's okay up here?" she asked, looking at Vin, the question clearly intended as a check on Trina. Vin nodded.

"Laugh's calling the police. The guy's walking away."

"I called 911," Vin said.

John came up to the dining area. "He's gone," he said. "You really don't know him?"

"No idea," said Vin.

"Well, I'm going back out to check on our magnificent grill." As John passed through the dining room toward the deck, Vin and Kim watched each other, Vin's arms around Trina.

"That man talked about a war cabinet," Kim said quietly.

"Yeah," said Vin. "What did he want?"

"No one knows," John said, just before he stepped back out on the deck. "He was a confused man."

"He kept saying he wanted to talk with you, Vin." Kim's face was flat, emotionless. "He said, 'I need to talk to that man who was here.'"

"Kimmy, everything okay?" Laughlin yelled up from the door.

"Yes, thanks, Laugh," Kim called back.

"He's gone," Laughlin said a moment later, as he walked into the room. "That was a bit of excitement."

"What did he want? What was that he mumbled at you, at the door?" Vin asked.

Laughlin laughed, "I think he said, 'I'm a buried man, clawing at the dark.'"

"That's creepy," Brant Spence said.

"What did he want?" Vin asked again.

"If anything, maybe just to talk. He said there was a ship in this house that he needed to get on, and that you were the captain. But then he started whistling and he staggered away."

WHEN THE POLICE ARRIVED, KIM and Laughlin had a brief talk with them. The strange visitor had given the evening a shot of adrenaline and energized conversation. After dinner, Vin spent about twenty minutes putting Trina to bed. Vin and Kim could both use their phones to listen in or watch her room, and their baby monitor would call them automatically if the volume in her room rose above a preset level. A couple of hours later, Laughlin was the last of their friends to leave, smiling as they thanked him for handling "the gunfighter" so diplomatically.

As they shut the door behind Laughlin, Vin said, half-jokingly, "And why so *Kimmy*? Is plain *Kim* not a good enough name for him to use?"

"Alright," Kim said, losing all trace of the jokiness with which she had seen off Laughlin, "that guy was one of them."

"One of who? What do you mean?" Vin was caught slightly off guard.

"He said someone was in his head, telling him to come here." Kim was almost accusing him.

"Okay, but there could be other reasons for that." Vin was remembering how difficult it was to influence people when he was in the crèche.

Kim said, "No," and when Vin hesitated, she said, "Remember, Mona said she could make people do things. You said you made that guy ignore the woman he had a crush on."

"I don't think it's the same. Bringing him all the way here—it doesn't work like that." Vin wanted to talk about Laughlin and didn't want Kim to use the crèche to avoid it. "That guy just seemed like a crazy person. Didn't he?"

"To show up at our door? Our door?"

"Well, we're near the base of the staircase to Marshall Park. There are all kinds of people up there. To be honest, I'm surprised more people don't randomly come to our door. Aren't you?"

"Random people with voices in their heads who come to our house looking for you? And a ship to ride?"

"I don't know—he wasn't *necessarily* looking for me. He saw me and decided, maybe for no reason, that I was the solution to his problems." Vin had committed to his interpretation.

But Kim saw his doubts. "Is there something I should know?"

"What?" he said, "What?"

"You know what I mean. Is there anything that I should know?"

"I don't know what you're talking about."

"What are you doing? What are you doing here all day? Are you going down there?"

"No. I work."

"No? You're not trying to go down there when it's not on the schedule?"

"No."

"You didn't try to go into that thing, today for example? You haven't gone in, or gone somewhere? You don't know that man?"

"No. No. No," Vin said, keeping his voice calm though he felt the fumes of his anger igniting. And then, suddenly, he was shouting. "Of course not. That was a crazy person. And now you're accusing me of something?"

Both their phones began ringing. The baby monitor was

alerting them to noise from Trina's room, but they didn't need the monitor. They could hear her yelling, "Daddy! Daddy!"

HE RAN TO TRINA'S ROOM and Kim watched him go. After he calmed her, he and Trina talked for a while. She was only reacting to the excitement of the evening, and then to their fight. As Trina lay back down, he sat at the end of her bed and rested a hand on the orange sheet above one of her ankles.

The room was dark and smelled of fabric softener and Trina's own warm scent. The stuffed elephant Trina slept beside was a bulky shadow above her large head. Trina said that Hanna liked pictures of the stars, and then they talked about the things Trina liked to draw, and at some point Kim appeared at the threshold of the room, looking wrung out. She didn't say anything, just watched them. After a bit more conversation, Vin and Trina agreed that Trina would go back to sleep and her dark eyes quickly closed. He kissed her and rose to leave. Kim had already gone.

Kim and Vin spent time wordlessly cleaning and then Kim went upstairs as he finished in the kitchen. When he reached the master bedroom, Kim was sitting cross-legged on their bed in underwear and a thin tank top, elbows on her knees.

"This place isn't right for us," she said as he walked past her into their bathroom.

Green tile on the floor, yellow and white stonework on the walls. A double soaking tub and a separate double shower. Just the taxes on this house could almost pay the mortgage on a home in a less expensive part of the country. He'd tried to puzzle out why Nerdean didn't keep the house if she expected to return. The best explanation he had come up with was that she figured the "house sitter"—whoever it ended up being—might not stay under other circumstances. He might want to get on with his own life, maybe take a job in another city. Which might mean a new house sitter, and another person who might learn about the crèche. But that still didn't make a lot of sense. Unless you also allowed for petulance, a knock on Joaquin for trying to undermine the contract.

He squeezed natural toothpaste onto the end of Kim's electric brush and the brand he'd been using since childhood onto his own and ran both brushes under hot water and started brushing as he carried Kim's to her. They went back to the bathroom and stood together in front of the mirror until they each dropped foamy spit into the tap water.

Kim said thickly, "There's a half-dead woman down there. This house is haunted. I can't keep working as hard as I do and come home to worry about this too. I don't feel healthy here. I'm going to dark places. Nothing feels right."

"Maybe you could work less?"

"My work is one place I know I'm doing things right."

"If you were to cut your hours . . ."

"We need to leave."

He walked into the bedroom and started unbuttoning his shirt. The deceptive cluster of electronics was long gone. A single corner of the bedroom hosted an office large enough for both of them, with expensive desks that had special cutouts and weighted springs to easily adjust their angles and heights for sitting or standing. But Kim rarely worked at home, and he'd gotten used to working downstairs where he could keep track of Trina.

"I don't want to fight anymore," he said.

Kim leaned against the bathroom door. "I have nightmares. I see her floating down there, under our house. How do we know that she can't choose whose head she goes into? What if she can get inside one of us? What if she can change our thoughts or what we want?"

"Do you feel like someone's doing that?"

When Kim didn't answer, he said, "She hasn't done anything. Mona is just a sad, lost person. She's more lost—she's possibly the most lost person who ever lived. She's not trying to hurt anyone and she doesn't care about us. I mean, she cares whether we keep the power on, but that's it. And why can't we do that? Keep the power on?"

"The most lost person who ever lived?" Kim said. "That's what you think she is? We shouldn't have anything to do with anything that rare. That's not who we are."

"We don't get to choose that kind of thing," he said. "Life chooses that."

"Life? What? Are you answering me with a *cliché*? Are you saying that *life has chosen* for us to live on top of that horror movie science experiment?"

Vin plugged his phone into its charger on his side of the bed. "I'm sorry you're scared. That guy was a real crazy, and I agree, it did sound like he might somehow have been referring to *it*. I'm sorry about how we—*how I*—kind of lost it. Look, it's Friday. Let's let it go for the weekend and think about it. If you still want to move on Monday, how about we talk about it then?"

"I'm going out of town Monday, to Chicago, remember?"

"Well, just let me know what you think before you go."

Kim sighed. "Yeah, I guess." She lay down and turned away from him. "I'm sorry too. I don't feel stable right now, though. This place can't be good for Trina. I just want—I know I want to leave. It's time." He peeled back the sheet on his side and lay on his back and then pulled the sheet across his legs.

Kim, with her back to him, said, "You're going to restock the fridge down there, and check on the systems tomorrow, right? You still do that just once a week, right?"

"Yeah." Vin turned out the lamp on his side of the bed and the room went dark.

"I want to come with you this time. I want to see it again," she said.

Kim had only been to Nerdean's office maybe three times in the last two years. "Sure. Okay," he said. "It'll be nice to have company. So, are you ready for the trip? Are you going to jump while you're in Chicago?"

"There's a site. It's going to be hectic but I may have time. If I do, I'll text you."

He said, "Let's both just clear our heads, and try to think of some way to improve things."

THE NEXT DAY, THEY MADE an effort to be more appreciative of each other. They decided to do extra housecleaning after breakfast and attacked it energetically, but a short disagreement over their plans for Sunday set them on edge. That afternoon, with Trina at a playdate, they went together to Nerdean's office. Mona hadn't left any sign that she'd been active. The robe might have moved from the back of one chair to another, but Vin wasn't sure, and the robe was dry.

While Vin was inspecting the apartment, he called Kim *Kimmy*, and that immediately revived the disagreement over moving. Kim fortified her earlier complaints by insisting the house was too big for only three of them.

The tension bled into Sunday, a subdued mutual resentment simmering through temperate, late-summer hours. On Monday morning they worked on logistics for the rest of the week, but with a baiting antagonism that left them both relieved when Kim finally set off for the airport.

ON TUESDAY MORNING, AFTER TRINA had gone to daycare, Vin received the email he'd been waiting for from the server operating system's support group. They weren't going to work on his problem. He called his manager to say he had an urgent errand and needed to take the afternoon off. Then he went outside and around the house to the apartment door.

He unlocked the second deadbolt and the lock on the knob, but the door wouldn't budge. The top deadbolt was locked again. He knew it had been unlocked on Saturday, when he and Kim had been down there. That meant Mona had come out of the crèche again.

He decided that he wanted to talk with her. If they were approaching a decision on whether to move, this was a chance to let her know. He didn't want to barge in, so he tried the walkie-talkie but she didn't pick up. He used the app on his phone to unlock the top deadbolt.

He called Mona's name as he opened the door, but she didn't answer. The living room light was on. He hadn't noticed it through the curtains. In the large bedroom, he stepped on the floor switch and after the slight hesitation the chute opened and light spilled up from below. Even though the chute was narrow he had a moment of vertigo when he looked down. He saw and heard nothing below. He called Mona's name again.

He was feeling even more uneasy than he usually did in the apartment. He walked into rooms and checked closets, turning on all the lights, but the apartment was empty. He went back to the chute and leaned over it, calling down one more time before he put his feet on the rungs.

As he descended, lowering one foot after the next, he called out a few times, "Anyone? Hello?" It was a mild relief to finally hear the whisper of the air conditioner. When he stepped off the ladder he saw that two of the crèches were activated. The first and the third.

He stood listening until he could hear his own heartbeat. He took a hesitant step toward the first crèche, took a breath, shook his arms. He walked up to it and put his hand on the transparent pane. The mist cleared immediately to reveal Mona floating in the blue fluid. He watched her for a few moments. Maybe she'd lost a little weight. Her skin had an odd, loose quality but he thought he might be imagining that. Maybe it was just because he was seeing her through the blue liquid, but he hadn't noticed it before.

He lifted his hand. The pane misted over and he walked to the third crèche. He didn't want to touch the transparent pane. He stood beside it, staring.

When, at last, he stretched out his hand and touched the pane and the mist cleared, he saw Kim floating within, naked, her body buoyed in the blue fluid, her beautiful black hair swept back from her face.

CHAPTER 12

The Bonfire

He carried a chair into the empty basement bedroom, tipped the hatch to close it, and sat down near the door. He waited in the dark and watched the floor.

After a while, the warm closeness of the room overcame him and he drowsed, filling the darkness with dreamy, elongated shapes. He imagined that any action was a possibility—that was what the crèche meant—there was no limit on behavior, absolutely everything was happening all of the time and he was simply a line of awareness trickling through the densely packed matrix of probability, his life an infinitesimal silvery trace, all but invisible within the morbid certainty of endless variation.

At the noise of carpet slipping against carpet he came alert. The square of floor, lit from below, lifted and then turned on one end, lighting the room. Kim's hand appeared first, flat on the carpet, the edge of the white robe sliding back from her wrist, and then her head rose out of the light.

She saw him and her mouth opened—an *O* of surprise. Her face hardened and she stared at him with open hostility as she climbed the rest of the way out of the floor.

"You lied to me. You said you didn't come down here more than once a week," she said.

"You remember that."

Her mouth tightened and she walked calmly past him. He rose and followed her into the small bedroom where she had flicked on the light and was pulling her black travel bag out from under the bed. He hadn't looked under the bed.

"Do you want to talk about what happened in there?" he asked, as she began laying her clothes out on the bed.

She shook her head *No.*

"Did you tell Laughlin you were sick, or . . ." He let the question trail off.

"Laughlin?" she asked.

"Your boss."

"Work is fine. I'm on sick leave." She pulled on her underwear and was putting on her bra.

"How long have you been doing this?"

No answer.

"How many Kims have I been sleeping with?"

"How would I know? More than one I guess."

"Alright. And, are—whoever you are now—what kind of work do you do?" he asked. "Are you a politician, or a janitor, or do you own a jewelry store, or a restaurant, or are you a short order cook, a waitress? What . . . what do you do for a living, Kim? Is that your name?"

"I'm the same person who left," she said, pulling on her jeans. "Nobody died while I was gone."

"Or came back to life? You're sure of that?"

"No, I'm not sure," she said while she was pulling on her green blouse. "How's Bill, Vin?"

"Don't pretend it's not reasonable for me to ask questions."

"I'm the same person I was yesterday."

"What's the name of our daughter?" he asked, and she froze, her fingers stilled at the bottom button of her blouse.

"What's the name of our daughter?" he asked again, his voice rising.

"The name—"

"The name."

"She's alive?"

Her head came up, her desperation a goad to the rage that filled him. Wherever she had come from, it had been less than this universe, less than what he and Kim had made here. In her world, Trina must have been miscarried. She had never happened. He held himself motionless, but the room blanked to red.

"Vin," she said, pleading. "You're not just saying that. Trina's alive?"

Which surprised him. She knew their daughter's name. She wouldn't if Trina hadn't been born in her world. She wasn't responding as he expected. This wasn't what he thought it should be.

She ran past him, barefoot, and slammed open the apartment door so it bounced against the wall. He shook off his astonishment and followed. By the time he reached the porch she'd already thrown the door open and was shouting—"Trina! Trina!"—her voice rising through the house.

Then she was rushing up the stairs, jumping two and three at a time, still yelling Trina's name. He chased her to the second floor where the yelling stopped. Kim had fallen to her knees in Trina's room. She buried her face in the neatly made bed and stretched out her arms and grabbed the blankets and pulled them toward her as she gasped and breathed in the scent on the sheets, the smell of their daughter.

Vin watched as her burst of energy decayed into sobbing. She climbed onto the bed and curled up in the blankets, crying. After a long time, when Kim was lying still on the bed, her eyes open, shocked and staring, he said softly, "What happened? What happened to you?"

Kim said, "Where is she?"

"She's at daycare."

Kim's voice became cold, quiet and firm. "I want a divorce, Vin. I'm taking Trina."

He rocked backward as if struck. He staggered, turned slowly away from her. He descended the stairs and sat at the dining room table, waiting for her to come down.

HER WORLD AND HIS COULD have been misjoined in any number of places. Anything could have been happening in her mind. He needed to consider the best way to talk with her about what she thought was happening.

He listened to her moving upstairs but she climbed to the third floor and there was quiet. With a spike of adrenaline, he remembered he had left the door to the apartment open. He went outside and around the house. The door was wide open, exposing the empty living room. He stepped in and closed it.

The hatch in the bedroom had closed so he stepped on the switch and it lifted. "Mona!" he called down, which didn't make sense if Mona was in a casket.

"Vin," she said softly, from behind him.

He spun, taking one short step backward, his heel landing on air, toe scraping the lip of the chute. Momentum from the spin carried him sideways into the hatch. He fell, bouncing against the side of the chute, fumbling to keep from dropping down it, then his leg exploded with pain as he lost consciousness.

· · ·

WHEN HE BECAME AWARE AGAIN, he was on his side at the edge of the chute but looking at the ceiling, his leg somehow both in agony and numb. He felt as though he was drowning in air. Mona's head came in sight, blurry and partial. The planets were actors and the moon was saying, "That's your cue." And then Mona disappeared and Vin blacked out again.

He reawakened in an ambulance, and again in a hospital room. He tried to imagine that the day had not happened.

HIS LEG WASN'T BROKEN, BUT both his knee and hip were badly twisted. Kim didn't respond to his calls and texts. He got an email that said she was sorry he was hurt. She said Trina was fine. The email included an apology and a link to the web page of a divorce attorney.

He had a phone call from his mother in Michigan. Kim had told her he was hurt and that they were getting a divorce. He had difficulty listening and was almost unable to respond through the fog of his anger. The next day, he got email from his brother, expressing concern.

John Grassler and Corey Nahabedian showed up the next evening to help him get home. John said he was sorry to hear that things were difficult between him and Kim.

Sophie still had food and water. Vin asked Corey to check if the door of the basement apartment was locked and Corey confirmed that it was. Vin had no idea where Mona had gone off to, and couldn't descend the chute to look. No one answered the walkie-talkie.

Because there was no one else in his home, a home health aid was assigned to check on him daily. The aid was a tall, thin man with a protuberant Adam's apple and an unhurried demeanor that frustrated Vin. He said he'd get Vin back on his feet and actually winked as he said it.

Trina texted every day from Kim's phone, a few words or an emoji or two, always preceded by "from Trina." Sometimes a few came on the same day. He replied every time, ignoring the fact that Kim must have been helping; just trying to tell Trina how much he loved her. He waited for texts throughout long, dry, day-lit hours while he was trying to read, or was staring at the water outside the picture window, or lying awake on the big sectional that the health aid had dressed as a bed.

He had no desire to work. He called Kim and alternately begged and threatened her, leaving a catalog of voicemails because she never answered his calls.

HE WAS IN A DREAM, standing on the sidewalk in front of a coffee shop, Caffé Vita on lower Queen Anne. There was a crèche inside, three caskets near the door to the restroom. He wanted to go inside but a man blocked his way.

The man's hair was tangled and greasy, his mouth loose, his lips sliding over crenellated teeth. He wore black jeans and a black T-shirt and his eyes were bright and sharp.

"I'm the old stag," the man said with cryptic dignity, extending his hand.

"My name's Vin."

"Oh, I know you Bambi," said the man, "but your name doesn't matter. I'm Buck, the old stag. I'm here to show you the ropes."

Vin reached to shake his hand but as soon as they touched the man pulled back and rubbed his palm on his faded jeans, as if rubbing off the contact.

"Psyche," he mumbled.

"My name's Vin," Vin said again, pointlessly. "What should I call you?"

"Buck. And devil take the *hind*most. Ha."

Then they were on Aloha street trying to merge south onto State Route 99, but they were on foot, not driving.

"JFC!" Buck yelled in frustration because he couldn't get into traffic safely.

"What?" Vin asked.

Buck glanced at Vin and his upper lip rose, almost a snarl. Then his face relaxed and he appeared thoughtful.

"What I mean is," he said, "it's simple, like ABC."

But Vin thought those weren't the letters he had heard. Buck was ignoring him now. Cars flew past on the highway. Buck's head jerked, his top lip and nose wrinkled upward as he drew in a breath. He leaned toward Vin. "The machines of the mind are more difficult to recognize than machines of iron and steam."

They walked back to Caffé Vita but not by a route Vin knew. They were moving silently, disturbing nothing. People didn't notice them. Birds and sunlight filtered through high treetops. Vin had a sense that the two of them were being stealthy and that all the small animals just out of sight were unaware of their passage.

High, layered apartment buildings rose on either side, and the street had gaps that descended to other levels of street. Their path reminded Vin of a place he once walked in Lisbon, on his way to a movie theater.

"What are you crying about?" Buck demanded, which felt unjust because Vin wasn't crying.

"How can I get back to where I want to be?" Vin asked.

"No telling." Buck was sipping his latte in a booth at Caffé

Vita. His face had a greenish pallor. "But in my experience, among the available infinities, there's always a higher proportion with you than without you, so odds are you'll find yourself again."

THE HEALTH AID STOPPED VISITING, which was just as well. Vin's cheek had started twitching when the man winked at him. Vin's doctor told him that he'd always limp. And then, in a moment when he was at the picture window wondering how many days in a row the sky had been blanketed by dark gray clouds, everything cheerful about the world disappeared. It only took an instant. Words became flayed skins of sound, meaning drained.

From that moment, Sophie stopped coming to him. She eyed him from a distance. He had stopped feeding her at regular intervals and now she stopped protesting.

He no longer saw a reason to turn on the lights in the house. He realized he had never really thought much about them. Maybe Kim had been turning them on and off when she lived with him. The city remained weather-stricken. He closed the curtains and lived in the dark.

He spent hours planning to regain custody of Trina, working through scenarios. Kidnapping was appealing, but as he thought it through, it was difficult to escape the high potential for catastrophic failure, if a neighbor happened by and got nosy at the wrong time, or if Trina chose the wrong moment to scream or run. No matter how he went about it, kidnapping would require a lot of advance work, scouting, and thorough planning, which also added risk. Another possibility that might be less risky was destroying Kim's reputation, after which he could appeal the custody agreement. There were reasonably secure ways to do that, starting online. He could connect her with unspeakable services. She would have to click a couple of links to make it all work, but he knew enough about her to hide the links in things that looked innocuous. Then he'd adopt aliases to build out a record of activity that he could accuse her of in court. He could even make pictures of her doing things, and forge browsing records. And he knew where to go for advice—the Internet was almost a push-button operation for harassment. And he could attack her finances. He probably still had enough information for that. Or hire someone to force-feed her Fentanyl. He did many long hours of research on the dark web. There were people who could help. But maybe Fentanyl was too elaborate. Simpler would be safer.

The big problem, however, that he kept running into as he gamed out his ideas was that they always ended with him being an unfit parent. And if he were unfit, that would mean that Kim had been right to take Trina from him. When he reached this point, he would start over with a new idea.

He would sometimes piece together enough resolve to phone a friend and beg for news about Kim, but he stopped making those calls because he kept threatening his friends when he thought they were withholding information. He started sending emails to Kim describing how wrong and unfair she was being, and then warning of consequences if he didn't get custody of Trina. It felt important to describe the consequences in detail. He got an email from an attorney who claimed to represent her and who asked for contact information for his attorney. He wrote that he was not going to hire an attorney but was avidly looking for an assassin.

John and Corey dropped by a few times. Vin tried hard not to lose his temper with them. One of them would sometimes accompany him on a short walk with the crutches. Weeks passed. On the day he finished with the crutches, he received a call from his new manager at work, who told him his projects had been picked up by other developers. When he was ready to come back, they'd review his options.

"Am I fired?" he asked.

"We're not saying that," said his new manager, with warm imprecision. Vin didn't mind.

When divorce documents arrived, they included references to threatening voicemails and emails. He didn't recognize most of the quotes but when he checked his Sent Messages, he saw they were accurate. The elaborate language he'd used surprised him and he couldn't bear to read it all. Life felt alien and he was unrecognizable to himself.

Kim wanted full custody and the right to determine when he could see Trina. She made no claim to any joint assets, including the house. The documents included a note that Trina had written saying she wanted to live with her mother because she was scared of him. He lay down on the sectional and didn't move for the rest of the day.

He had locked infinity in a vault in their basement and it had exploded into Kim's life, and then her life destroyed his. He didn't know whose fault it was, but what they were suffering had to end. The day after he received the documents, he found an inexpensive attorney and signed everything.

TWO DAYS AFTER THE DIVORCE was finalized, as he was idly scanning job ads, his phone rang. It was Kim. "Vin," she said when he answered—she was crying—"I had to do it because I know what you're capable of. I'm sorry. I'm sorry, but you need help."

"You never trusted me. I don't know you," he said, feeling

clearheaded, "and you don't know me. You're a stranger who's living in my ex-wife's body. One day, I'll come for my daughter. You shouldn't get in my way. Don't call me again."

"Vin," she said, panicked, "I know what you're thinking. I know. Don't do it, please. We didn't love each other. We really just didn't. Vin, we were only together, weren't we, because of what happened with Bill? And yes, I did this. I did. But I was thinking about you, too. I thought, maybe there was a chance if I went into it, then—I thought someone else might come out, someone who could really love you, and forgive you. But I got so lost. I saw things . . . I went through hell." Kim sobbed softly as Vin waited in a wash of confusion. "I was trying to find her. When I realized I'd come to a world where Trina was still alive—"

"What do you mean, goddamnit,"—he shouted, blowing out his voice—"why the hell are you saying that? What happened to my daughter in your fucking, shitty world?"

There was only the sound of breath from four lungs, two throats, two mouths, breath finding its way between worlds. Kim said, "Oh, Vin, you have to know. You can't guess what happened?"

"No. How the hell would I be able to do that? You weren't here. I was here. The whole time. You were someplace else. Somewhere else." He shouted again, the last phrase.

"No, it was all the same. Everything is exactly the same as here. But, where I started, we had a party, and, a man came. He was a military, army or—anyway, he was wearing a gun, and he was yelling. I think he was looking for Nerdean, her office. You got angry at him." Kim cried softly for a few moments. "You got so angry. I watched and I couldn't stop it. You started a fight but he had a gun. And he shot Hanna. She was okay. But—Trina . . ." And she couldn't say any more.

Into darkness and distance—through the space a phone line crosses that is filled with every possibility that never happens—Vin strained to hear more. Anything that might start on the other side of that gap but would come from a world he recognized.

"No, Kim," he said at last, "that's not right. That didn't happen."

"It did."

"No, it didn't. You're *confused*. That's what happened with your brother, Bill. That's what happened to you and to him. But it didn't happen here. Trina didn't die."

"I know. I know it." She said, and hung up.

THE LAW IS A FROSTING of cyanide and judges are bitter, small people, angered by their humiliating yoke of stunted ambition, drunk with their smeary quarter-ounce of power. Lawyers look at you and see a meal. Judges see another measure of the drug that feeds their habit. No one saw him. The world he had believed in had tried to poison and kill him and sell off the parts. She had become evil. How could he have behaved differently than he did?

Kim. That was her name. But it wasn't her. She had taken herself away from him. Whoever this woman was, he didn't know her.

Before this, Bill was the person he had relied on. They could talk about anything. But this "Kim" was here now instead of Bill.

He could learn to murder safely—a poison that broke down completely or a neatly staged accident. Make it look like suicide. Who would investigate a death if it clearly looked like suicide? Who would really do that? And what if she died in an underfunded county in some bankrupt state where working people are shitty at what they do? He could plan that out, make that happen. He was patient. He was good at fine detail work. He knew how to use log-less proxy services to hide activity online. He knew how to scrub a hard disk to make it truly unreadable and then how to drill it and smash it.

And if things went wrong? He could escape through the crèche. It was the perfect safety valve. Someone else would land in the problems he created. Did he care about that? That one other person?

Although, if the crèche was what he thought, he would be creating the same situation an infinite number of times—infinite variations across infinite worlds. But, if Mona was right, that problem already existed.

He could just use the crèche to leave. Find another world. Was there such a thing as a better world? He could find a place to be with his daughter. He was a good person who had gotten lost among infinite possible worlds.

The crèche was an alternative to staying in this universe and finding out what he would do. And among the infinite possibilities there must be at least a single world in which Kim loved him. It had to have been possible for her to love him.

Mona was gone. She had walked out of the apartment into the physical world and disappeared. The office was his now. The house was empty. All the caskets were empty. The dead had risen.

HE SOMETIMES WOKE IN EARLY morning hours without his anger and lay like a stain in the bed that possessed the memory of Kim's body. In that other world, the one that the present had deprived him of, her arms and legs had stretched out beside him and he would brush against them and gently lean into the smooth warmth of her skin, igniting and intensifying their delicate radius of safety. Now he turned from side to side in the densest darkness or lay on his back keeping his eyes closed and the house sometimes creaked or popped as houses do and he was seared with the useless hope that the sound might be Kim or even Trina—a footstep, an inadvertent bump—one or the other of them out there, near him, one or both returning.

NERDEANISREAL—THE FILES ON THE SYSTEMS in Nerdean's office were completely different when you logged in with that password. The *Nerdeanisreal* account was the administrative account for everything in the *Neardeanisafake* account, so you could see and edit all of the *Nerdeanisafake* material, and a great deal more.

It occurred to Vin that there might be other accounts, so he logged out and tried to log back in with several other passwords:

Nerdeanisanasshole

WhatthefuckNerdean?

ShitfuckshitfuckshitfuckNerdean

FuckyouNerdean

Nerdeanistheabsolutelycruelestfuckeronthisicymotherfuckingplan-etofhell

Nerdean?Hello!Nerdean?, and a few more. None worked.

When he tired of pounding out frustrations on the keyboard, he read further into the new documents, the truer explanations. The files under this account assured him that time and chance were both—as Mona had said—illusory. Everything that had or could exist always did. The human experience of life was the result of a kind of channel created by and filled with awareness. The mind moved; the world didn't. The mind's path formed as the alchemy of observation slipped through the unimaginably vast and otherwise static structure of everything, the mind trickling, ever in motion, pulled toward states of greater entropy.

Sure, I'll buy that for a dollar, Vin thought. Why the fuck not? He logged off. He sat in the eggshell chair looking at the dark screen and imagining Kim there. He imagined Kim reading that same drivel before giving in to her weak, frustrated, middle-class despair and then throwing all of their fucking goddamn lives onto the bonfire of pure chance.

Although—and here he dynamited the roaring train of his own furious musings—she did that only after he had done the same thing. And after he had done it a few times. And then told her about it. And admitted to her that he was sometimes tempted to do it again.

But she had always been so frustrating in that way, always drawn toward the things that frightened her.

And so, if he knew she was always that way, shouldn't he have been able to recognize the risk? How much of her had he missed? Did he know her at all, or had he just been filling in an outline with his own ideas? (And if ideas were things a person could contain, could the crèche measure them?)

AS FOR LUCID DREAMING, THE new files only referenced it in a passage that said the crèche was so revolutionary that its capabilities should be disclosed slowly, or new subjects might be too frightened to test its full potential. Vin had difficulty wrapping his mind around the savage arrogance that passage betrayed. Its author was willing to camouflage the nature of the device, hide its ability to wreak havoc on a life. And for what? To experiment?

Also surprisingly, this "truer" documentation contained only a small number of well-constructed, coherent passages. Most of it was a jumble of mannered terminology, excess, and slapdash notes sprawling under hoary titles like, "The Second Law of Thermodynamics and Attributes of the Structural Relationship Between

Event Contexts that the Human Mind Interprets as Probability." It also included many obscene drawings of massive genitalia variously configured with faces, brains, and deformed bodies. They looked as though they were drawn on paper, scanned, and then pasted into the files. Beneath many were neat, numbered captions—like "Mind Fuck Series"—as if they were items in a formal display. They seemed to be interspersed without a pattern throughout the files, their creator ensuring a record of comprehensive disdain.

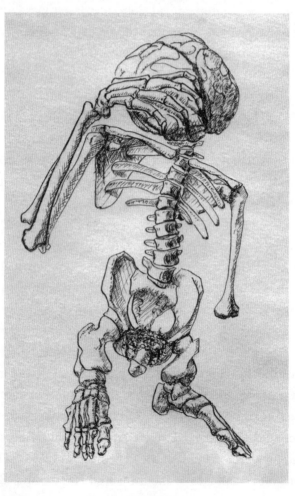

A file titled "Exercising Causality Through a Surrogate Awareness" had a tutorial on how the "subject," a person in a crèche, could influence the actions of a "surrogate," a person whose mind the crèche was "compositing":

> *The subject may only directly affect the surrogate's internal dialog . . . Broadly speaking, the subject has two options for taking action:*
>
> *1) develop trust over time by aligning with a surrogate's perceived self-interest. The subject becomes a trusted advisor to the surrogate . . .*
>
> *2) Bombard the surrogate with hyperbolic emotional messages, either strongly positive or strongly negative. Sudden, unexpected shifts from one extreme to another can enhance this approach, which may generate emotional disruption intense enough to interrupt the surrogate's motor response system, thereby creating opportunities to exercise direct control.*

It went on. There was nothing about whether the techniques should or should not be used, only how to use them.

A large document named "Unforeseen Risks" began: "Original assumptions were that the crèche technology was essentially risk free. Subsequent extrapolation from empirical results suggest the following list of possible risks." And then a long list of nightmarish scenarios, such as:

> *4) Double-Loading: New probability models predict an unmeasurable possibility that two affiliated awarenesses may be simultaneously recalled to the same body, creating*

a highly volatile and possibly lethal encrustation of pre-explanatory awareness.

There was no explanation of what "pre-explanatory awareness" might mean, and:

9) Shot-Stuck: a process by which a subject becomes immune to the potential for a return shot. This risk has been confirmed, but is probably highly improbable.

At the end of the list, he added:

Maybe Nerdean is an unhinged sadist and anything is possible.

Vin learned that aiming of the outbound shot was very crude. Because all constraints bracket infinite possibilities, the initial "throw" of a mind from the device was less "aimed," and more "guided"—almost random, no matter what parameters were set. The "return throw," on the other hand, had a clear target: a crèche. "There are infinite possibilities for the return, but all include a crèche prepared to receive a specific mind.

"The crèche terminates a shot by collapsing the field that sustains dislocation of the subject's basis (his or her awareness). Acute local perturbation in the field of consciousness resolves and consciousness reinvests the subject. However, any motion of a basis requires a transition through a probability state, including the inescapable influence of all entropy (necessary uncertainty) attached to relevant contexts. Entropy ensures an incongruity between the basis and the subject. Put plainly, there is infinite likelihood that a 'person' will not return to their originating body."

PART V Worlds Within Worlds

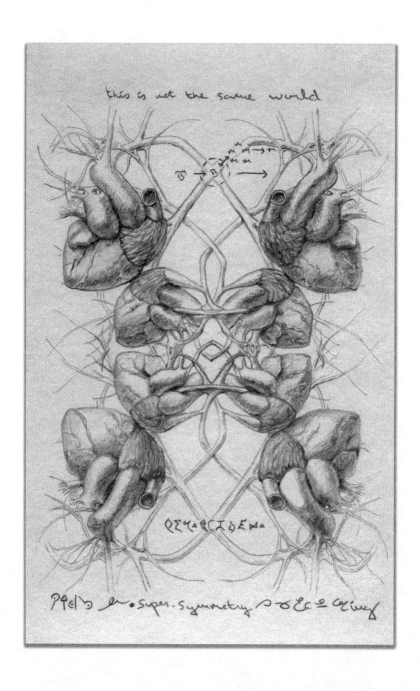

CHAPTER 13

Within Worlds

Vin is in the crèche again and a buzzing in his head is getting louder and more painful. Then it ceases. He feels a release of tension and a wave of peaceful absence, no sensation of any kind, no light, no smell, no sense of touching anything and he's not sure whether or not his eyes are open.

A voice, which he experiences without hearing, says, "Welcome to this event context, designed for the temporary storage of unanchored awareness. The meta-causality you have attempted to establish is unauthorized and is associated with a protected awareness. To prevent permanent damage to your consciousness resulting from immersion in simulated oblivion, to avoid ethically compromised outcomes, and to promote greater self-awareness, you will experience this context with an appropriate number of affiliated awarenesses."

Vin hears a brief sequence of high-pitched tones that seem to originate inside his head, and then the voice continues: "Please understand that your influence on other, nearby awarenesses is limited in scope to methods that simulate verbal communication. You will have a simulated experience of speaking and hearing, as will other awarenesses in your context. You may move freely, but your perceived location will not change. If your experience becomes trying, we suggest that you protect your own coherence by adopting the conviction that you are experiencing a dream.

"You will be returned to a context closely related to your origin point within a period determined by the construct that has attempted to establish meta-causality. To preserve mental health, your storage facility is equipped with a utility that displays a best estimate of perceived time remaining in this event context. You may view your remaining time by making a verbal request. Simply say, 'View Time.' You will now hear a series of tones, after which you may have limited congress with affiliated awarenesses."

Another short, high-pitched tone sounds. It has a color as well: red. Then a slightly lower, yellow tone sounds, followed by a lower, blue tone, and finally a green tone, a very comfortable sound.

At first, Vin sees only darkness, but that slowly fades until the world in all directions, including above and below, is no longer black but dark gray. At the same time, a set of evenly spaced points within the darkness begins to grow lighter. The points thicken and slowly take on the shape of human bodies until all about him, positioned as if at the eight corners of a cube and the midpoints of each edge and the middle of each side, are twenty-four lines of bodies, with Vin at the center. Each line extends to a vanishing point, with a new body floating in darkness at roughly every ten feet. Each body is naked and looks exactly like Vin. Several nearby are watching him.

"Hey," one of them says, from above him and to his right. He sees the man bending toward him, hears the man's voice directed at him. "Don't freak out. This place is completely safe. You're safe here."

"What is here?" Vin asks.

"I know what you're thinking," one of the other men says, then he and a third man laugh at the joke.

"This," says the one who spoke first, "is like a holding cell." The man isn't being loud but Vin can hear his voice clearly. He can hear the breath that's creating it. "Your crèche tried to throw you forward in time, to a future when the technology Nerdean invented is pretty common. They made this place as a defense against people jumping into other people's minds."

"So, this is the future?" Vin asks.

"Well, that depends on where you're coming from," says a version of him with a stubbly chin.

"He's from the same place we are, nitwit. Look at him, he's our age. Use some common sense. Jesus." That version of him punches the air. He has longer hair than the others.

"Oh, really? Half the time I come out of the crèche I've landed in some crazy place I don't know where the hell I am. So how does common sense apply?"

As Vin turns about, he sees each naked body—each version of his own body—with a level of detail that increases when he focuses. The darkness between them seems flexible, expanding or contracting in response to his attention, and the light is uniformly clear, the shadows always what he expects them to be. He realizes that a few of the men are crying—apparently inconsolably, because others are trying unsuccessfully to console them. There are versions of him shouting, barking angry orders, cursing. Almost all those around him—all the versions of him—seem to be having an intense emotional experience of some kind.

"Hey, hey. Concentrate on me. On me," says the man above him and to his right, who looks exactly like Vin, even the cut and length of his hair. "It'll make this all easier."

Vin tries to, and the voices rumbling about him—the grumbling, the mad wailing, the waves of conversation—recede into a background murmur. It's weird and distracting to see a naked version of himself standing about fourteen feet away. The man's feet rest on nothing but are angled as if they're supported by an invisible floor. He's crouching, so when Vin looks up, the two of them are facing each other.

"Thank you," Vin says.

"Don't mention it."

"Are you bending your legs?" Vin asks.

"What?"

"Are you actually bending down, or am I only seeing that?"

"I mean—I don't know what you're seeing," says the other man. "Are you frightened?"

"Yes."

"Me too. I always am. But this place is safe. The strangest thing about it is the lack of smell. And how my sense of touch feels muted. But don't worry, I've been in your position before."

"You mean that literally, don't you?"

"Yeah. I do."

"Was this a mistake?" Vin asks. "Going back into the crèche again?"

"Probably," says the other Vin. "Or maybe. I don't really know. I'm on the same journey or, whatever, that you are."

"This is it, isn't it? I mean, I'm finally, really going crazy."

"You mean you think this is all just a figment of our imagination? That you're just unable to tell the difference between this and a dream? No. The crèche threw us into the future, that's all. And this particular future is defending itself. I've been in this place before, or maybe other places with similar defenses. I've been in other futures, too, that don't have defenses. Things can get hairy. On a cosmic scale, you know, there's basically zero difference between one generation of humans and the next."

The intensity on the face of the man looking at him—which must mirror his own intensity—surprises Vin. It feels as if he's being prodded by it, as if it's demanding something of him. He takes a breath and imagines that this other Vin probably doesn't know how his look affects people.

"So, if you've done this before, then you must be a future me, right?" He glances around at the endless versions of himself, then back at the one he's talking with. "Because this is my first time here. So, if you told me what happened to you, I could try and do some things differently, make different choices and things could get better."

"Not really. I could tell you a bunch of stuff, but there's so much happening, so many different interactions and possibilities. Things are just different for each of us. I mean, I could—look, the truth is, I tried that. I came to grief."

"So trying might bring me to grief too. Well, what else do you have?"

"No, I'm not going there. Really. And you don't want me to. Trust me."

"Can you at least tell me why all these variations"—Vin motions at the lines of himself—"why are so many crying?"

"Or why are some furious? Or why can you and I have a civil conversation? Chance, I guess. Just random, dumb luck."

A very small number of the other Vins look relaxed or bored, even while standing naked on the non-floor in non-space. One or two are cackling mad. Some are shouting at each other. A few are whimpering.

"I actually find this place painfully, painfully boring," says the other Vin, the one he'd been talking with. "So damn boring. I hate when the crèche drops me here."

"Really?" Vin asks. "Really? Boring is about the last word I'd use to describe it."

"You haven't traveled much, have you?"

"This is my fourth, um, do we call it a shot?"

"Oh." The other Vin becomes somber, sad. "Did you abandon Trina, then?"

And Vin can't help himself. He leaps upward, though his position doesn't change at all. "Do you know what happened to my daughter?" he demands. "Do you know where she is? How can I get to her?" He is wrenched by anger. He can feel himself overheat and sees his spit flying at the other Vin, lit with glinting clarity as it arcs through the non-space.

"Hey, hey. Calm. Calm. Your daughter is back there, wherever you started from," the other Vin says, his voice softening.

"Kim took her from me," Vin snaps. "I can't reach her. Kim took her."

"Ah, shit," says the other Vin. "Look, I'm so sorry." And with a deeply pained expression he turns away.

"Kim completely fucked you over," a Vin near him yells out, one who's leaner, who looks almost starving.

"Fucked me over too!"

"Me too!" A Vin with a mustache.

"That bitch!" yells another Vin.

"That fucking bitch, Kim!" yells someone else.

"Ah, fucking bitch!" A loud chorus of voices swells around Vin.

"Kill that bitch!"

All around him, legions of different versions of himself are erupting with obscene vitriol, but he's shouting as well, forgetting himself, joining them.

He yells for a long time. He froths. When he feels his energy wane he remembers Trina and the injustice, remembers she's deprived of his love and protection and nurturing and he's furious again and curses and howls.

Time passes. A moment arrives in which he realizes that he hasn't shouted recently. Dizzy and nauseous from the strain of his galloping anger, he says, "View time," and immediately sees a digital display counting down from two hours, fifty-eight minutes and seventeen seconds. He waits for what seems a long time, his anger boiling back up, and then says, "View time" again. Two hours, fifty-two minutes, one second.

YOU LOOK UP AT THE sky, the stars endless and isolate, distances so vast that your only defense—the only way to exist in your single body that feels less amid all that span of darkness and light than the fading warmth from one curling breath—is to imagine, imagine you are there, everywhere, as everything, and by imagining, by dreaming, allow yourself to continue. And then, as nebulas bloom and grow smaller with an outward rush of perspective—of time and scale—your specific experience becomes integral to the whole, a mystery whose integrity is set in motion by a living world and the passions it inspires.

WHEN VIN WOKE FROM THE crèche a fourth time, his world was both too small and too large for him. Above the underground office lay the basement of the house and above that the surface of the earth and then the sky, and the only way to live was by being a part of it all, so that imagining became a survival skill and dreaming the foremost skill of every individual who is alone.

And as for companionship, Kim and Bill had lives of their own; all companions did. They were swept up in their own dreams, the consequences of their own decisions, directions of their making that must be different from his because there is just too much raw possibility in the universe for any two lives to follow the same course. Possibility was the stuff of the universe; difference the material of time.

When he exited the casket and left Nerdean's office, he left his limp behind in another world as if it was a sloughed-off skin. He walked around the huge house that he had just that very day inherited from a likeminded creature, a man with his same name who had also conveniently left a body behind for him to inhabit. Sophie lay on her bed near the dining room's picture window, alertly watching small birds in trees just across the street, her long, cream-colored fur catching cloud-filtered sunlight, her mouth quivering in ecstatic, predatory anticipation. "Ah, ah, ah," she said, in her cat voice.

It was nine-thirty in the morning and her dish was empty. When she heard him opening a can of food, she jumped down two levels from her perch and ran across the dining room to join him in the kitchen.

He didn't check his phone. He didn't want to know how people he loved had fared within this particular sliver of eternity. He was only a stranger here, and would travel further afield.

FOR THE FIRST TIME, HE attempted to stay in the crèche for more than twenty-four hours. After arranging for Corey Nahabedian to feed Sophie for a week, he set the system to start what the files described as a "multi-shot," the same mode Mona was using. In a multi-shot, the subject had a short shot, returned to a crèche, and then was briefly revived. If the subject exited the crèche, the cycle aborted. Otherwise, the subject went back into partial-torpor, and took another shot. He didn't quite understand how a multi-shot could work, given the shell game that the crèche was playing with bodies and minds, but he had decided to try it.

DARK, MUDDY GROUND SPINS AS if the whole world were a thrown disk, then hits him in the face. Soft and heavy sludge pushes into his mouth, his cut lips and cheeks. His teeth hurt. Face down in muck near the splinters of something, he shudders and angles his chin up, leaving his forehead embedded while opening a gap to breathe from the side of his mouth. The world shakes and booms. He waits.

He must pull his face from the earth. Pain lancing neck and shoulders, the furrow of a sharp edge crosses his jaw—a helmet's chinstrap—these things press him as he raises his head. A man, craggy and broken, is gibbering in his mind. The man tugs the muscles of the body Vin inhabits, makes them spasm.

Vin moves jaw and tongue as regions recover from numbness. Sound of gunfire. A high, deafening whistle comes and goes. The air shakes with distant thumps. The broken ground he is on is a mix of bodies and dirt. The crèche has sent him to another bad place.

He is breathing, this body whole but hollow, as if abandoned. He finds its owner, the madman who is now begging him—begging anyone—to act, to move. The madman is searching in the firmament of his own mind for a hole to crawl into. He will give over the reins of his body if Vin guarantees a crushing defeat of all enemies. Or if he doesn't. Vin pulls and pushes their shared body up to its knees.

The body aches with cold and injuries. Vin stumbles to standing. The air hums. A great fat sun with fiery cheeks strolls over distant hills. The corpses may rise up to dance in rhythms of sky. Is that his old friend opening a bloody breast to let in the raw wind? He is a good friend. A fine, generous man. Sadly, his name is shattered. Vin should splash a bucket of water on his filthy head and clean his crusted face and close his split mouth. If he can find the pieces of his jaw.

Fields turned by battle lose their place in the world. These might be fields anywhere. This is no place. Oh, my brothers, Vin thinks as he staggers, why such a mess? Why carve such bits and pieces off your bodies to strew all around, so careless with meaty arms and gut, or this toe that should be tapping stones or this face with paled lips puckering to whistle songs of grief?

He bends to touch the face, squats and presses its bony forehead, draws three fingers across a mud spattered eye, tries to close it but it won't. Instead, he scrapes grit into the eyeball and the helmet falls backward, pulling off the crown. Vin and the madman reflect on the lack of discipline. Any man would be disappointed to make a show like this at the end. The madman takes the reigns of their body and lifts the helmet, filled as it is with skull and brains. He digs within to ensure no one is hiding.

No one is, but the tiny, bristly hairs and the bloody gunk and bits of skull are frightening. The madman has little schooling, but Vin knows that each of the billions of cells of blood and brain includes a unique string of DNA, the double-helical chain that was this man's signature on his contract with eternity.

"I know it now," the madman yells, triumphant. "I saw it in my own mind. You are saying that these numberless, twisting worms have already eaten him. Poor love."

"No," Vin replies. "Those twisting worms are proteins that are a part of him. They are his blueprint, his design."

"Oh, I am a fool for words," says the madman, who feels grubby and abashed before Vin's angelic knowledge.

Time to walk. Most bullets fly out of one direction and into another. Is it better to go where bullets come from, or where they're going to? Questions. Going where they come from may put you behind them, which has benefits, surely. Going where they're headed may offer company, if you could walk beside them. So, which direction is the better choice? The madman makes a worried sound and grabs his tongue with his filthy left hand.

Vin makes a choice. He has died before within the crèche, and survived it.

"Oh, you have, have you?" demands the madman, his broken head popping up like a gopher in Vin's thoughts. Vin doesn't answer. Making the body move is hard going. He doesn't have a lot of energy left for being thoughtful.

Staggering and falling and rising ensues. Vin is in Africa, in the body of a mercenary fighting EPLF rebels in a conflict he knows nothing about. He's never been to Africa before. ("Born here," corrects the madman.)

He's dizzy and in great pain. The body he's in is insane, and the world is spinning and stopping. The hours begin to drag by.

HIS SHOT WITH THE MADMAN ended during a firefight—bullets twanging through humid air and into thick plants that sprayed green shrapnel. When he awoke inside the crèche, he was too stunned to summon the presence of mind to exit. He slid into a second shot . . .

. . .

. . . IN WHICH HE EXPERIENCES A lot of sex, with many different people. The shot begins as a tessellation of bright sensory
moments, a musk of bodies and perfumes that gently unstitches
him. There are soft chests and others firm and geometric, wide
caramel aureoles and pink-rimmed, vanishingly small buttons,
gooseflesh along slick lengths of skin leading to innies, and
others to outies. He lies on his back and things happen. He rises
to his knees and acts. The first time he begins to organize a full
sense of himself his prostate becomes a ringing wave and he gets
lost again.

Vin has only had a few partners, and has never had sex with
men. There are many men and a few women here. But when his
host runs a palm over a bearded face and pulls it to him, Vin's
understanding of himself is irrelevant. Elian, his host, is alert
and more than happy, is expert in responding to and intensifying a coupling. Elian's delight is already faceted and Vin only
adds another lens. During pauses, recollections of Kim form
and fade, smells recall her, the weight and feel of bodies and
limbs evoke ghostly memories.

Elian is lying on his back, exhausted, his limbs over
other healthy limbs. He stretches and stands, makes a joke
that Vin doesn't process. He's on a large yacht in a lovely,
island-bound cove, a young body that feels most comfortable wrapped around other bodies and that's now clothed in
a mild breeze. He may be a prostitute, though Elian bridles
at the term. After Vin's day in combat, the surrender of this
shot and possibly the drugs in Elian's system make surfaces
tilt and slide unexpectedly, lips stretch and then relax, bruise-
like circles around eye sockets swell and recede, voices waver
as if jostled by bubbles that are wishing themselves toward
breathable air. Elian seems to be keeping Vin at a distance,

as if Vin were a crawling sensation that could lead him to a bad trip.

For hours Vin doesn't try to influence Elian, just tries to remember that he's a separate person. It's difficult to decode Elian's perspective. There is drowsing, then more nuzzling, drinking and snorting, straining and smoking, a return of other naked bodies.

A flock of vivid green parrots are loose on the yacht and in slack moments when Vin sees their curious faces or startles at their piercing cries he wonders whether they might be phantoms. A gray wire-haired dog sits on a green cushion beneath two of the green parrots. If he is hallucinating, Vin might be seeing the ghost of his dog Xiao Hui, Gao Cheng's doomed companion.

Elian has a terror of mixing the wrong drugs and dying at an anonymous anchorage. Between the bouts of confusing sex with roaming packs of hedonists, Vin tries to make various pills, powders and pipes on offer seem unappealing, and tries to keep Elian hydrated. At one point, as Elian drifts in and out of sleep, Vin experiments with suggesting that he change his life, maybe steal away with a companion and settle down. Elian seems to be ignoring him, until—just as Vin is wondering whether direct communication is possible—Elian says aloud, but softly, "Okay, but without fucking what are we for?" Which might be a response.

Though Elian's love of sex is genuine, he wants other things as well, he's just unsure what. He wants desperately to be away from the yacht, but he has trouble thinking of other ways to live. Vin tries to envision alternatives but the drugs are still making it difficult to maintain his own coherence. In the end, Vin can't overcome the nihilism of Elian's commitment to partying, even though it limits and may kill him. Again, Vin is in a person he couldn't imagine without the crèche, a person who doesn't think about the questions that obsess Vin. For example, Elian never asks himself what's "real" and what isn't.

CHAPTER 14

The Freedom to Choose

Vin dragged one of the wooden chairs from the dining table over to the picture window and was watching things move on Puget Sound as he tried to define a word that appeared and disappeared in his mind—*equilerium*: a balance of reality and dream in simultaneous tension and compression.

He had spent what felt like a long time with the madman, and had a lot of bloody fighting in recent memory—with enemies, friends (mostly accidental), rats and at least one spiky plant. He might have fought with himself near the end. Then there was the yacht. First, brutality and pity, and then a world full of bodies that were healthy, sinuous, inviting and hungry for him. And his own frail self stretched nearly to vapor connecting those places.

When he came up from Nerdean's office, he might have remembered to lock the apartment behind him, but maybe not. He looked for Sophie. He wanted to show her a rat. She would have scrapped with it like a tiger. But he didn't bring any rats back with him and couldn't find Sophie.

Why did he make such enormous jumps from one shot to

the next? He was the common element. The shots connected through him in some way, but the device didn't seem to register any of the kinds of differences that human beings valued. And contemplating probability was useless. If there were infinite worlds that contained Churchill and infinite infinities that didn't, what were the chances that he would land in Churchill? Arithmeticians might say, divide the single infinity inhabited by Churchill by the infinite infinities without him. But how would that work with real things? You could pair up moments with Churchill and moments without him forever. Was probability a trick that only worked with numbers? And if a shot didn't narrow probability (because the crèche always pointed at infinity), then what did it mean for the crèche to "aim"? Did the surrogates he inhabited reach toward him—were he and the surrogates aiming at each other, the crèche connecting them through rage or despair? He watched the lovely light and gentle scatter of activity beyond the big window and concluded that the crèche wasn't a place to attempt romantic self-discovery.

"Hey sweetie," the house said, in bird talk. "Hey sweetie."

It was a friendly sound but it startled him and his hands and arms shook with sudden, nonspecific fear. He tried to calm himself. This house was safe. He would be okay.

"Hey sweetie," the house said again. It was friendly.

He stood and walked across the room, then down the short flight of stairs, and opened the door to find Mona outside.

"I see you're surviving alright," she said.

"Am I?" He felt like poison soup.

"Looks like it to me." She stepped past him into the house.

He returned to his chair and lay down in front of it. He could hear Mona moving around behind him.

"Bad one?" she asked.

"That's all it is, isn't it? A bad trip."

"Yeah, I guess," she said. He heard her moving around in the kitchen. She said, "I mean, I think that's a pretty self-involved way to look at it, but, yeah, sure. I'm not going to argue with you."

"You almost killed me. You nearly pushed me down the chute."

"Oh, c'mon. I didn't push you. And to be clear, you and I have never met before. You just showed up in this world, just now. Anyway, let's say I did scare you, how was I supposed to know how jumpy you were? And think about how I must have felt. Shit. I was as shocked as you. One minute you're hopping with surprise, which is delightful to watch and makes me happy, and the next you're wriggling over the chute like a terrified chihuahua. At least you lived. In this world. I must have called an ambulance."

"I thought Kim did that."

"Maybe. Who knows? I probably did too. Anyway, you're not the guy I scared and neither of us were in this world when it happened, so, bygones, right?"

"I can't talk about this." He propped himself up to a sitting position.

"Sure. Get something to eat. Maybe take a nap."

"I'm afraid to sleep."

"Oh." She walked to the window. "Anyone in the crèches now?"

"No. Why are you back?"

That surprised her. "You don't mind if I camp here, do you? I need a place to live. Maybe in one of the bedrooms, upstairs?"

"Why don't you stay in the apartment?"

"Because you can lock me in."

"You told me you might be dangerous." Vin felt a little defensive on this point. "*You* were the one who warned me."

"Well, anyone could be dangerous. Jesus. I probably didn't think you were going to put me in a damn cage. You've got to trust *somebody*. When you lock me in I have to go back into the crèche just to step outside."

Vin hadn't thought of it like that. "Why didn't you use the walkie-talkie then? That's why we put it there."

"I shouldn't have to ask."

AT SOME POINT HE SLIPPED to the floor and drowsed off. Then he heard paper unwrapping and smelled greasy takeout and shook himself and pulled the forest-green sheet over his shoulders as he stood. Mona was at the table with a large hamburger in both hands, a paper carton of fries in front of her.

"Hey," he said.

"Hey."

"I've been thinking. I'm really lucky you're here. Did you have anyone to talk to?"

She made a sour face, as if the burger tasted bad. "I'm not your confessor. I'm not here for you." She chewed for a moment, then said, "It wouldn't have done any good. But I could have talked to one of the others if I wanted to."

"I haven't seen any others yet."

"I thought you said there was another woman when you first found it."

"Nerdean," he said.

"Oh, right. Sure." She waved the idea away.

"Why do you say it like that?"

"Nerdean? No one I ever met has talked to Nerdean." She took a bite. "And I would know."

"What do you mean?"

"Nothing."

Vin pressed his eyes closed and walked to the table. "How many shots have you done?"

"Lots. I usually changed every couple of days."

"You stayed in a long time. You were just traveling?"

"Yeah." She set down the burger and picked up a glass of water.

"But if you didn't come out you couldn't know whether your kids were alive."

She took a long drink from the glass.

"If you were looking for your kids, like you said, you would do short shots, the shortest possible. Then each time you would come out and check how the world was different, whether they were alive."

"Maybe."

"But you didn't. So, what were you doing then?"

She shifted her weight in the chair. "That's pretty fucking personal. Fucking intrusive."

He pulled around a chair and sat at the end of the table. "Maybe you've been waiting for someone to ask you about it."

"Don't try to rescue me," she said. "And it doesn't matter, does it? I had a life, and now I don't. Now I just go out into whatever that is. I'm never getting my life back. Even if I found my kids, I'm not the same anymore, am I? I'd be a shit parent now. And I'd be taking them from someone else." She bent to her left and fished a quarter from her jeans, pinned it on its edge on the table, and flicked it with an index finger, making it spin in place. They both watched. She waved a hand over it as it fell. "I can go to the other side now. I see through all this."

"So, you haven't looked for your kids in this world?"

A big sigh. "No. I'm afraid to. Just get reminded, you know, over and over—in every new place—of the damage I did. Sometimes, I can't face it. You know how that feels."

"Um, no."

"C'mon. You say you're looking for your daughter. A world where you share custody, or where your wife hasn't divorced you. But think about this, maybe even though there are infinite versions of you, maybe every single one of them is an asshole."

"Nice," he muttered. Since that first conversation with Mona, he'd been thinking about multiple universes, remembering stories like *The Chronicles of Amber*—his favorite books in the seventh grade—and turning over the idea of "infinite versions" of a person. Most "same person but different" stories—*The Merchant of Venice, The Prince and the Pauper*—pitted a "good" version against a "bad" one, or "happy" against "dissatisfied," or asked, "What if I changed one important thing in my life?"

The crèche implied infinite variations though, a smooth function through all possible differences, like a calculus of personality that would progress from one person to another. And if you could evolve through infinitely small variations into one other person, then you could go through similar steps to reach any person; and, if time was an illusion, you could do the same thing for every other person who ever lived. Every individual would be a single point in a function expressing all of human possibility, and then, in infinite steps through the multiverse, humanity would also be joined to every other living thing. But he hadn't thought of it the way Mona had just put it, that maybe there was an infinite number of universes that each contained a minor, meaningless variation on the same person, the very same asshole everywhere, and that person never gradually morphed into anyone else.

"Or ask yourself this," Mona said, "if there's a version of you that lives in a world where he's happy, why would he go into the crèche? Even if he doesn't know that the shot will change the world around him, he knows he's risking his life. A mysterious little box that fills with blue liquid? Why would someone who's happy get into that?"

"Ah," he said, "fuck."

"That's right. And for a long time, every time I went in, I told myself I was looking for my kids. And then later, when I knew I wasn't, I still told myself I was."

He put his head in his palms.

"Okay," she said, "now you can have a fry." She gestured at the food.

He bent forward and took a few. Salty, greasy, reassuring. He felt hungry and light-headed. He stuffed more into his mouth, as many as would fit, and pulled his chair toward her as he chewed and swallowed. She eyed him resentfully and chewed her burger.

"Consider it rent," he said.

After the second handful he stood up and went into the kitchen for a glass of water. He leaned on the edge of the island as he drank. "I was in a huge bloody battle, in Africa, I think."

Mona placed the last quarter of the big hamburger into the carton and wiped mustard from her mouth. "I've never been in one there," she said. "It always sends you to such fucked up things. Infinite worlds but all of them are in crisis. Oh, and by the way, all that's a common refrain among shooters. Like talking about the weather. Something everyone agrees on. If you meet someone else, just complain about how shitty all your shots have been. Then go do more." She smirked.

His experience had been so far beyond the words she was using that it deadened him. He said, "The man who was . . . *hosting* me was not all there. In his head. I made decisions. I did things. He just tried to hide."

She said, "I have a weak feeling, a nagging feeling that won't go away that says that people I land in want me there. That they're willing to do whatever they need to do to get something or do something. They're desperate for something as simple as maybe just a feeling of security and they're willing to blow up everything else in their lives to get it. They almost invite me. Almost all the people I've been with were thinking about something obsessively, and were desperate to get it. Mostly they're angry or scared. I was in a monk once who was driving himself insane. He was absolutely fixated and bitter because he couldn't change the way his little house, this little house he'd built on a mountainside, was settling on the ground." She moved her hands up and down, palms turned out, as if balancing them against each other. "The house only had a main room and a bedroom. The settling was throwing the angle of the door to his bedroom off of square, so the door wouldn't close all the way. He had to leave it partially open all night, the front edge just touching the jamb. He pulled the door off its hinges and planed it down. But he went too far and then there was a gap. He tried to stuff a towel into the gap but the door kept moving the towel around. He knew the problem was really the whole house. By the time I got there the house had shifted some more and the door started binding in a different place. He was so angry. It was frustration, but it was this thing that was boiling out of his marrow. Like his bones brewed anger, as much as anyone I ever spent time with."

"Wait a minute," said Vin. "The crèche put you in a man?"

"Uh huh. That was when I realized that I might have some influence over how it aimed."

Vin was tired again. "I want to hear more about that after I get some sleep." He turned to leave. He wanted to get dressed and go buy something of his own to eat.

"You're going to need someone to house-sit," Mona called.

"Am I?" he asked as he reached the stairs. "Sophie doesn't seem to be here. In this world."

"If you're going back in there, then I'd be doing you a favor by staying. Having someone in the house keeps the neighbors from asking too many questions. Besides, why not let me stay? You'll never be back."

She was right. He yelled over his shoulder. "Just tell whoever lands in my body whatever you want them to think."

VIN RECOMMITTED HIMSELF TO ACTUALLY finding Trina. He decided to stick to a schedule, to do three twenty-four-hour shots in the crèche each week for a month. Each time he came back from a shot, he'd look for Kim. If she hadn't divorced him yet, and if they had Trina, he wouldn't go back in. If he got to the end of the month and hadn't found a world where he wanted to stay, he'd re-evaluate. He wouldn't end up like Mona, deadened and doing it just to feel something. He'd stick to a plan.

In the first week, he spent a day in Indonesia in the late sixties, and one in China in 1953. Both times he returned to the same situation in the house, with Mona drifting around, no Kim, no Trina, no Sophie. Mona was keeping to herself and every time he saw her she was eating—peanuts and beef jerky, then lumpy nachos from the convenience store—and watching sports or soap operas on television.

He delayed his third trip because his mind felt like jelly and he worried the world that he had believed in might just be an obscuring mist. His thinking was so jumbled that he found it difficult to keep focused long enough to do simple things.

On what he took for the seventh day, he did manage to pull himself into the crèche for a third shot. Off he went to Luxembourg. He landed in the head of an investor named Roland Schroeder in a bright boardroom at a glass table with four people whom he loathed. The others were trading loud insults around life-changing financial losses while Roland was trying to remain calm. He stared down at his blueberry poppy-seed breakfast muffin and focused on a rhythm of inhaling and exhaling. It was 2008. The chairman of the board, Jukka Pekka, called a board member named James a hyena and then the locked door splintered open. Arne, a major investor, hove in with a long kitchen knife. Roland/Vin quickly disarmed him. (Arne was in his midseventies and Roland was a body builder.) Roland was very open to Vin's influence. Within a few moments, they had punched a board member called Max in the throat and slammed Jukka Pekka's face into the corner of the transparent tabletop, knocking out teeth that left a wash of bloody slime on the shimmering glass. Then Arne had a stroke.

It was only minor violence after his experience with combat and his day on the march in China, but for the first time he felt a real satisfaction in it. Roland's mind was a warehouse of efficient techniques for causing swift injury and Roland suspected terrible things about the other people in the room; he believed that his attacks on them were physical expressions of a deep and incontrovertible moral logic. Vin knew he would be safe no matter what happened to Roland. To enjoy it, you just had to get past the question of who deserved it.

When he exited the crèche for the third time that week, he

was clearheaded and felt invigorated. This most recent brutality had almost cleared his lingering sense of oppression from the previous shots. He wrapped himself in a robe that had been draped over one of the eggshell chairs. It felt cleaner and fluffier—newer and made of higher quality material—than the one he had brought down to Nerdean's office.

He remembered a song called "Itsi Bitsi" that Roland considered the lead cut on the soundtrack for his life. It had a Dylanesque melody and lyric, and a chorus in a language that Vin couldn't pronounce or understand any longer but that he remembered was an invitation to a sweetheart to go far away together, to distant Nepal. He hummed his way up the chute, slurring through a few lines.

At vi er inviteret til lamabal
Så Itsi Bitsi ta' med mig til Nepal

He found Mona in the family room, stepped in and nodded to her. She glanced over but didn't acknowledge him. She turned back to her show, a daytime soap. He went to the master bedroom and took a shower, singing in the warm water; then dressed and felt refreshed. For the first time in a while, he had a good feeling about how things were going.

He sat for a bit in a big leather chair in the master bedroom (a nice addition, he felt grateful to himself in this dimension) and stared out the window at the same panorama of Puget Sound that he'd contemplated in so many of the worlds he'd bounced through. The same water. The same hills. The same yellow sunlight. It seemed odd to him that people and events changed but topography stayed the same. But, of course, he didn't know whether it actually did stay the same. There could be any number of changes and they'd all be invisible to him, because he didn't really see what was happening out his window. He saw what he expected to see. Water, hills, marina, boats, and no real details. Nothing specific. He saw an idea of what was there. It was all probably completely changed from the last time he had come out of the crèche, but to him it all looked the same. With the world as with people, you know only the tiny percentage you pay close attention to.

Feeling restless and energetic, he returned to the family room where Mona lay sprawled over the sofa. The dialogue from her television show, a melody of actors' voices in a stylized rhythm, was weirdly mesmerizing.

> *"If Jake finds out how Angela has been lying to him, he'll come to me, and he'll ask me what to do next. He won't ask you. Because he trusts me."*
>
> *"And you'll tell him about my relationship with Angela, is that it, is that what you're saying?"*
>
> *"Yes, yes, I will. Because I love you. I love you, Donald. Even though you don't see it. You can't or you won't. No matter how often I try to show you. No matter what I do. You throw yourself away on that creature, that lying, scheming woman who cares more about her shoes than she does about you."*

"Mona," he said loudly.

She looked annoyed at the interruption.

"Have you heard anything from Kim?"

"Who?"

"Kim?"

"I don't know that name. You sure she's in this world?"

He had forgotten what he was doing. He hadn't been thinking about where he might be or the specific steps he needed to take.

He pulled his phone from his jeans and scrolled through the list of contacts. Bill was on it.

Mona was watching him. "No Kim?" she asked.

"No." His voice caught.

"I hate that," Mona said.

In a daze, Vin walked into the kitchen. If Bill was in this world, then maybe the sequence of events was different here. Maybe this was the place Vin was looking for at first, where neither of them had died. There still might be a chance to salvage his life. He pressed Bill's name on the contact list.

"Yello," Bill answered. His voice sounded different. Peppy. "This is William Badgerman."

To Vin's knowledge, Bill had never before referred to himself as William. He'd always been Bill. Since third grade, at least. "William?" Vin said.

"Yes." There was a pause, then Bill said. "And, who is this? Who's calling?"

"Bill? This is Vin."

"Wha—? Vin. Oh, Vin. Hey, man. Sorry. It's been so long. I didn't, ah, I didn't recognize your voice." A quiet *heh heh heh* laugh. "Well, hi. How are you?"

Vin prepped for a nanosecond and then plunged ahead, saying, "Okay. Bill, I'm, I'm looking for Kim."

There was a much longer pause. Bill said, "What do you mean, Vin?"

Just in case, Vin said, "Kim. Your sister. I'm looking for her."

"Vin, what's going on? Are you doing okay?"

"Yes, I'm fine. I'm sorry though, sorry to bother you."

"No bother at all. But, it's been so long. After Peg and I helped you with that seed funding you sort of disappeared."

"Peg?"

"Yes. Vin. Peg."

"Bill, I'm sorry—"

"My wife, Vin. And why do you keep calling me that? I haven't been Bill since—and why were you asking about Kim?"

"Because—is she—do you have her number?"

"What do you mean, her *number*? Do you mean the number of her plot at Mount Pleasant? Or maybe you mean the zip code of the cloud she's laughing at you from?"

"Okay, look, I'm sorry. I shouldn't have called—"

"Maybe not. But now that you have, I think we should—"

Vin ended the call. Hung up. He flipped the phone onto the island as if it was scalding him and then leaned on the counter. The phone rang, the same music he had chosen from the "Floe" movement of *Glassworks*. Even though Bill had called himself William, the phone screen said "Bill Badgerman." Maybe they weren't that close in this world. Vin reached over and pressed to decline the call.

Mona wandered into the room, stretching her neck.

"I helped somebody," Vin said hoarsely, without turning to look at her. His throat was dry. "In the crèche, this last time."

"That's good," Mona said, her voice flat, indifferent. He was conscious of the fact that this was Mona, but a different Mona. The same woman, but maybe taller, and with a face that seemed a little lumpy, something he didn't remember ever thinking about Mona before. She wore a green velour sweat suit, a fabric that had a mild sheen. He hadn't seen that before.

"What about your children?" he asked.

"Hmmm?"

"Your children. Are your children here? Mona, do you know how to use that damn thing to find people?"

"Oh. I guess not. Is that what I told you? Children?"

"Yes," he said. "Two of them. You said they burnt, in a fire. A fire. That you set. Is your name Mona?"

"That's why I was going into the crèche, huh?"

"Yes."

"Hmm. That sounds really bad." They stared at each other for a few moments and then Mona said, "I'm going to watch TV," and raised a hand to point over her shoulder toward the family room. She made a face, a grimace as if to say, "See how fucked up all this is?" Then turned and shuffled out of the room.

THE "HEY SWEETIE" DOORBELL RANG early the next morning and when Vin answered, a short and stout dark-haired man with fair skin and irises almost as black as his pupils was standing on the porch, wearing a finely tailored blue serge suit and clutching a leather portfolio to his chest.

"I have informed you that you need to vacate." He spoke rapidly, while the door was still swinging open.

"Joaquin?" Vin asked.

"What?" said the man.

"Are you Joaquin?"

"*Jason*, Mr. Walsh. As always. Are you prepared to vacate?"

"What?" said Vin. "This is mine."

"Yes, you have said that, and I have reminded you that it most certainly is not. I purchased it at auction and, as I have said, I now own it. Homes are repossessed and auctioned if you do not pay your taxes, Mr. Walsh. Surely, even in your . . . condition, you must be able to understand that?"

"You own it? The crèche—"

"Yes?" Jason's gaze sharpened, concentrated, like a raptor spotting a rodent.

"Show me the title."

"I have done that. You have seen the title in my name. Tomorrow, I will bring the police. Please pack and remove your things. Tomorrow, I will be back, and I will search this house from top to bottom. I will find everything that is here. I am tired, tired to my death of your reticence, your confusion and your secrets. I will find everything. You have my word."

"Then I won't leave anything."

Jason smiled, a perfect segment from the radius of a large circle. "I am sure you will leave significant things," he said. "Though whether or not they were ever yours in the first place would be debatable. What a terrible mistake it was to bring you into this. I trusted you and you lied to me. I know there are substantial secrets here, even if I do not know just what they are. You will not remove them. You probably do not understand them."

"Is Nerdean real?" Vin asked.

"Of course she is."

"You've met her? You've talked with her?"

"I have had direction from her, clear direction. And she pays her bills. People who do not exist, do not pay."

"It's been years since you've heard from her though, hasn't it?"

"I will be back tomorrow. You should be gone. Or I will call the police to have them remove you."

"I'll go."

Jason was looking past him, at the interior. He turned, stepped off the porch and walked around the house. Vin followed him toward the apartment. Jason stood in front of the locked, yellow door, staring at it.

"You know, I have had a private detective watch this place," he said, while considering the door. "I thought you were going to be living alone, but my detective has spotted a woman who appears to have come out of this apartment. He tells me that her name is Mona Chanson and that she was involved in an incident. What is your connection with her?"

He waited a moment for a response. Vin shook his head, a tiny little negation, and Jason turned abruptly and walked away. At the curb, he opened the door of a root beer colored BMW sedan and said loudly, not looking at Vin, "It doesn't matter. To hell with the both of you."

VIN DESCRIBED HIS ENCOUNTER WITH Jason while Mona was watching a soap, splitting her attention. When he had finished, she picked up the remote and turned off the TV.

"So, he's going to come in here?"

"Yes."

"Then I'm leaving."

"You once warned me about Joaquin," he said.

"I did?"

He nodded.

"So, here's the thing," she said, "He's the bad guy."

"Always?"

"I don't know. Infinity, right? So, I guess not always. There must be some places where he's good. But it doesn't matter. In our world, here, right now, he's the bad guy. And you can bank on it. He may seem reasonable, kind or generous or even romantic, but he's not at all. He wants everything. He'll take the house and crèche."

"Okay."

"But not just that. From what I understand, Joaquin is the worst. James is really bad. I don't really know this Jason. This is the first place I've heard him called that."

Vin said, "Okay, you need to actually explain things. I get

it. He's bad. But why? Wake up from your goddamn television shows."

Mona blinked, pulled back a bit, put her hand behind her head and pulled thoughtfully on her hair. Then she turned away from him. "Vin, you've got a bad temper."

"Yes. I know. Don't tell me things that I already know."

"Alright," she said, lifting her hands and leaning forward on the couch. "I'm going back into the crèche. You too. That's how we get away from this situation."

"What?"

"He's getting the house and he'll control the crèche." When Vin just stared at her, she added, "Or do you want to be stuck here, in this shitty world for the rest of your life?"

"But, you'll still be in that crèche when he takes over the house."

She slapped her hands on her thighs and stood. "Nope. Somebody else will."

"Yeah. Who is you. They're all you."

"Look, screw them. There're an infinite number of me and I don't owe any of them anything. You should see some of the shit they dropped me into."

Both Mona and Vin went into caskets.

CHAPTER 15

Ban

Aggad is calling to a crow, "Ta, ta, ta," fast, an angry call, a warning. The bird is high in a tree, but if Aggad wanted to, he could spear him. The bird watches Aggad and Ban with one eye, bends his head toward them and caws. Ban, whom Vin has landed within, feels a particular closeness with crows. He always has. Birds are other creatures with two legs, like people, and crows have always struck Ban as among the wisest of birds, rather than the tricksters his uncle believed them to be. The truth is, most stories of crows can be heard either way. Ban thinks of it as a test of the listener—can you understand the crow's wisdom? He and Aggad have never agreed on that point. Aggad thinks crows are foolish.

"If he keeps following," Aggad tells Ban, "then he's a spirit and I'll have to fight with him."

"Don't do it," Ban says. "We already have enough trouble on this hill."

Aggad is a young man, but a bad listener. The people say Aggad may be possessed one day. He reminds everyone of his father's father, Duan, who wrestled with a leopard and lost. By his recklessness, Duan angered the spirits of their old home and brought the ants. When the ants arrive in waves like they did, you have to move. Because of Duan, the people have had to look for a new home. This place they came to a few days ago looks good, but everyone is worried that Aggad will make the same kind of stupid mistake. Angering black birds like crows, maybe even bringing them swarming to rush and storm through the treetops and blot out the sky, that's the kind of stupid thing people would have expected from Duan. If Aggad does it, no one will be too surprised.

"We have to defend ourselves in this place," Aggad says. "The birds we ate have probably already planted sorcerers in our people."

Sorcerers? Vin's response is reflexive. He knows that magic isn't real. By communicating with his host, Ban, he might actually be able to help these people. So he thinks—he suggests—as much to Ban, but when he does he feels an immediate, violent response, a forceful wave of fear and aggression. Ban's mind centers on Vin and batters at him. Vin is stunned. Ban seems to be able to clearly perceive Vin as a foreign presence in his mind, something no other host Vin has visited has been able to do. Ban is alert to his own awareness in a way that Vin hasn't felt before. As the assault continues, Vin realizes that not only does Ban understand him as a separate entity, Ban is unwilling to share space in his mind or concede even a single note of agency. Vin hides. He's not sure how he's doing it. He's emptying his mind, trying to feel what Ban feels, think what Ban thinks, and not create independent observations.

Vin has no idea how a fight with Ban from inside Ban's own mind would work, but Ban seems ready for it. Vin's brush with Ban's awareness suggests that Ban would be ruthless. Vin wants to retreat further, but thinking about retreat might be enough activity to draw Ban's attention.

Ban's body is rigid, still, his eyes closed, and Vin imagines that Aggad is watching him and waiting patiently. Trying not to think is a task whose paradoxical nature becomes immediately apparent to Vin, but it seems to be working. Ban seems to have lost track of him. Vin doesn't allow himself to judge or suggest. He simply accepts Ban's understanding of who and what Aggad and Ban are.

They are the people who walk on two legs. They wear the skins of animal people and plant people. They are homes for the spirits of those who came before them. Vin is aware of other whispering inside Ban's mind, conversations happening without words like the movement of wind through the limbs and leaves of a forest.

Ban jerks his head to the left and then the right and then pounds on the back of it with the heel of his palm.

"Something is changed," he says to Aggad, and Vin can feel cold worry stiffening Ban's lanky body.

Aggad looks away, not willing to challenge Ban by staring when Ban's mood is so serious. "What is it?" Aggad says quietly.

"That crow." Ban nods toward the tree limb where the crow is perched and now watches them with a brotherly concern. "He's warning us. There is a very dangerous spirit here, who is mocking us, and who has come into me through my eyes."

Vin tries not to react, tries not to be anything, tries to melt into the flow of Ban's perceptions.

"The forest is singing," Aggad says. And it's true. Many spirits—a tricky one like a leopard, an irascible spirit like a boar, or a thoughtful but dangerous spirit like a bear—any of those would quiet the forest before possessing a person, but Aggad and Ban can still hear birds, breezes, and the movement of small animals creeping and scrabbling around them, and there is no smell of fear. That means the spirit is not something they understand. It must be a sorcerer.

"I don't know why the forest is still singing," Ban says. "The spirit inside me is angry. He's trying to hide right now, but he's a large spirit. Larger than us. Maybe a sorcerer, so the forest can't see him. I can't see him right now, either. But I smell him."

The crow caws loudly, agreeing with Ban, then spreads his wings and rises into the treetops with the *fllup*, *fllup* sound of heavy wing beats. He pauses for a moment on a higher limb before flying away.

"Alright," says Aggad. "Do you know what it wants? Will it stay in this place if we leave?"

Aggad is asking something else entirely. A thing that he cannot say. "I don't know," Ban says carefully.

"I hope it does," says Aggad.

Ban has known Aggad since he was a child. They both know what Aggad is really saying. Ban nods, and Vin is absolutely certain that if Ban perceives himself to be compromised, to be influenced by sorcery, he'll warn the other people and they'll have to kill him and put his body in the fire so Ban's spirit has a weapon, and so no one else becomes possessed by eating his body. Vin tries to clear his mind. He tries not to exist.

A FEW BLACK BEETLES—INDIFFERENT to the attention they're offered as they scrabble over dark root tangles and through moist green leaves that hug the ground—point Aggad and Ban toward the bear scat they've been harvesting. Beetles have no guile.

From there, Aggad and Ban track the lazy bear's path to a

heavy berry patch, her clumsy trail through the stiff twigs that combed her fur and over the supple buds she crushed in mud, her estrus vividly staining the air where she paused or rubbed her bottom on undergrowth.

Beside the berries, there's a scarred tree at the end of a long line of thin trees with bright leaves that have a yellow tinge. It will be easy to tell the women which trees to ask for directions.

It's getting late. The hunters will be back at their fires soon. As long as the trees don't tell one of the big bird flocks about them, then there's not enough time for this whole big berry patch to be eaten. There will be a lot left tomorrow. It's a good find. The bear must have been in a hurry to leave so much. She must have been chasing her lover, which would make her a bit crazy.

Ban is tired and uncertain. Aggad wants to keep hunting, to find more meat, deeper in the forest. That seems reckless to Ban. They don't really need more and the forest may be hiding relatives of the birds they killed. This is a new place and two-legged people like Aggad and Ban, who can house so many spirits, need to be particularly cautious. They have meat at their fire and soon they'll have these berries. There's too much at stake to push their luck.

It's only right that Ban make the decision. After a short conversation, Aggad agrees to go back. Ban is elder and Aggad's line is weak after Duan's mistake. Aggad knows people are suspicious of him, but Aggad is proud. He doesn't mask his resentment that Ban has assumed the right to choose. As they start toward their fire, Ban reflects on how often mistakes flow into other mistakes, how difficult it is to stop poisoned water once it starts moving. He hopes Aggad will begin to listen. Aggad has a lot to learn from the voices around him.

. . .

AGGAD AND BAN SMELL THEIR fire long before they reach the meadow, the odor of fat from the cooking birds lying heavily on the slowly shifting air. That restless bear is well fed, so she probably won't be drawn by the scent. Then they see the distant glow of firelight through the trees and soon hear fire crackling. The ground is still moist from yesterday's heavy rain, but there were no clouds today. They'll probably see all the sky fires tonight. It might be a good night, with everybody celebrating, singing and dancing.

In addition to the meat, they found many ferns and mushrooms on the bodies of fallen tree people. The astonishing truth is that this new place may be even better than the home the ants took. They'll have to consider how they might convince all their dead ancestors to join them here. If this place continues to give them so much food, it's possible that Duan's folly may ultimately be revealed as guidance, and then Aggad's line might return to leadership.

Their fire circle is the first one, and closest to the trees. When they come to the edge of the forest, Aggad squats and does a rocking dance, leading Ban back into the circle that the two of them share with Naf. The feathers in Aggad's hair shine with gold as he becomes a squirrel and shakes his head with urgent news in the fading evening light. It's a bit showy for Ban's taste. Aggad wants to take credit for finding the berries.

Naf lies beside the fire, his three women—Tatsi, Bejis, and Amnir—cleaning bird hides nearby. Naf's face is pale and sweaty. He was the only one hurt in yesterday's fighting and he's been getting worse. The people surrounded the birds and took them by surprise just before sunrise, killed many of them quickly, including their young. But a few of the strong ones fought back. Every kind of person, even a bird, is frightened by the voyage to the spirit world. One of the birds in particular had been very courageous. Now his courage and strength will feed the people, fortify them against whatever threatening magic might live in this new home.

"Tatsi," Aggad calls proudly to the oldest and strongest of Naf's women, "we found berries for you to pick tomorrow."

"Alright," she says. She grins at him. She's bending around Anja, a boy who might be strong enough to stay with the people. Tatsi's arms encircle him as she uses a thin stone to cut strips of hide. "That's better than nothing." Tatsi is a natural leader and has always had a sharp tongue. Aggad's confidence drains away and he looks sulky.

The smell of the roasting meat is irresistible. Ban is hungry. It's Naf's women who are doing the cooking though. "Where are my women?" he asks Tatsi, and she grunts and points with her chin in the direction of the creek.

"What about my woman?" asks Aggad.

"Same," Tatsi says.

"When did they leave?" Ban asks.

"Not long," Tatsi says.

If it hasn't been long since they left, they probably won't be back until all the fires in the skies are lit. A few are visible already, but most of the sky people are still out hunting.

"Naf is looking tired," Ban says, making the story easier, less threatening. It's a courtesy—you create the possibility that a person may just be tired, and not badly wounded. But Ban can see that his old friend is fighting to stay in his flesh.

Ban's limbs grow heavy as he squats beside the fire. He and Naf have always agreed on things. Naf is a sensitive person, and is strong in Ban's mind. Naf's eyes are always red from thinking too hard. Bejis and Amnir look up from their work and Tatsi shakes her head sadly.

"He isn't doing well," Tatsi says now. Ban winces, wishing she could be just a little more subtle. Then she says, "You can have some of that meat."

That's a very bad sign for Naf—his women bartering for new men. It almost implies that Naf was just waiting for Aggad and Ban to return so that he could say goodbye before leaving for the spirit world. Ban likes Tatsi, and won't mind if she wants to be his woman, but even though she's strong she can be so tactless.

Ban hopes that Naf won't leave to the other worlds right away, that he'll stay for at least a few seasons in this new place. It's a little dangerous to hope for a thing like that—if you hold them back, the dying can turn bitter and cause sorrow—but Naf is kindhearted and has been a good friend. And Naf has a good nose for sorcery. After today, Ban is sure Naf's advice would be helpful. The sorcerer who came in through Ban's eyes might have even followed them to the fire. If it did, then if Naf does die, maybe he can help Ban kill the sorcerer.

Ban reaches out for a stick that's holding a hunk of meat above the fire. He lifts the stick and looks the meat over. It's charred on the underside and moist above. Tatsi has a talent for cooking meat. Her line works well with plant people and she's expert at coaxing leaves into changing the taste of cooked things. The truth is, she's good at making most things. Ban pushes a thumb into a greasy split in the meat and separates a tender chunk and drops it into his mouth, closes his eyes as his mouth fills with water. He chews slowly, savoring the smoky richness of the charcoal sear. But the worry for Naf is heavy on him.

"What about me?" Aggad asks. He's making a fair point. Naf isn't dead, so Tatsi is still with him. If Naf's women are sharing meat, they need to share it with everyone at the fire. Ban glances at Tatsi and can see she agrees. Bejis, Naf's middle wife, will probably go with Aggad. Everyone likes Bejis, so it will be important to keep Aggad happy.

Seeing their agreement, Aggad says, "Yeah," with a grunt. He pulls out the largest skewer that's hanging over the fire, which is very rude. That should be Naf's, or Tatsi's. Aggad notices Ban glaring at him. He looks away and pulls a hunk of flesh from the skewer.

"A sorcerer went into Ban," Aggad says.

"Oh?" Tatsi's voice and manner remain neutral as Aggad openly challenges Ban. The hair on Ban's forearm prickles. The other two women are paying close attention, but no one pauses in their work.

"Yeah," says Aggad. He returns Ban's unblinking gaze. "Is it gone?"

The breeze turns and the smoke rising from the fire flows directly into Ban's face, making him lean back, away from the heat and ash. He grunts. He doesn't have many good options. The accusation from a man who shares his fire could limit his influence for years, maybe forever. But what Aggad said is true, and—what's worse—Ban isn't sure the sorcerer is gone. He still feels a thing that he can't identify. No matter how badly it harms him, Ban must be calm, for the good of the people.

He eats the last morsel from his small skewer. He stands and stretches, flexing his shoulders under the old leopard hide and scratching his ridged belly. He's bigger than Aggad, and stronger. A better hunter. He looks toward the sky where more fires are lit for the night as the sky people gather in tribes.

Ban doesn't want to eat any more of Naf's food. He decides to cook his own meat. His women will appreciate it when they return with water. He steps to the line of trees, where his cache hangs from the branches. He unties the grass twine that holds the heavy bundle in place, sets it on the ground, then pulls open the thin hides. On top is the roasted forearm and hand of one of the birds, the bones of two of its five fingers showing. A child's forearm and hand are underneath. Ban moves those away. He wants a cut from the good meat under the arm.

Vin convulses, his disembodied presence tightens and curls up as he remembers the delicious, greasy meat that Ban was just enjoying. The limbs in Ban's cache are human. Ban stands and freezes. Vin feels the iron of Ban's mind encircling and squeezing him, an airy, crushing pain.

Then Naf, who had been lying quietly and breathing shallowly as Ban finished off his meat, makes a loud sound—a single, extended gasp as he sucks in breath, followed by a long, slow sigh. Ban is distracted, his attention swings to Naf.

Tatsi throws down her work and throws herself across Naf's body. Tatsi, Bejis and Amnir let out rolling, ululating wails and then from the plains all around them other cries begin to rise, growing and climbing toward the sky fires until the clear night is stormy and wracked with the rising and falling winds of grief. Naf has died.

Ban's own grief transforms him. He falls to his hands and knees and arches his back and shouts. He wants his brother's spirit to know that he'll help him find the path to the spirit world, that he'll do everything he can to help guide him. Only Aggad is silent, watching with moist red eyes from across the moving firelight.

In the midst of the erupting cacophony, Ban becomes still

again. Naf has come into Ban's mind. He is sharing it with Vin. Naf—thick-chested, broad-shouldered, his newly emptied spirit pouch hanging from his neck, his limbs heavy with etched muscle, is watching Vin. Curling, graying hair circles his broad, severe face.

"You don't belong here," Naf says.

Vin can't believe that Naf can see him. Naf is looking directly at him. They are in a place where the ground is flat, even and lifeless. There is nowhere to hide. Vin can feel Ban watching and listening.

"Go," Naf says.

"Aren't you dead?" Vin asks. Is this really Naf? Is it Ban's imagination?

Naf's shoulders come forward and his eyes narrow. His hands crawl up his sides and his fingers splay near his hips like poison barbs. He takes a single, deliberate step toward Vin.

"What?" Vin asks, "What have I done?"

When Naf opens his mouth to speak Vin sees a flame within it. Naf's tongue is fire. "You have come where you're not wanted. You bring sickness."

"I didn't choose to be here."

"You chose to leave your own place." The fire from Naf's mouth is spreading along his lips. "Sorcerer. You chose sorcery."

Naf takes another slow, high step forward, his fingers lengthen and curl, sharpen.

"I'll go," Vin says.

In the world outside Ban's mind, Aggad shrieks, lofting a cry of fury high above the broken wailing of the mourners. He is pointing at Ban, his arm stabbing at him over the crackling fire.

"Ban is possessed," Aggad yells. "Sorcery. Ban is possessed."

The darkness begins to move. Other people, drawn first by

cries of mourning, have come from nearby fire circles. Above, the night is full of fierce sky hunters—crows, dogs, leopards, bears—all the clans peer down at the people, watching in judgment.

"Ban is possessed," Aggad yells again. "He brought this on us. He brought sorcery here that has killed Naf."

"Yes," Ban howls, admitting the evil. He raises his hands and arches his neck, exposing himself because what Aggad says is true. Ban has carried a sorcerer into the fire circles of the people. A javelin flickers out of the dark, its point diving into the grass near Ban's feet.

In Ban's mind, the long talons of Naf's right hand flash and dig into Vin's side. Aggad's javelin, thrown weakly over the fire, slips its needle-sharp point between Ban's ribs. Ban gasps and leans as its hanging weight pries his ribs apart. The angry cries from the people outside the circle of fire and then the judgment of the sky hunters rains on Ban as javelins bristle and swarm out of the darkness.

"Sorcerer. Evil," shouts the dead cannibal, Naf, as he leaps on Vin's image of himself, sinking his talons into Vin's bare body and pulling away ribbons of flesh, breathing the roaring fires of his own truth into Vin's face.

PART VI

Everything Is Possible but Very Little Happens

CHAPTER 16

Wait, Who Are You?

c£¨c L a life that 2008 0109
0015 2111 1316 0415 1114 3204 3203 1329
someone else 0714 2517 1325 1523 1500 1012
2912 0202 15

The lid of the casket was open, the interior only slightly moist. Vin stirred and faint traces of oily residue and crystalline grit prickled under his arm and on the back of his scalp where his head rested against the device's supporting armature.

He felt as if he was still returning from the shot, his mind pulling itself back together. He remembered details about himself, the uniform of jeans and shirts that identified him, the smell of his hands, the presence of his daughter. Information was structure and a human being was a kind of information, even arms, heart and bones were structure, information. But each mind was a different world, like a different dimension, both isolated and connected—integrated with the world around it as a unique embodiment of a shared pattern.

Each time he went into the crèche he risked destroying himself, as if becoming aware of a new pattern required a new kind of mind. He could feel it happening, the same emotional entropy that he'd seen in Mona. How long would it take to claim him? How long had Kim been lost before she'd found Trina and destroyed his world? Even now, lying in the dormant casket, he was suppressing a memory of enjoying the taste of roasted human flesh.

HE NEEDED TO RELIEVE HIMSELF and vestigial self-respect set him into hurried motion. As he poked his head out of the hole in the bedroom floor, Sophie stood up, a foot away from the chute, and stared at him. She looked away but stretched her front legs toward him and yawned. Her paws were dark at the ends and she looked like the cat he remembered from the short years they lived together as family, Kim, Trina, Sophie and him. Sophie stepped forward and head-butted his face. He climbed so his arms were out of the chute and petted her as she purred and pushed against him.

In the bathroom, he wondered at her presence. When they'd added the apartment, they'd removed the staircase to the basement.

In this version of the house, the staircase was where it had been before the remodel, and the downstairs wasn't an apartment yet. The old card table and folding chairs were huddled against the island. He took a breath and sprinted to the third floor, to the master bedroom and the blinking cluster of electronics that were piled around the huge flat screen television, just as they were years ago.

On the second floor, his old inflatable mattress looked worn, covered by faded but familiar green sheets. He dressed in his other self's clothes, found his phone and wallet and fed Sophie, but he needed to get away from the house. The world outside felt both familiar and fresh. He was walking, moving the same way he always did, speeding his pace over ground that he'd covered endlessly in a city that enclosed most of his life, a life of short sequences repeated through clusters of ragged flourishes any of which might grow into a new variation, a fractal structure of a life spiraling through fading sounds and colors. The air had a distinct taste of salt water skimmed from the mist above Puget Sound, the vanishing scent of ocean.

NEAR THE PIKE PLACE MARKET, he stepped into a small restaurant with a handwritten sign crowing about ZESTY CALZONE. He ate slowly, suppressing memories from the crèche that crowded and tugged, including smells and tastes that simultaneously repelled and comforted him. Food had been the uncomplicated part of his life. Now everything felt alien.

He remembered being in his father's backyard the summer after Kim died, on a lawn chair of woven plastic bands that stuck to his skin, and feeling almost dizzy with a grief he didn't understand, his father barely aware that he was present, let alone wounded. Vin kept telling himself to be practical, her death wouldn't change anything in his life. His feelings were a fantasy, his claim on them false.

Then his teeth bounced on sausage he was chewing in a way that reminded him of the resilience of the flesh that Ban had pulled from the smoking skewer. He flashed on opening the bundle of darkened, fragrant leaves and the hand with two fingers roasted to the bone, the child's hand beneath. He choked to prevent himself from spewing chewed food. He closed his eyes and lowered his jaw, breathing carefully, deliberately. A person moved away from him.

He put his feet flat on the floor and slowly straightened his legs. Still bent at the waist and shoulders, he staggered to the counter while staring at the floor. "Bathroom," he managed to mumble. The cashier came swiftly, took his hand firmly and led him to a door that she unlocked. He rushed to the toilet as she shut the door behind him.

BY MIDAFTERNOON, HE WAS WALKING into a stiff wind that shook the trees on Second Avenue and cut itself on the cracked edges of Belltown's low brick and plaster buildings. He had wandered in circles, and then watched foot traffic in front of the squat Westlake Center mall, then started north with a vague idea of resting at the Seattle Center.

His phone felt solid. He might not be wearing his own body, but this was his phone. He brushed through contacts, finding Bill's number. Kim wasn't listed.

"Halloo," Bill's voice. A happy version.

"Bill?"

"Hey, Vin. Hi. What's happening, man?"

"I need to talk."

"Well, that sounds serious."

"It's not, I just—"

"Yeah?"

"I'm confused and need to talk with someone."

"Okay." Bill's voice was lower, concerned. "Listen, I could get out and come by pretty soon. Meet at Pagliacci, maybe? The one near your house. Would two-thirty work?"

"Not pizza."

"Now you're worrying me."

"Do you know where the Lucky Diner is, in Belltown?"

BLUE JEANS, A T-SHIRT, A leather jacket, and sneakers—Bill was wearing his standard uniform but everything had the tailored, slightly glossy look of higher quality materials and extra cost. He looked happy and energetic as he pushed open the glass door. The waiter near the door stopped in surprise when he spotted Bill. Then his hand rose as if to touch him. Bill gave the waiter a half smile while looking about for Vin, who was as far away from the door as possible, nursing a coffee with a milkshake and a cold order of French fries untouched on the flecked Formica tabletop. Bill smiled broadly and Vin was momentarily overcome by the reality of seeing him again.

"Hey man," Bill said. "What's this?"

"I'm sorry. It's just good to see you."

"It's good to see you too, but I'm probably not going to cry about it." Despite his grin, Vin's eyes had teared up. Bill dropped into one of the red cushioned, chrome-framed chairs.

Vin said, "What year were we born?"

Bill reached for a French fry. "Really, man? You've been acting pretty strange recently."

"I have?"

"Yeah. Crying at the sight of me, for example, is strange. And that question."

"Okay." Vin stared at the tabletop. He put a hand on his sweating glass of water and shook it, the bits of ice ringing lightly. "Then, let me ask about"—he took a breath—"do you know someone named Peg?"

"Are you joking?"

"No, but I might be losing my mind." Vin's voice cracked and slipped.

The approaching waiter stopped. Bill glanced up and shook his head, asking the waiter not to interrupt.

"So, tell me what's going on here," Bill said. "Are you high right now? Do you want to go to a hospital?"

"No. No. I'm not going to hurt anyone, or myself. But I'm just losing track of—it all. Nothing is holding still." Vin whispered this last, twitching as he said it. "Have I ever been married?"

Bill frowned but said, "No, you never have."

"Are we still friends?"

"Yeah, sure we are. Of course, man. We always have been."

"And you bring me drugs."

"I don't—well, sometimes. I mean, I have in the past, but I don't anymore. You know, we're both a little older. A little wiser."

"But, I'm not married?"

"I think you'd know."

"That's the thing. I might not." Vin was speaking quickly. "Don't assume I'd know things. I ask because I am married. Divorced. With Kim."

"Who?"

"Your sister."

Bill sat back and bit his upper lip. Outside the window a young man and woman were standing by the curb, staring at Bill. The woman—short, dyed black hair and round cheeks, pale skin—was trying to catch Bill's eye. She shyly raised a hand and waved at him.

"Do you know them?" he asked.

Bill didn't even glance. "Fans. You are saying some crazy

things. You have a barrel of monkeys in your brain right now, man. You're scaring me."

"Do you know someone named Peg?"

"Do you mean *my wife*?"

"I need to show you something."

BILL WAS DRIVING A MATTE-BLACK Lamborghini Aventador, a sculpture of motion tricked out with shining wheels. "*Speed Racer* car," Vin said, walking to the passenger side.

Bill watched him as the doors lifted skyward. "Yeah," he said, "those old cartoons were the best, weren't they?"

As Vin flattened himself into the low-slung seat, he had a moment of panic. How could this be Bill? Was this car—with its smell of fresh leather—a different kind of crèche?

"It's nice," he said quietly, as the vehicle purred to life and glided away from the curb and onto Second Avenue.

"Yeah. Thank you, again."

"What do you mean?"

Bill glanced at Vin. "Dividend from Sigmoto. We've taken this one out before, haven't we?"

"Sigmoto did well? For you?"

"Yes, it did well for me." Bill laughed. "Broke the galactic bank. Is that what this is about? I thought you got past all that."

"So, do I have a lot of money?" Vin watched the world outside as the car drifted to a stop at a light.

Bill said, "People pitch stuff at me now. You wouldn't believe how many crazy ideas there are out there. Actually, I kind of like it, but, right now, you sound a little like one of those people, and not to frighten you, but I mean that in the most alarming way. You're asking questions that I don't know whether or not I should take you seriously."

"What I'm going to show you will help."

"Um, so, I'm still clean. You know that."

"It's not drugs. For now, humor me."

Bill let out his breath, his index finger tapping the steering wheel. "Well, if, by *a lot of money*, you mean by government standards, then yes, you have quite the fuck-ton of money."

Vin looked out the side window. People were staring as they passed. "Those people watching you at the diner, you said, fans?"

Bill glanced at him, measuring his disorientation. "Yeah, from the movie. Which I also have you to thank for."

Vin closed his eyes and sank further into the leather seat.

Bill said, "I'm a little scared right now, but only a little, okay? So, I don't mean to pry, but is there a medicine, or—I mean, do you have everything you need?"

Vin's phone rang, the music from *Glassworks* he'd chosen years ago. He dug it out of his pocket. The screen said, "Alina," and showed a slim woman with straight dark hair and narrow features, wearing a green halter. Gorgeous.

He asked Bill, "What do you think about Alina?"

"She's great." Bill was uncomfortable.

"What do you think about her?"

"Really?"

"Yeah."

"This isn't a test? Because you're pretty out there right now."

"I want to know what you think about her."

Bill made a sour face and shook his head. "Not good for you. Smart, but a party girl. She's in it for what you can do for her."

Vin declined the call and rested the phone against his leg. "I have bad judgment."

"Maybe. Sometimes. We going to that weird house you use as an office?"

. . .

WHEN THE DOOR OF THE chute opened, Bill whispered, "Holy shit. What the hell, man? Why did you never tell me about this? Fuck."

"I can't. There's a notebook. It's complicated."

"Complicated? That sounds like an understatement. You couldn't tell me because there's a notebook?"

Vin went down the chute first, Bill following, showing the same fear that Kim had shown the first time she climbed down. The same fear Vin had felt.

CHAPTER 17

Do You Need a Moment?

none of it happened here

They sat at the card table, open cartons of Thai takeout spilling onto the paper plates. Bill was still a sloppy eater. Vin had finally been able to keep something down—a little tofu Pad See Ew because, despite his leather jacket, Bill was inexplicably vegetarian. Vin was nursing a beer.

Bill said, "I think about this sometimes, how I could have been born as anyone else. But then, I think, everyone feels like they're dealing with a load of terrible shit, so all things considered, things could be worse."

"No, you couldn't really be anyone else. Your body, your specific relationship to time and space makes you who you are. You're bound to your circumstances."

"Alright, man. That's a lot more literal than I was taking it." Bill poked through the wide noodles before spearing a chunk of tofu. "You know, without that stuff in the basement, none of your story would be even remotely believable."

"Yeah."

Bill stared at him and grinned.

Vin laughed. "You know, you're better here."

Bill's smile began to fall away. "Meaning what?" he asked. "Better how?"

"Well, just . . ." He looked down at the food cartons.

"Oh."

"How did you do it?"

"Stay sober? You're asking me . . . What *I* want to know is why I didn't get sober in your other world."

"I don't know—you kept trying things. Maybe something happened there, or you were more broken, or . . ."

"Wow. I've never felt so good about being an addict in recovery before."

Vin was looking at the stained mess of food on his plate again. He couldn't look at Bill.

"Okay," Bill said. "Well, I'm still finding it hard to believe in travel between dimensions, no matter how many DIY home dungeon recipes you followed out of your old Maker magazines."

Vin laughed. "You're more sarcastic here."

Bill set down his chopsticks. "So, in this *other* world, Kim was alive?"

"Yeah."

"But, *I* was dead?"

Vin nodded.

Bill shifted in his chair. "And you married her?"

"Yeah, but she was unhappy."

"You didn't make it?"

"I tried. I don't know what it's like between you and Peg. I thought everyone must be a little unhappy, you know? She didn't think we really knew each other." Vin listened to the quiet in the room. "We both felt guilty about you. I didn't see how important that was. Just how hard it was on her. I—"

Bill started up but then slumped back into his chair and closed his eyes. "Yeah."

The room was quiet, the big house empty and haunted as though only desire could live in it and only alone. Bill said, "You're right, though. I mean, I killed her."

Vin couldn't look at him.

"But, you're from another world. And there are worlds where it didn't happen. That's how it breaks down, what you're saying. I just got myself into a shitty one."

Vin lifted his beer but didn't want to drink. He set it on his knee. "This world doesn't seem shitty."

"What happened," Bill asked, "in the other world? How did I save her?"

"I don't know what happened here . . ." Vin hesitated, then told him the whole story. When he was done, Bill said, "Your phone was dead. You said you didn't charge it."

"It could have gone any other way," Vin said.

Bill stood, looking around as if unsure where to go. "To be clear, in every world, in every other world you went to, I was an alcoholic and a drug abuser?"

"Yes," Vin said, seeing the terrible weight of the word as it pressed Bill.

Bill turned his head, but wasn't looking at anything in particular. "Yeah. I was going to ask whether maybe I could use that thing. But what you're saying is, what's the point, right?"

"I don't know. Everything that's possible happens."

"So you said. Look, I'm glad you called. It's always good to talk, man. And I want to find out more about this. All of it. You've been there for me, I know, and I almost believe you. Batshit crazy. But, right now, I think I should call my sponsor, so I'm going to leave. I'll call you back and we'll talk again, okay? Alright? I'm going to go."

"Bill, you can't tell him about this. Your sponsor. I'm not telling anyone. Goddamnit, I'm so sorry. Bill, this stuff can't be known." When Bill stared at him, Vin said, "Nerdean didn't make it public. She didn't want people to know about it."

"And who is Nerdean? And why should I care?"

They looked at each other. This version of Bill was very different. Less afraid. "Okay," said Vin. "I'm the one who's not ready to make this public. Yet."

THAT NIGHT, AS HE LAY awake on the air mattress and felt the bellows of his chest manufacturing moments, he imagined a crèche that would allow a person to simply sleep, to pass decades of life dreaming peacefully while the world changed outside the box. Maybe there were worlds in which he was the one who died, rather than Bill or Kim. In those worlds, someone else might have found the crèche.

He needed to confront the question he had been avoiding: what next? He was restless. He rose and dug in the closet for a change of clothes, discovering a small safe hidden inside a cabinet. It looked like the same safe he'd had in the master bedroom when he was living in the house with Kim and Trina. He tried his combination and it opened, revealing a small, bright chamber that contained five thousand dollars in cash, his .38 caliber handgun, some design documents and a shoulder holster.

He called out for Sophie but she didn't respond and he didn't hear her moving in the house. She sometimes slept on an afghan near the television but he didn't remember if the afghan was in this version of the house. He decided to look for her. When he got downstairs, a thin woman with iron-gray hair was sitting at the card table. She appeared to be waiting for him. She was wearing a T-shirt and what looked like a pair of his jeans. They were baggy on her. She'd strung a sheet or pillowcase through the belt loops to keep them up on her spindly frame.

It was the woman who had been in the crèche the first time he saw it, years ago, in a version of the house very much like this one. She smiled, her teeth perfect despite her apparent frailty.

"Sit still and go far," she said, her voice crackly and high.

"Nerdean," he said.

"No," said the woman, suddenly agitated, her smile disappearing, brows coming together. "I don't know her."

She might have been in her midthirties, her skin clear but with deep lines. The gray in her hair looked premature. She watched him with birdlike wariness, her eyes tracking him, her head twitching to align with her drifting gaze.

"You're not Nerdean?"

"No." She moved her head back and forth in an exaggerated, slow negation.

"Would you like something to eat? Or, some water?"

She nodded, another exaggerated motion. He went to the kitchen, trying to keep an eye on her.

"You've been traveling a lot," he said.

"Yes. She gave up on faster-than-light travel and started working on weirder-than-light travel."

"Who?"

"I would have thought my goal would be obvious," she said. "I want to live horizontally in time."

"Is that possible?"

"Move between universes with the changing increment of time's most meager fragment, from universe to universe at the governing rate of change." Her voice creaked like floorboards. "My awareness would ride the wave, the transition out of one single unit of time, one moment to the next, ride that ripple of time through eternity and travel forever in a single moment. I would live sideways through infinite lives, live forever without becoming older, live forever an infinite number of times."

"Did you?" he asked.

The woman smiled, a mysterious, empty expression.

"I've been in your mind," she said. "Remember?"

"Yes. The words that came to me." He ran a glass under the tap. "You told me, 'The switch will be in an appliance.' I saw those words in my mind."

She looked pleased and almost shy, as if he embarrassed her with praise.

"I do remember," he said, and thought about several other times when strange ideas had appeared in his mind. He had some trouble turning off the tap. It might need maintenance.

"Good," she said. "You're going to see Kim again. And Trina. Everyone."

"Nerdean," he said.

"No. Never. I'm not that person. I'm everything that can be made from starlight."

She stood, lifting her arms, her smile lengthening and the room behind her darkening. "I'm not Nerdean."

The house shook. An earthquake. He'd lived in fear of one for decades. He tried to set the glass down but it fell into the sink and shattered. He reached out to keep his balance and grabbed the refrigerator door, pulling it open. A few containers dropped

out, then a few more fluttered from the top shelves as the house
continued to shake. The fluttering things became dollar bills
and even more fell out, and then coins as well, a stream, a river,
a torrent of money.

He took a step backward as a wave of clear plastic containers,
the kind meant for leftovers, followed the money. They clat-
tered onto the floor and more money poured out between them.
Each container was filled with meat, red and bloody, and he saw
fingers and pieces of limbs through the plastic, the butchered
bits of people he loved.

"Look over here," the woman said. Vin looked up from the
piles of things and saw the wall and the picture window it contained disappear. Night sky and stars drifted behind her.

"You think this is a dream, don't you?" she said.

He woke up. He was in his inflatable bed on the second floor.
He lay still. The house had stopped shaking. He was at the tail
end of a mild temblor. His bed was getting softer, the air mattress slowly deflating. So much air had gone out now that the
edges of the bed began to curl over his arms and legs, covering
them and then binding them so he couldn't move. He strained
to pull himself free, his teeth grinding, until he finally did. And
he woke again.

But he still couldn't move his limbs. He was still far under
the surface of sleep, held down by a force that pressed on him,
a weight that felt endless. He pushed against it, tried to rise,
to cross the heavy layers of dream and rise above the plane of
sleep. He woke again, and woke again, each time forcing himself up further, again and again and again.

HE WOKE A FINAL TIME out of a series of dreams that had filled
him with euphoria, dreams that had showed him days and events

that seemed possible, things that might have happened in this world but that he hadn't experienced. It was Saturday. Rattled and tired, he lay in bed until his mind ticked over to thinking about being rich. He considered finding the place where he actually lived—Bill had mentioned a condo on South Lake Union. But everything he needed was in the house and it all seemed well worn. As he fed Sophie, he wondered whether the person who had made his life in this world had spent much time at the condo.

He took a long walk through the Uptown neighborhood, stopping for a sleepy meal at the Mecca, a bar and diner with a twenty-four-hour breakfast menu where he ate waffles and hash browns under the motto, ALCOHOLICS SERVING ALCOHOLICS SINCE 1929.

Things were as he remembered them—the concrete—and plank-covered Counterbalance Park that sprang to unexpected life at night when its LED lights raised colored curtains along gray concrete walls; the orange logo of the coffee shop; the movie marquee above the pet food store that was across the street from the marquee above the old cinema; the Greek, Thai, Japanese, Mexican, and Indian restaurants; the old world pub, the pizza place. He stepped into the used bookstore and browsed, sampling paragraphs.

He took a circuitous route back to the house, climbing the wooden staircase above the tennis courts and realizing that the thing he appreciated most wasn't the odd new awareness of being wealthy, or the feeling of knowing the place well; it was the place itself—the air, the slope of the hill, the trees he was passing that may have been different than those he'd passed on other days but which looked similar enough. The phenomenal world and its reliable consequences were all here, slowly transforming in obedience to mysterious fundamentals but offering the familiar cool breeze, the generous leafy canopies and limpid sunlight even among the infinite possibilities that branched endlessly away from each choice, each action.

In this world, Sigmoto had worked. He had stayed on as a technical lead. Rather than fighting to keep his job as CEO, the version of him here must have agreed to be replaced. It was a scenario that he'd considered but in his own world his fight to keep his job had created real acrimony. So, that was a thing he clearly had gotten wrong. Although, if there were an infinite number of worlds in which he stayed as technical lead, that same decision would have been a mistake in some of them. What he knew for sure was that there were worlds in which he'd accomplished something meaningful, and that he was getting a do-over.

He pulled his phone out of his pocket and typed *Buys Sigmoto* into the browser and stood under a massive fir tree halfway up a wooden staircase as he read about the purchase by a company called Peerteq. The unconfirmed price was eye-popping. There was even a quote from him saying Peerteq was the kind of perfect strategic opportunity that only comes around once.

Buoyed by the good news, he decided to check his email. At the top of his inbox, his financial advisor, someone named Edgar Wylie, had sent a status update on a couple of transactions. Vin had a lot of money. The second email was from a name he recognized, John Grassler. Its subject was *Got it* and it said:

> *Vin, we found it, and you were onto it. You were close.*
> *But there's really no question anymore. The security*
> *breach was the result of a bounds-checking thing, but not*
> *that simple. It's only possible because of the way you put*

*together the core. It's a spot I was supposed to refactor but
I de-prioritized it during diligence. I'm so so sorry. Come
in today and I'll walk you through it.*

As he was reading, an email arrived from samwelltarly99q9@
hottymail.com, with the subject: *You Moth4rfucking Life Sucking
Poisond Sack OF Ball Sweat.* It started,

> *You lied lied lied, and then you fucked me over when you
> didn't have to.*

He couldn't read any further. He was surprised it got past the
spam filter. He deleted it and turned off his phone.

WAS HE IN LOVE WITH her? That was the question that waited
for him as he opened the door to the big house, and he knew
that he was asking himself about Nerdean, and not about Kim.
He couldn't have loved Nerdean, though. He couldn't even be
sure that she existed. But wasn't it Nerdean, above anyone or
anything, who had truly offered him a new world?

Sophie came padding into the dining room and made a
quiet yowling sound that tapered into a long, low growl. She
often seemed angry with him, as if each day began with a ritual
of him neglecting her. He walked over to pet her but she ran
from him and then waited near the island.

As he forked the contents of a can into a bowl, chopped and
mixed the oily pâté, he was aware of a thought trying to shape
itself just out of the reach of his awareness. He bent to scratch
Sophie's head and stroke her back as she pushed her face into
the bowl and purred.

No matter what else was happening here—the wealth, the

security breach that could jeopardize what he had built (a breach he, uniquely, might be able to mitigate), Bill's happiness—no matter what else was happening—Trina and Kim were not here. He sat at the table until Sophie walked away from the bowl then got his laptop and sent Bill a short email. *I couldn't imagine a better friend.*

He walked down to the basement where he half expected to find that the switch in the carpet and the chute to Nerdean's office were both gone, and that everything he thought he had experienced since moving into the house had been a dream. But the switch was on the floor near the wall, maybe eighteen inches from where he remembered its original position. It might have moved in different versions of the house, but it was always there.

When he got to Nerdean's office, he woke one of the monitors and at the password prompt he typed *I am Nerdean*, including the spaces because he wanted to make a statement. He had only wanted to prove to himself that he could type those words, but a moment later the system cleared to show a desktop he hadn't seen before.

He searched the account for additional files, more information, greater access, but found almost nothing new. Almost. There was one thing. In a directory that had previously held only a text file, he now found a small application that ran a crude user interface with a single control, one horizontal line stretching between the labels NEAR on the left and FAR on the right. A gray box, a crude slider, sat halfway between the two labels. He moved the slider all the way to right, as close to FAR as it would go.

CHAPTER 18

And What Are You Looking For?

He's in the crèche, but in this shot he is himself. He's not inside anyone else's mind. He's standing in a great, spreading meadow that's filled with activity. He knows he's on a shot because he has a clear memory of being clipped into the crèche's wiring and submerged in broth just before blacking out and then waking here.

A soft breeze plays against his cheeks and he finds himself facing Mona. She's smoking a cigar, a half-inch of ash hanging from its tip, the cloying smell of sweet tobacco smoke wafting about her.

"Well, sleeping beauty joins the party," she says, in a growly, throaty version of her deep voice. He turns in a slow circle. There are people in every direction, moving swiftly here and there, most wearing what appears to be heavy, metallic armor. A few are in military fatigues, a very small number wear silver and white gowns, one person in the far distance appears to be wearing a tall hat. As he watches, an androgynous couple who may be identical twins float by trailing long orange-and-black trains of shimmering fabric.

A hovercraft zips past overhead, oddly quiet. In the distance, a convoy of heavy trucks is rushing across the field. There's motion everywhere.

"Hey, over here," Mona says. "Look at me."

Mona's face is scarred, her nose flatter than he remembers, as if it's been broken more than once. She is also encased in what looks like heavy armor. She pulls a two-handed, cannon-like weapon off of her back and holds it in front of her.

"What's going on?" he asks. "Where is this place?"

"This is the future," Mona says, her lips dexterously moving the cigar to the left side of her mouth. "So, 'I am Nerdean,' huh? You figured that out? Well, welcome to Armageddon. You good now?"

He shakes his head and says, "No."

With the right side of her face, Mona says, "Alrighty then." Mud splatters from beneath the heavy metal boots she's wearing as jets fire under them and she starts to lift off from the ground.

"Where are you going?" he asks.

"Back to the fight," she says, her voice humming with satisfaction. "I've spent enough time being your nursemaid."

The jets in her boots roar and screech and she drifts upward. He lifts his hand to shield his face from heat that crisps the hair on his arm. She accelerates as she rises and soon disappears into the sky, leaving a faint, curving contrail.

He recognizes many of the people around him. Several are

other Monas. And a dark-haired woman about forty feet in the distance is walking away from him. Kim. Even in her armor, he knows it's her and the sight of her provokes a lumpy pain in his throat. He steps forward, but a man in armor with a helmet held under his right hand comes between them.

The man says, "Hey."

"Do I know you?"

"Hey, motherfucker, it's me."

"Is that—Bill?"

"Yeah, man. Always good to see one of you join us."

"Bill, you're black."

"And in my world, you are too."

"I—" Vin is stymied. The man's face is almost composed of Bill's features, but slightly different. The look in his eyes though, and the sound of his voice, are Bill's. He stands with his chest forward, as Bill's would, with his weight shifted toward the balls of his feet. His chin is high, hiding his fear the way Bill does.

This Bill says, "I see, you haven't been here before? That's too bad. I was looking for a partner for an attack. But, you should probably get oriented first. Sorry, I thought you might be cycling through a second time or something."

"No."

"Well, okay, I can give you the basics, anyway. I don't think anyone can actually explain all of this." He laughs. "This'll be sort of an *ad hoc* thing, but that's really all most of us get. So, first, I guess the fact that I'm black is important. You can tell I'm not from your world. You may know me, but don't make too many assumptions. That's good as a general rule for people here. Second thing is, obviously, this place is different than most of the others. I think that this is a far, far future. They've had crèche technology here for a long time, and are good at it, very good. You are actually in this place and if,"—Bill's face suddenly screws up as if he's in terrible pain. His head starts to swell, it happens quickly, skin weirdly separating from bone until his skull pops softly—his skull explodes—slapping Vin with a spray of blood and sharp bits of bone. Bill's headless body rolls onto itself and falls to the meadow. As Vin is gasping and spitting out the taste of blood, another Bill, also black and also in armor, hurries over.

"Shit," the new Bill says.

Vin can't speak. He bends to put his hands on his thighs and turns away from the bloody mess that had been a neck. One of his hands is moving on its own, wiping at sticky brains and blood that plaster his soft cotton shirt to his bare chest.

"You okay?" asks the second Bill.

"What was that?" Vin manages. "Is he going to remember that?"

"Remember?"

"When he gets out of the crèche?"

"Oh. No. You haven't been oriented, huh? No, he won't remember. If you're killed here, then you're dead, okay? You die back in the crèche. So that version of me is dead. Are you alright?"

Vin shakes his head. Vomits. Bill puts a hand on his shoulder as his body shakes. The vomit is oddly gold-colored, shining. Vin is leaning forward, hands braced on his legs.

Bill says, "I can see you can't help it, but we need to be quick here. We're always under attack. Even right now. It's kind of like archery coming over castle walls. The enemy's trying to soften us up by sending waves of random death events at our causality shield. Every so often, one gets through. And—" He nods toward the mess that was the other Bill's body.

"Who is the enemy?"

"He didn't have a chance to cover any of that with you? Before he got hit?"

"No."

"For now, I guess who the enemy is probably isn't that important. And, just so you know, we're doing the same thing to them. First things first though. We need to get you into some armor."

Vin stares at the heaped body—veins and hints of structure, maybe a chip of spine—but he's also starting to pay attention to the efforts of his right hand, which is still swiping at the remains on his face and chest. And he's trying to spit out bits that are dripping from his upper lip, and not allow more into his mouth.

The new Bill touches his shoulder. "You've got to put yourself back together. C'mon. Follow me."

Vin straightens, muscles and joints slowly unclenching. He walks in shock past Monas and other Vins, other Bills, and other people he doesn't recognize. Of course, this means that Bill used the crèche. That would be Vin's fault. But then again, if it were possible for Bill to use the crèche, he would have. Somewhere.

There are also several of the thin, gray-haired woman whom he first saw in the crèche, and many Kims. Many people are wearing metallic helmets. Vin can't see who they are.

The Bill walking beside him says, "Okay, man, here's what I think is going on, but the truth is, I don't actually know and I don't know that anyone does. People say this place was created in a future—a far future from our time. And, one thing they did was build it big enough to accommodate any number of travelers, maybe like, literally infinite people. So, then, maybe what they didn't understand was that because of its sheer size, it created this huge radius of probability, a probability sinkhole that attracts people who try to shoot themselves into the far future. Maybe that was what they wanted, though. What's really, completely cracked, is it took on its own reality. Because the technology was manipulating—ah, I don't know. Shit. But now it's a real kind of place, a manufactured fork in dimensions and out of control. They say it doesn't split the way normal dimensions do but just adds to itself, so it's, like, eating other dimensions. Try to get your head around that. We call it Armageddon. Maybe you gathered that."

"But, why are you fighting?"

"The fight? Well, that's simple. Survival. I mean, when I first got here I realized this is what I've always been doing. It's just more honest here. It's kind of what life's about when you factor out the living."

"That's terrifying." Vin isn't sure he's hearing Bill correctly and is yo-yoing between states of panic and numbness, his heartbeat surging painfully then slumping into fatigue.

Bill says, "Funny though, some people feel better here than in worlds like ours."

"Those people are terrible."

Bill looks like he's about to say something, but doesn't. The sounds around them seem almost unsynchronized from the movement they see, like a video with a fractionally delayed audio track. But Vin can't be sure. It's slippery. Anything he pays close attention to becomes synchronized. It might just be his general feeling of disorientation. He says, "Do you talk with them, the enemy? Why do *they* fight?"

"Same reasons, I assume. But I haven't been on their side. I don't think."

"You *don't think*?"

"Well, yeah. You know how it is. It's confusing. I think maybe their side looks like ours. When I come here, everything is always the same. And, you know, infinite people, or so many you can't tell the difference, flying up into the sky to fight infinite people. Everyone in armor. I mean, you might not know who's who."

"You *can't tell the difference* between them and you. That's what you're saying?"

"I said maybe."

"So, people appear in this world. There's a fight. No one knows *why*." His voice trails off and they walk in silence. A small cluster of helmeted and armored figures is having a conversation. One of them flashes a thumbs-up at Vin. As a group, their boot jets fire and they begin to ascend. "And death here is real," Vin continues, watching them rise, "and we can arrive on either side. Maybe, side A. Maybe, side B. And human beings *made* this."

Bill makes a kind of growling noise. "It's almost like you're purposefully not getting it."

"Okay. What if you and I were to just start fighting, right here? If I were to attack you right now, what would happen?"

Bill stops and puts an armored hand on Vin's sticky, bloody chest. "I suppose that would make *you* one of *them*. Look, man, don't freak out here, okay? It doesn't help. Not at all. This place is actually as fucking deadly as you think it might be. I've been here a lot. I know. Your job is to get out alive."

"Alive?"

"Yeah."

"But you just said this is what life is about, when you factor out the living."

"Yeah. I believe that."

"You *choose* to come back here."

The distance between them doesn't actually change but feels

as if it may be twisting. Strong, unknown scents are turning on and off in the air. Bill says. "I'm trying to find something better, like everyone. I don't avoid this place, though. Look, you have to kill to eat. You kill things to build. You kill to protect your family. This place is just uncomplicated about it."

"Bill that's—some fucked up death cult shit."

"It's just survival, man. We're all part of something that pits us against each other. When it's hidden, I just feel despair. People may have made this thing, but there's a reason it grows on its own. It's a *clarification*. And that word, *survival*, maybe it's like *infinity*, or *probability*, words that are just the sound of your brain giving up, in English."

"No, those are ideas. We can work with those things, we can understand them. They're math."

"Jesus. See, you're such a fighter, man. If it doesn't make sense to you, you fight it."

"This is *bullshit*. We don't have to do this."

"I thought that too, once. But you know that's just another kind of fighting, right? Resistance. And it can be infectious too. So, if you resist, you end up on the other side, and the people here kill you. It's true no one knows how the sides get made. Maybe Vins are always on our side. Maybe you guys get split up." Vin has a sudden moment of blankness as he realizes that he's hearing a threat in Bill's voice. Bill says, "I should warn you, man, a lot of you Vins die here. A lot."

Vin's eyelids are getting stickier as blood dries on them. He rubs them. Bill waits, says, "Armor?" Vin, feeling sick, nods, and they keep walking. The field is covered with a tough and vivid green grass, moist, a few inches long. It folds under their feet but doesn't seem damaged by their tread and they don't leave a trail.

Despite the many vehicles, some wheeled, some flying, there

are few sounds of engines about them—primarily the loud, Doppler-stretched whines of rapid motion, and a constant uneven surround of many voices. Beneath the odd fragrances that seem to come and go, the field mostly smells of freshly cut grass. Sunlight sparkles like poured gold between standing and walking bodies.

Vin says, "Nobody seems bothered by what's happening."

Bill stops walking again. He's making a *tsk tsk tsk* sound and shaking his head as he looks away from Vin. "You still don't get it, man. You have to stay buttoned up or you will die. I just saw *my own head blow up*. There's plenty of people suffering, but we don't show it. Weakness gets you and people you love killed. The Vin from my world understood that. And, by the way, that's not the first time I've seen myself killed. How do you think I *should* react to something like that? What would satisfy you? I'm doing what I can, and right now, I'm helping you."

As they're facing each other, Vin sees the Bill he knows, the Bill he has a history with. And he also thinks he notices a subtle thing about the air. Breathing it is sending little micro-jolts of panic through him. It's not just the smells that stop and start. It's almost as if all of the air, even the air in his lungs, were blinking out of existence for microseconds and then returning before its absence changes anything, but his body can feel it. Why build that into a manufactured dimension? Could it be a bug?

"This place, the fighting is pointless. There are no answers here."

"No, man. That's not right. There are two sides. That's an answer. The fight."

"It doesn't *explain* anything."

"I love you man, but this fight is happening. Pick a justification. The fight is what matters. You Vins have your heads in the clouds. You have to focus on your game here, or you won't survive."

AT A FREIGHT TRUCK WITH its rear doors rolled open, Bill and a woman Vin doesn't know find him armor and a weapon—a long, shiny gray tube with metallic protuberances. The parts that stick out have triggers on them. With the safety on, Bill shows him how manipulating the triggers can cause the tube to fire a variety of lethal ordnance. The tube clicks with magnetic certainty onto a flat area on the rear of Vin's armor, leaving his hands free as needed. The armor fits as comfortably as loose cotton clothes and doesn't feel as though it has any weight.

Bill talks Vin through what's expected of him. Assuming he survives this shot, if the crèche ever sends him to Armageddon again he'll be expected to suit up on his own, find others willing to accompany him to the front, then go there and fight. Most of the people around him are veterans of the environment and can answer questions. Bill suggests that he connect with a Mona, if he can get one to talk with him, as they're generally considered exemplary warriors of Armageddon. While Bill is helping, Vin is only half paying attention. He is distracted by the repeating mental image of the first Bill grimacing in agony, his mouth stretching open, cheeks and forehead knotting down over his eyes as his head begins to expand.

Bill points out that Vin's armor includes jets and suggests Vin practice flying before going into battle. Then he fires his own boot jets, and before he streaks away, tells Vin that the armor will protect him from enemy fire and random death events, which means that for safety, Vin should always wear his helmet.

From the inside, the helmet is invisible and the world looks exactly as it did without it. It seems to fit poorly though, and slides a bit across the back of his neck and knocks against his nose when he moves his head quickly.

Vin curls an index finger into his palm to fire up his boot jets, as Bill showed him. The pressure balances across the soles of his feet as he lifts off the ground. Bill told him there were stabilizers in the armor.

Vin isn't sure whether he actually has a body in this place. His "real" body must be in a crèche in some other world, and so he's not sure whether he's wearing any actual armor at all, in any sense he'd understand. But, whatever is happening, the flight feels true— joyful, liberating—and he doesn't have any trouble directing it.

No one seems to be paying attention to him. He spends the rest of the shot flying from place to place across the field, trying to convince himself that no one cares that instead of contributing to the cosmic battle of *us* versus *them*, he's just playing with his equipment. And he thinks Bill has it wrong. No matter how overwhelming the reality of the place, there is more to living than a brutal and arbitrary fight for survival. There is flying, for example.

HE LEANED FORWARD, COMING PARTIALLY out of the casket. Dumbfounded again, scrambled and worn by the shot. His limbs felt drained. His mind was active but deadened, a dizzy zombie. The crèche was a trauma marinade. All those people fighting. A warm bath would have been a better vehicle for changing the world.

This variation on Nerdean's office was cool and dark, an unusual gloom shrouding its corners. The light was weak and fragile, portions of the glow-strips on the ceiling were off and he couldn't hear the AC.

He stepped out of the third casket, the one furthest from

the chute, and put on the white terry cloth robe that was hung over an eggshell chair. He turned toward the rack of servers. Only two appeared to be on; there were no lights on the others. On the back wall, the lights of some batteries were green but some were yellow, a few were red, and some bezels had no lights.

He picked up the notebook and flipped through it quickly, looking for unexpected entries. It all looked familiar. Only one computer screen would turn on. He logged in with *I am Nerdean*, and looked for clues that might explain why this office was different, but could find nothing. He considered going back into the crèche and leaving this world.

The third casket, the one he had just left, began its cycle of rejuvenation, its exterior lights blinking in the gloom. No lights illuminated the other two. But the transparent pane on the middle casket, number two, was oddly shadowed.

He opened an empty document on the only computer screen that worked, turning the screen white, then found a button to increase its brightness. He tried to angle the screen so its light would fall on the middle casket.

Something large and dark filled the interior there. Straining for detail, he saw that the thing inside was partly transparent, had a blue hue, and contained a deeper shadow that might have the form of a body. He traced a roll of darkness—an arm—to its end—a hand, fingers curling in. The blue broth had hardened around a person, sealing them in.

A breaking clangor, the sound of metal raking across metal, rose from the casket he'd just exited, followed by an extended thrashing noise. The lights under the lid turned red and started blinking. As he watched, all the lights faded and went out and the noises ended. Silence washed the room. Then the crèche seemed to restart the cycle of rejuvenation. Its lights came on at the beginning of their sequence, but the device also made muted squealing sounds.

THE LID OF THE CHUTE made a sucking sound as it lifted and a briny smell with a familiar tang of iron dropped into the narrow space. The room above was dark. He placed a hand on the rug outside the chute but pulled it back immediately. His fingertips were wet, bloody.

He pushed himself back so he was leaning against the wall and took a slow breath. Should he go up or down? He couldn't hear any sounds above. He pulled himself up and peered into the basement room, gagging softly. He turned to his left and almost fell back down the ladder. There was a body lying on the floor, staring toward the chute. Kim, eyes open and lightless, the lower half of her face a reddish-black blur.

He retreated. He hung on the rungs in the dark shaft until the smell of death filled it and he could not be still any longer. He climbed out, keeping as far from the corpse as possible, but spotted a child's body tumbled on the carpet in the back of the room. He closed his mind. He knew who the other body was, who it must be. He closed his mind and floated. And found himself upstairs.

The dining room was dark, heavy curtains drawn across the picture window. Mona sat at the long dining table in a white robe like the one he was wearing, her elbows pressed on the table, her hands covering her face. She didn't look up as he approached, as he paused to steady himself on a chair.

"Mona," he said. She turned to look at him and shook her head in incomprehension.

"Do I know you?" she asked. She shook her head again, startled.

He walked into the kitchen and pulled a long knife from the wooden block. Her gaze flicked to the knife then back to his face.

He said, "Downstairs, did you do that?"

"No. No." She drew back in shock. "I would never do that."

He walked to where she was sitting and brought the knife close to her cheek, the blade just below her eyes. "But you have done that at least once before, haven't you? To your own family."

She looked up at him. She wasn't scared. She didn't care. Why should he believe anything she said? He brought the long blade to her throat, just below her chin so that when she breathed her skin pushed against it. It was a sharp knife. The cut would be firm and fast.

"They were shot," she said, her voice level. "I don't have a gun. I don't even know who they are."

He tried to remember how Kim and Trina were killed. Kim's jaw destroyed, perhaps the back of her head gone. He took a step away from Mona and suddenly the lightness left his limbs. He sucked in air until his chest felt like it might explode. He lowered himself onto the edge of a chair, slipped into the center.

"I could never do that," Mona said, hatred straining her voice. "But I think you're someone who could, aren't you?"

The words stilled everything else. He didn't know. His body vibrated, struck by passing seconds.

"Maybe you did do it." Mona's voice was throaty. She spoke slowly but she wasn't accusing, only evaluating him, reading him as if what he was were plainly written in his face, on his body. "Here or in another world, you could lose your temper. Just like that. Couldn't you?" But then her head sagged again as if the room were filling with all of the disappointment of life. "And after that," she said, "you'd just go on, wouldn't you? Because what choice would you have?"

A wire broke inside him. A machine in his mind that enraged and aimed him, automated decisions, would defend itself by destroying her and him. He placed the knife on the table between them.

NEITHER OF THEM HAD MOVED and Vin had almost regained control of himself when they heard the front door open. Mona was tilted forward, staring blankly. Vin felt welded to the chair but his head could turn. He said, "Joaquin?" and Mona looked up.

Joaquin was staring, unblinking, at Mona. At his side was an enormous revolver, the kind that doesn't fill a hand as much as consume it.

"I'm sorry," Joaquin said to Mona. "Please. Please, come back."

Other than the look of loathing frozen on her features, Mona hadn't moved, but everything about her was different. She was alert.

"You know each other?" Vin said.

Joaquin's mouth tightened in acknowledgement of Vin's presence. "I asked you to stay in this house, Vin, in the hope that you would find her. We are married. She killed my children." As Vin struggled to reshape his past around this new information, Joaquin continued. "She was a general contractor. She built this house. She introduced me to Nerdean. Through email."

"It was an accident." Mona's voice was low, controlled. "They weren't supposed to be there."

Vin said, "What about my daughter? And Kim?"

Joaquin's mouth fell open slightly and he took a longer breath.

"I am sorry, Vin, about Kim and . . . I am truly sorry about them. I needed Kim to show me the machine. You lied to me, Vin."

"*I* didn't."

"You *did*," Joaquin shouted the second word, his face flushing, eyes clenching, spit flying from his mouth. He regained his balance at the edge of the stairs and said with effort, "I wanted you to find my wife so I might *help* her. Because she is dangerous and I did not want this"—he stopped talking, stared at Vin and said—"or anything like this to happen. But you would not stop lying to me. Even when your pretext was transparent, you lied. You did this."

The gun was aimed at Vin again and an asymmetry caught his eye. A single coppery glint showed on one side of the big revolver's barrel.

He caught a blur in his peripheral vision. Mona had risen and was flying toward Joaquin.

It was not a sound—more a cataclysmic motion of the house. The gunshot blew the air out of the room and threw the three of them together into a new world, a universe birthed in that shaved second of violence. Blood sprayed from Mona's back and the huge picture window behind her cackled and shivered into an obscuring web of stilled moments.

Mona straightened. It was as if she had been cored, the back of her robe red from the spasm of blood, but she didn't even look at her wound. She took a staggering step toward Joaquin. A tinny *crack, crack*—the sound of the gun's hammer falling on empty chambers.

Mona had the knife in her right hand. She swayed away from Joaquin, almost tipped and fell backward, but then miraculously swayed the other way. She took three more falling steps and shoved the knife deep into his gut.

His face went taut. Mona pressed forward and jerked up on the knife, pulling the long blade through him. As they pressed into each other, their bodies held upright by their opposing weight, Joaquin's face paled and the stalk of his neck wilted.

Mona made a sound, a soft chuckle of blood bubbling from her mouth. Vin ran to them as they sank to the floor, leaning into each other. He kneeled in the spreading pool of their blood, reached a hand to Mona's shoulder. She blinked as if returning to life and looked at him, her eyes rolling, head not moving.

"Vin," she said, struggling to form the word, her shallow breath seething between bloody teeth. She and Joaquin were fused in a gory mess. Vin couldn't see what had happened to her.

Vin said, "Let go. Let go of the knife."

She didn't let go, and as he strained to pull Joaquin away from her, tendrils of viscera came too, spinning apart at the knife's edge as it slid out of his gut. Joaquin's body collapsed to the side and Vin pushed it away. Then he pressed on Mona's wrist and gently took the knife from her.

She folded to one side and he helped her onto her back. She was wide-eyed, staring upward. "I'm going to die."

"Yes. I think so."

"I used accelerants. My babies weren't supposed to be there."

"What can I do?"

"It's okay. It was a fight I needed." Her eyes closed but she was still breathing.

VIN WORKED QUICKLY. MONA WAS not a large woman and adrenaline lent him strength. He tore strips from the robe, which separated cleanly, and used the robe's sash to tie the strips tightly against her wounds. As he carried her into the chute, remnants of the robe caught on its lid—he simply tore them apart and continued with his fireman's carry.

She hadn't spoken since he'd picked her up. When he laid her in the first casket she was pale but still alive. He could see her shallow breathing and as he removed the sash and pieces of robe he felt her pulse whispering through her cool flesh. Nerdean's office was busy with muted scurrying sounds, scrapes and squeals from the damaged third casket that was still battling through its cycle of rejuvenation.

"You didn't call the EMTs . . ." Mona came to as he was finishing his frantic work on a keyboard. The third casket entered a quiet phase in its cycle and her voice was a hoarse whisper. He stepped quickly to the side of her casket.

"Thank you," she said, twisting her head slightly to look at him. Her eyes were clear but her voice was fading.

"I don't know if this will work."

"That's okay," Mona said. She was going to embark on a shot, one way or another. He found the sedatives and bottled water and she managed to swallow a pill.

"I found another password," he said.

"Yeah?"

"Yeah, so I can set how far—"

But her eyes drifted slowly shut and he knew she had been pulled under. She was still breathing. He ran to the computer and pressed a final key to fire the shot. The lid of the first casket lowered with smooth precision and sealed her in.

HE DIDN'T KNOW IF SHE'D make it to Armageddon, didn't know if she'd even survive until the shot started, but it seemed possible. The crèche was designed to incubate, to support, nurture and heal the body, no matter what else it might do.

He sat for between ten and thirty minutes with the third casket grumbling through the end of its cycle of rejuvenation. Shortly after it finally fell silent, he recalled himself. He stood and walked to the first casket and placed his hand on its transparent pane. The mist cleared and he saw Mona floating peaceably in the slightly rust-tinged broth.

On the desktop, Kim's phone buzzed. He had retrieved it and placed the baby monitor outside the front door. It was notifying him of noise. The casket's transparent pane sighed and misted as he lifted his hand and hurried to the desk. He heard the shriek of police sirens and closed down the monitoring app, silencing it. A police forensics team would definitely find the chute, and Nerdean's office.

In the urgent quiet, he peeled off his bloody robe, sat at a keyboard and opened the controls for the third casket. He keyed in a command and the third casket's lid lifted with a squawk. At least it could still open. That was a good sign.

More of the batteries along the far wall had gone dark. He wasn't sure whether the casket would work for even a short shot, and he didn't know of any way to use it without landing another version of himself in the mess that he was running from. Maybe even infinite versions. But he hadn't made this mess. Did he have a responsibility to stay in it? At least Mona's body might die, so no other version of her would end up in this shithole. Her death would free her from this particular world.

He checked the duration, and then pulled the slider for the third casket all the way to the left, as close to the label NEAR as it would go. He had the presence of mind to worry for a moment about what *near* might actually mean—might the crèche project him into a version of his own mind? But he left the slider alone.

Mona may have chosen to go down fighting, but Vin did not want to return to Armageddon.

IT'S LATE AND CHILLY AND he's sitting on a concrete staircase looking out at the glittering Seattle skyline from the south shoulder of Queen Anne Hill. His name is William Marigold and he's thinking about smoking a cigarette. He used to smoke and he misses it.

The *sarcococca ruscifolia* is near the end of its bloom but still managing to spread its delicious, spicy vanilla scent. The smell might not be so bright if he hadn't quit smoking when he did, many years ago.

Fragrant sweet box is the plant's common name. It was one of his favorites when he cared about things. The flowers are small and humble but when they're in bloom they can pack a breeze with a scent so fine it can stop a jogger cold. He's seen puzzled, spandex-clad runners halt midstride and then follow their noses around the foliage, sniffing nearby plants, looking for the source of their pleasure. The flowers are so modest that sometimes people don't think to smell them. Once you know the secret though, you look for them. If you still possess that magic feeling of giving a damn.

William looks up at the shadow-clotted sky. He's been thinking a lot about eternity and how close it always is. One single motion can take a person from useless to infinite.

Vin is in William's head and the dull, burdensome sense of being in a place—the almost unendurable weight of the sky above and the weight of being in a body and pressing down on cement and dirt—alerts him to his existence. The crèche did this to him.

"The crèche?" William thinks. "What's that?"

"Oh no," Vin thinks. "He can hear me, like the cannibal."

"No, I'm a vegetarian."

"Oh. Like Bill."

"No, I prefer William."

William stands—a prickling pain in his left knee. He rubs his right elbow to check that the bump beneath his flesh hasn't gotten any larger. His doctor says it's benign, only a fat deposit embedded in the flesh near his joint. It may be, but it's also an intrusion in his body, a thing that shouldn't be there.

It's a warm winter night. *Unseasonable* is the old term. *Presaging doom* is the new, more accurate way to think about it. Thirty to thirty-five billion metric tons of CO_2 emissions per year. Probably more now. Warming the surface of the earth as if it were a green pea in a convection oven. But William stopped tracking all that long ago. He stopped seeing the point. Any one person is able to recognize and avoid danger, but the human species as a whole is incapable of responding to it effectively. The human species will defeat life at last and the earth will sizzle under the solar lamp until it becomes a dry shell.

Once he stopped caring, the world opened a great distance between itself and him. Even the air, mild against his skin, reaches him now only by crossing a gulf. As he walks up the slope toward the basement apartment that he rents near a park, he sees himself walking as if he were hovering above and behind his own body.

He's imagining the perspective. Of course, he knows that. But if he could actually see himself from that perspective, he would see that the crown of his head is shiny with grease and thick with embedded flakes of dandruff. It's like that no matter how often he cleans it or how well he grooms himself. It's a sad fact that the memory of only a few sneering rebuffs from people you might have loved can leave permanent, grimy streaks on your self-image.

Though the globe is warming, a warmer winter is pleasant for most people. In that way, temperature change is like a helium balloon, very nice, inspiring even, when you first notice it—vivid and colorful, defying gravity—until it pops. Then it becomes an elastic environmental poison.

At the top of the hill he turns back to look at the skyline while he catches his breath. Vin notices that some buildings are missing.

"Oh?" thinks William. "Why is that?"

"Well, I guess they must not have been built yet. But you shouldn't listen to me. I think you have enough to worry about."

"Okay," William responds meekly.

"Do I frighten you?" asks Vin.

"No. I'm much too frightened by real things to be frightened by an imaginary voice in my head."

"I'm not imaginary."

"That's what they all would say, I'm sure."

"You have other voices?"

"I might have. But what I mean is, all psychotic voices would tell you that they're real. That's a part of the illness, isn't it?"

"Are you psychotic?"

"I suppose I might be. I'm talking with a voice in my head. You might be a psychotic break. I suppose. But I don't really care. One more reason to kill myself."

Vin is silent after that remark, but William doesn't care whether Vin responds. William sniffs and places the palm of his hand against the end of his nose, which is cold and starting to drip. He wipes his palm against it, then wipes his hand on the side of his parka and keeps walking.

"Don't kill yourself."

"Why not?"

"I don't really know you, but—"

"Interesting."

"—I can tell you that this has been a particularly shitty day—"

"Yes, I agree. Another one."

William doesn't so much dismiss Vin as just move on, as if Vin were a thing that should dissolve when neglected. William begins to think about the question of weight, and how much exactly is pressing on him. He steps through a lengthy back-of-the-envelope type of estimate, figuring the weight of the atmosphere at sea level in the mid-Northern latitudes (excluding the vast exosphere, whose contribution would be negligible), the height of Queen Anne Hill and the resulting height of his shoulders above sea level. He concludes that roughly 2093.5 pounds per square foot is bearing down on his head and shoulders, which confirms his expectation that simply standing up in this world is a burden.

Observing William working through his mental estimate, Vin is impressed, but can't help remarking, "That's a whole lot of work to shave off a total of only twenty or so pounds per square foot from the standard atmospheric weight at sea level."

"I do it because I'd really prefer not to exaggerate," thinks William. "Once more, the truth is frightening enough."

VIN DOESN'T BRING UP HIS real concern until they reach William's apartment, a dank claustrophobic studio in the basement beneath a large Craftsman house that squats across the street from the West Queen Anne Playfield. William flips on the overhead light as he enters but the bulb barely wakes the comatose room. The apartment's small windows are covered with blackout curtains, the furnishings old and abused—a faded, light-blue, broken-backed sofa; a recliner covered in a frayed floral pattern, its cushions pancaked by years of reckless flopping down. Slips of paper spread like a scatter of severed wings over a small breakfast table, glossy magazines in a slumping stack beside the couch.

"Are you still there, voice?" William asks himself.

"Yes," says Vin.

"What's your name?"

"If I'm in your head, shouldn't I have the same name you have?"

"Well, do you?"

"Vin. My name is Vin."

"I see. So my suspicion was correct. You are a robust enough hallucination to have your own name," thinks William. "That is depressing."

"No. No," Vin thinks. "It's not fair to trick me into saying things that will make you feel worse. And I'm not a hallucination, I'm real."

"There is no conceivable way that you could be anything other than the kind of short circuit in my mental function that I've been anticipating now for years."

"Yes, there is," Vin says, surprising himself with a decision. "And I'm going tell you exactly how. But first, I want to get something straight with you. That whole thing about estimating the weight on your shoulders, atmospheric pressure doesn't work that way and you know it. It presses in all directions, it doesn't just drop a ton of weight on your shoulders. You just calculated a single vector to validate how you feel, but it operates in a system."

William opens a stained green refrigerator and extracts a

nearly room temperature Budweiser. When he pushes on the refrigerator door it drifts closed, barely sealing.

He thinks, "Okay, Vin, I did exaggerate and you caught me. But every answer is an estimate, and my *feeling* is genuine. So now that you've proven to be a more perceptive voice in my head than I expected, can you tell me why you're not a hallucination? Maybe your story will help me sleep."

VIN SPILLS IMAGES AND EVENTS as if he's confessing and everything he says will be forgiven. William is attentive, and Vin feels him waking mentally, slowly rousing himself from what had been a profound and lengthy funk to pay closer and closer attention to Vin's story. William is a good listener, and from inside William's head, it's easy to convey emotion. William's rare questions are thoughtful and sensitive and they test Vin's awareness of Kim's feelings, and Trina's. They test his awareness of his own resilience.

"It seems to me, Vin," William says at one point, "that you and Kim treated each other well while you were together."

"Thank you," Vin says, dizzy from their many beers.

William is horrified by Vin's trip to Armageddon, and when Vin reaches the bloody climax he has just fled, William gasps at each grisly development until, as Vin relates how he loaded Mona into the first casket, William is sighing noisily. Vin has been afraid that William would challenge his decision to use the crèche, rather than call an ambulance. Maybe Mona could have survived. But survive for what? Her phantom responds.

"You made the right choice," agrees William.

Throughout the story, William is an accommodating surrogate, allowing Vin to move his hands and mouth so they can take turns drinking beer. The two of them have kept each other going and drained many of the bottles in William's sickly but well-stocked refrigerator.

"Ah, god. It's so sad," William thinks as Vin explains how he landed in William's head.

"I know," Vin agrees, and then he's gasping, weeping without restraint in whatever way a thought process can.

"We're so cruel to each other," William thinks.

And Vin thinks, "William, please don't do it. Please."

Vin can easily hear thoughts that William intentionally directs at him but the deeper layers of William's mind are clouded under a mordant, almost fungal coating, a powdery glaucous bloom. Contact with them drains Vin, makes him feel grimy.

William thinks, "I know a girl who calls herself Nerdean. She's only fifteen though. We play Go at the Queen Anne Library."

"What?"

"Hey, stop poking around in my thoughts."

"But if you *know Nerdean*, and she's *young*, and I just told you about the crèche, then you might tell *her*. What if *I'm responsible for her creating the crèche?*"

William is appalled at how thick Vin is being. "Isn't that just the point," he thinks. "Isn't that just what we've been talking about? Shared responsibility? And, anyway, don't get too excited. There are other ways of looking at it. Infinite worlds is just hand-waving. Infinity isn't really a number, after all. It's the distance between math and truth, and I mean that literally. And maybe the crèche, maybe all of technology really, is an expression of an as yet unknown multidimensional geometry of causation, systemic effects we can't fully perceive. I mean, none of us really *invent* any of this any more than we *discover* things.

When conditions are right, maybe things, ideas, just grow. Like mushrooms."

William has been sitting for too long. He blinks with blowzy insensibility and then hawks up phlegm from the back of his throat. As he cautiously levers himself upright, his mood clears.

He staggers into his dingy bathroom to pee. "You know, for a bubble in my temporal lobe, you're actually okay. Interesting even. I thought you were going to warn me about Area 51, JFK and the CIA. Tinfoil hats. It's nice to have a conversation with my ideas though, rather than just have them pop up. Collegial."

William flushes the toilet. He runs his tongue across the outside of his upper and lower teeth as he steps up to a stained bathroom mirror.

"You," Vin thinks.

"What?"

"You. I know you."

"You *are* me." William spits into the sink. "No matter what you think."

"Do you recognize this?" Vin asks, and he thinks of a black military jacket with yellow piping and gold buttons. He feels a flicker of pleasure vibrate through William.

"Sure. And you know about the rest too, right?" William plods to a long closet and opens a sliding door on a collection of uniforms. He finds a black jacket with yellow piping that's hanging over blue slacks. "You mean this one. I collect them. My fingers are too long, my knuckles are ugly and knobby, and I have thin shoulders, a wide rump and a roll of fat around my waist. Uniforms hide all that."

"I need air," Vin thinks. "Can we walk?"

"I was going to sleep, but okay, I guess." William grabs the uniform's jacket. As he steps outside, Vin convinces him to draw in a deep breath. The dark, fresh breeze feeds him but also makes him dizzy. He sways for a few moments then starts walking west, toward the water.

Vin thinks, "This is you," showing William his memory of the man who interrupted the barbecue.

"Yes. I suppose it is. So what?"

Vin doesn't know how to have the conversation he's desperate for. In some worlds, William merely interrupted the barbecue, but in others he wounded Hanna and killed Trina.

William thinks, "You know, I'm hearing you think about all that. You're saying all of those things inside my head."

"Okay."

They walk. In his thoughts, Vin can't help connecting Trina's death to Kim's journey in the crèche and to the destruction of his own marriage.

William thinks, "Okay, I get the picture."

"I'm sorry. I can't help it. My thoughts just—"

"No, I understand. You're saying I'm going to murder a little girl who I don't know but already love."

"Given your state of mind, I wasn't going to tell you."

"Well, that's not one-hundred percent true. You were thinking about hiding it from me so I wouldn't feel worse about myself. Which I appreciate. But you probably would have told me, if there was a chance that it would stop me from hurting her."

Vin realizes that William understands him too well for even subtle deceptions.

"Yes," William thinks at him, "that's right. I do."

WHEN WILLIAM/VIN REACHES MARSHALL PARK, he sits on the bench and watches darkness begin to loosen its grip on the breezy reaches above the water. William has been planning to kill himself because he views humanity as a plague, an animal with the same narcissistic perspective as every other animal, but one that has uncovered the protean pliability of the material world and is rapaciously and incontinently bumbling through oceans and forests, smugly convinced of its own transcendence from the systems responsible for the creation and nurturance of all life, an animal that "discovers" components and attributes of the natural world as if they were separable from the circumstances they inhabit.

"I know it's depressing," William thinks. But the thing he feels is more urgent than depression. It's more like the despair Vin felt when Bill dropped a bag of meth on the folding card table. William feels it toward the species. He earned graduate degrees from MIT, won awards for his research. "But the species that honored me, or at least its inevitable idea of progress, is a toxin." William says this out loud. "And that's how I ended up here, feeling this way."

"But can't you find a way through your depression? Can't you fight it?"

"Like Mona did?" William thinks. "Like Armageddon? Run from the black dog of depression the way Winston Churchill did, or Teddy Roosevelt? Did you know that Roosevelt felt the same kind of overwhelming anxiety and fear of the future as Churchill? Should I be like them and keep myself so busy that I don't ever have time to think? Blunder through the world breaking and killing things because I'm trying to outrun my own depression? That would make me a part of the illness."

"I don't know. Is that your only choice?" Vin suddenly feels a surge of frustration. William is a sad sack, lost and damaged, a man Vin shouldn't give a damn about. But he's unique, specific and alive, and being here in his head, even with his depression—he's beautiful. Vin wants him to live.

"By the way," William is speaking out loud again, "Sophie was right about you neglecting her. It seems to me that animals we don't care enough about to kill, we sometimes adopt."

And William and his depression are now part of Vin's life. There's nothing Vin can do about it. He might even be happy about it, the strangeness of it. No matter whose mind he's been in, it's always been his life. The shots are *him*, not side lives where he can dodge reality.

A brisk chill from the water sweeps over William, silencing both his thoughts and Vin's. High above, the black fabric between clouds is rent by the closest, most energetic and violent stars. They fade as dawn restores the limits of the visible world.

HE HAD FELT THINGS THAT William felt but he wasn't sure he really understood William. Maybe William would kill himself. Maybe he wouldn't. These were Vin's first thoughts when he woke in a mild, air-conditioned version of Nerdean's office. Waking there meant that he had survived the shot, which meant that in the world where he left the corpses of Kim, Trina, Mona and the person sometimes known as Joaquin, the police hadn't ended his shot prematurely, and the crèche's battery power had lasted.

With his first step outside the casket, he felt a familiar stiffness in his leg. As he walked to the terry cloth robe heaped on one of the chairs—a midnight-blue robe—he became reacquainted with his limp.

His thoughts were darting, restive. He was trying not to reflect on his experience, didn't trust himself to draw conclusions. But his mind wanted answers, its default intoxicant. He would have to make an effort to deny himself at least for a while. If he didn't do that, he might pass more time searching, traveling from one world to the next, and his life would all be lived in Nerdean's office.

There was no one in the other two caskets. Upstairs, the card table wasn't in the dining room, but neither was the beautiful big table that he and Kim and Trina had lived with. Instead, there was a modest maple table with rounded ends. The chairs that surrounded it were functional, squarish, with cushioned seats. There was a sectional in the same place that Kim had once placed one, but not as nice. There were a few other uninspired furnishings. On the largest wall in the dining room hung a big canvas he didn't recognize, a painting, the outlines of a car and driver in spreading black strokes, defined and slashed through by playful geometric scrolls and a collision of faded prime colors.

There was no cat food under the sink. He realized with a pang that Sophie wasn't in the house. The odd cluster of electronics was not in the master bedroom, but he did find a phone charging on a black, wrought iron bed stand beside a queen-size bed. He unlocked the phone with his PIN and looked through the contacts. Bill was there. Kim wasn't. John Grassler was in his list, as well as Corey Nahabedian and even Brant Spence. He was surprised to see Hanna Dawkins—Kim's co-worker who had come over for their barbecue—in his list of contacts. When he checked his recent calls, there were several to and from her.

He sat on the bed and stared at the shiny phone screen. Outside his window, unfiltered morning sunlight was sharpening its bright knives against the slate-gray waters of Puget Sound. He thought he should probably read his email and try to catch up on how events developed in this world. Instead, he took a deep breath and called Bill.

THEY ARRANGED TO MEET FOR brunch at the restaurant in the Space Needle. Bill's idea. On their phone call, he'd told Vin that after finally receiving the largish check for their small investment in Sigmoto, he and Charlotte had been discussing what they should do next. She wanted to buy a few acres on one of the islands and start a small organic farm, raise their own food to sell at farmers' markets. Bill wasn't so sure.

Bill's voice was relaxed, and he laughed with an oblivious, unforced ease. Vin decided to save the in-depth questioning for their face-to-face. After hanging up, Vin spent several moments appreciating the fact that Bill was apparently sober in this world. He walked the distance to Caffé Vita, warming up his trick leg.

Trina had liked this walk. They'd often passed dogs leading drowsy owners who carried blue plastic baggies of poop. She called the route, "Going down the hill the long way," in her child's voice—the sound that was the unique cryptographic hash that had once authenticated his life. But there was no contact number in his phone for childcare.

The crèche was a technology that could change the world, disrupt culture, but technology followed its own logic, indifferent to the human arithmetic of suffering. Believing in it, relying on it was like worshiping a volcano. He had knowledge and skill. How should he use them? What good could he do?

He was walking by a line of ants that were shuttling pieces of something yellow past a watchful crow.

AS HE WAITED FOR A barista whom he didn't know to make his drink, he thought of a question for Bill. He took the latte outside, sat in one of the metal café chairs and called. A wall of dark clouds began to draw itself up against the blue distance.

"Hey, when was the last time you talked with Hanna?" he asked.

"Your Hanna?"

That would explain the calls on Vin's phone.

A shock of memory tore open the mild day, splitting it in two while somehow leaving it whole. Kim and Trina's bodies in the dark basement. Vin saw himself pressing the silver blade against the soft flesh of Mona's throat, saw the deadness in her eyes as they stepped to the precipice of her murder. But he hadn't hurt her. As a part of her own story, she had saved his life. At the world's terrifying edges, the rumors of endless shadow worlds trembled. Vin squinted into radiant air, felt sleeping moisture on the slow-moving wind.

"Vin?" Bill asked again, his voice bringing Vin back to himself.

"Yeah," he said.

"Well, yeah, Hanna called me after you guys broke up. Said that you were going through a hard time, and that, knowing you, you might not reach out."

Vin was fighting to regain a place in his body. A heavy bulldog stepped toward him and began licking the bottom of his jeans. Thick-necked, pug-nosed and gentle, the dog's flat tongue maneuvered like a separate animal. The bulldog looked up at him, grunted or sneezed, then turned to enter Caffé Vita. Its owner nodded as he followed the dog in. Vin wondered whether he knew either of them in this world.

"What do you know about the crèche?" he asked Bill.

"Did you use it again? You said you were done with it. You said when you came out your cat had disappeared, along with her scratching post, all her cat food and her dishes. Sophie, I think you said. You were freaked out."

"And that was all?"

Bill laughed. "Yeah. But that seemed like enough, right? You said you liked that cat."

"I did. I miss her."

"Okay, but like I've said every time you bring her up, you never had a cat. Right? That thing has bad mojo, man. Really bad. I think you should turn it over to the university. You're never going to figure it out on your own and you have the money from Sigmoto. It's not like you need the house."

"No. I probably know everything I need to know about it."

"See you in a little bit?"

"At the Space Needle's elevator. Sure."

"Yeah. Okay. And, hey, I'm glad you called. You know, that you reached out. I know how hard you and Hanna tried. I know how hard things must be for you right now. You've never really wanted to talk about this stuff though. Like I said, I'm glad you called."

"Thanks Bill."

"Oh, and hey, I saw Kim this morning. She told me to say hi."

There was a pause before Vin managed to say, "And, how's she?"

"Great. That paper she coauthored? It got accepted. Her first publication. I bought her a new pen and a scientific notebook to celebrate."

HE WALKED WEST ON ROY Street, aiming by default toward what he still thought of as Nerdean's house. He had mumbled something to Bill and hung up, ending their conversation, too stunned to keep talking. Wasn't this what he had wanted for years—all three of them alive, and Bill healthy? But what did he and Kim mean to each other now, in a new world where they were barely friends?

He wouldn't go back into the crèche, at least not anytime soon, but not because Kim and Bill had both survived here. Trina was still missing. Living in the same world as his daughter was what he wanted. But he didn't believe he could find her without destroying himself and possibly her, and he wanted a life, whatever that might mean. His feelings might change or they might not but for now, knowing what he wanted was enough.

At Counterbalance Park, sunlight was soaking into the teak decking and warming it so that steam rose in thinning spirals. The air was fresh, cleansed by the recent rain. Gray and rose canyons and bright buttes of cloud drifted above.

He decided not to go directly back to the big house. Instead, he turned up the hill, walking fast so that he ran short of breath and felt his body laboring. In this world, he hadn't taken very good care of himself.

THE SUN HELD OUT ALL the way to the top of the hill and then the day cooled as he turned toward the park and the daylight turned blue-gray. What are the forces that transform a person? What makes one thing possible and another impossible and what moves those limits? Beyond the obvious, what was now out of his reach and what was within it?

The house across the street from the West Queen Anne Playfield looked to him exactly as it had when he and William left it, only a few hours before and years ago. But this wasn't the same world, and that wasn't really the same house and Vin didn't know what to expect. Ghosts? Or violence? Ordinary people with unanswerable questions? He walked up the broad concrete stairs and turned left before the wooden porch, walked to the side of the house with the dull white door at ground level. Blackout curtains like he remembered at William's place. He knocked twice but no one answered. He waited and knocked again.

He decided to try the upstairs apartment. The owners, or whoever rented up there, might know where William was. He stepped onto the lawn and had another moment of panic, stood breathing and watching small birds in a large chestnut tree.

The front porch was spacious and clean, the paint recent. He walked up and pressed the doorbell and waited. A thin woman in her late sixties answered.

"Hello, Vin," she said. "How can I help you?"

And so here it was again, a question, what are your intentions? What do you mean? And once again, Vin wasn't sure. His mind was completely quiet. There were no words to borrow, no voices speaking through him. He could imagine responding in any number of ways and he tilted his head as he thought about the fact that he might not understand what she was asking, which could mean he was overthinking things.

He took a breath and glanced over his shoulder toward the green park across the street. He was an animal in a world somewhere, on a white porch, facing a similar creature. And she was waiting for him to say something. All of his questions remained and all of life lay before him. He answered.

ACKNOWLEDGMENTS

If this is being read, the odd experience of making *Side Life* is over, and what's left is to thank many people, starting with Bruce Oberg and Annette Toutonghi, who made this book possible. It wouldn't have happened without them and I'm profoundly grateful. Dasha Bertrand's illustrations gave Nerdean's elliptical presence a sensitive visual expression. Including illustrations was one of many excellent suggestions made by Mark Doten, who is brilliant and wonderful to work with. The whole team at Soho Press is absolutely the best. I want to thank them all, and especially Bronwen Hruska for taking another chance on my work. The interest and insight of my agent, David Forrer, helped prevent a collapse into an early draft. He also offered a box of chocolates when that was exactly what was called for. I'll always be grateful to David Vann for his confidence in my work.

Seeing phrases like "sugar is the devil's jerboa," in my file of "ideas" is humbling. I'm grateful to Ruta Toutonghi (*liels paldies*, Ruta!), Judi Linn, Bob Shaw, John Shaw, Carolee Bull, Tom Fillingim, Gary Knopp, David Shettleroe, David Zitzewitz, Geoff Pfander, and Alec Leslie for reading and commenting on early drafts. K. M. Alexander offered many useful comments and helped me believe the story was worth reading. Pauls Toutonghi is an inspiration and a generous and thoughtful friend. Thanks to Aaron and Karen Davis, Anthony Hsu, Osnat Lustig, Hsu Hsun-Wei, and Gary Murray for help with specific questions.

Research for *Side Life* went in several directions. Edward Burtynsky's breathtaking work, via the film *Manufactured Landscapes*, provided key details for Gao Cheng's shot. William Manchester's biography, Churchill's writings, and correspondence between H. H. Asquith and Venetia Stanley influenced the Churchill shot. Books and films about Tobias Schneebaum, descriptions in Carl Hoffman's *Savage Harvest*, The MET's Rockefeller collection, and interviews on YouTube helped with Ban's shot. Paul Nunez's writings, among many on the brain and mind, were very helpful. Donald Hoffman's ideas influenced revisions. Charles Johnston's work and example inform the book throughout. Errant speculation is all mine.

The Danish movie *Steppeulvene* was one of many SIFF films that contributed. Several lectures at Seattle's Town Hall were helpful. For years, you could purchase *Faux Museum* T-shirts from Tom Richards, proprietor of Portland's authentic *Faux Museum*.

To Mason, Michael, Danny, Anna, Phineas, Beatrix and Angelina—apologies for what I participated in doing to our world. We all have to try harder. Thanks to Joe, Mike, Alyona, Gabrielle, and Mary Toutonghi, to John Greene and to Peyton Marshall for their support.

My wife, Monique Shaw, has been everything to me, including an honest critic, for close to three decades. She helped in many ways, large and small. We recently lost a family member, Steinbeck, a dear companion while I wrote, who died unaware that he'd contributed to the character of Sophie. We miss him.